For Ma

Happy reading to a dear
sister! Hope the contents are
as interesting as the jacket
promises.

Love,
Cathy and Kevin

THE
PHILOSOPHER'S DAUGHTER

A **BOOK**

By the same author

CHARMED CIRCLE
IN THE COOL OF THE DAY
SUMMER'S LEASE

Previous Novels

MADAME CLAIRE
NOW EAST, NOW WEST
THE GALAXY
THE PROSELYTE
ANGER IN THE SKY
THE PRODIGAL HEART
INVITATION TO FOLLY
MARY HALLAM

The
Philosopher's Daughter

SUSAN ERTZ

HARPER & ROW, PUBLISHERS
New York, Hagerstown, San Francisco, London

FIRST U.S. EDITION

Library of Congress Cataloging in Publication Data

Ertz, Susan.
  The philosopher's daughter.
  "A Cass Canfield book."
  I. Title.
PZ3.E737Ph   [PS3509.R6]   823'.9'12   76-5537
ISBN 0-06-011253-0

76 77 78 79 80 10 9 8 7 6 5 4 3 2 1

CONTENTS

CHAPTER I

The Little Prologue

She was sitting in the front seat of the car that belonged to her father's lawyer and oldest friend, Mr Beallby, who was driving them slowly behind the undecorated hearse through streets that were wholly unfamiliar to her. She had known and been fond of Mr Beallby from as far back as her memory would go, and she called him, though it seemed childish to continue to do so, Uncle Hugh. Mrs Tronsett, who had attached herself to father and daughter twenty-two years ago at the time she became a widow, sat in the back seat saying nothing, keeping her thoughts and her grieving to herself. Mr Beallby spoke now and again, remarking that they would soon be out of the worst of the traffic – their destination was one he knew all too well – that they hadn't many miles to go now, and that the driver of the hearse had undoubtedly chosen the best route. It was early May, and at one point he made the comment that if you wanted to see beautiful flowering trees you could hardly do better than pay a visit to the suburbs of London.

Sibyl was thinking how often she had seen these sad little processions – though theirs consisting only of the hearse and the one car following it could hardly be called that – passing through the streets; she would quickly avert her eyes from them, hating to be reminded of loss and of the briefness of life; then, like most people, she would forget about them quite soon.

Not that it was easy to put death from one's mind. She had remarked to her father only a few days earlier that she wished 'the media', and that included the morning papers, had not reversed an old saying, changing it to 'Good news is no news', disaster being their daily menu.

'Why must they tell us,' she had despairingly asked, 'of
the horrible deaths of children in a fire in Winnipeg?
It isn't as though we could *do* anything about it.' Her
father had given her a long look and shaken his head,
comment being useless.

They did not own a television set, Sibyl being content
with hearing the main news on a small portable radio in
her bedroom. Her father spent his days writing, reading,
seeing a few friends, walking about London for which
however much it changed, he had a Johnsonian love,
sometimes spending an hour or so in the National
Portrait Gallery or a morning in the British Museum
Reading Room. As for her, ever since her childhood she
had been eager to learn, learn, learn. In the evenings, if
both were in – she of course went out far oftener than he
did, wearing a pretty dress and being called for by some
admirer – they played records, for both were music-
lovers. It was a peaceful, perhaps too cloistered
existence, and she sometimes accused them both of
selfishness, though each cared deeply for the well-being
of the other. Her father's need of her, his dependence on
her for his will to live, weighed greatly with her. Her
happiness, her good were his tenderest concern. For her
he would have put everything aside, even his deep
involvement in philosophical ideas and the quiet renown
his own had brought him, willing always to say, 'Enough;
I have someone close and dear, someone whose claim
upon me outweighs all other claims.'

There had been one occasion five years earlier, when
death, for the first time in her remembered days, had
come close. They were in Switzerland together taking long
walks which included a certain amount of mild climbing.
Mild though it was it had been too much for a sedentary
man of over sixty, for he had suffered a heart attack
described by the doctors as 'of more than medium
severity'. He had had to spend three weeks in a hospital
in Lausanne before he was well enough to travel home.
She had been warned that it might happen again but

most of the time she had been able to put it quite out of her mind because he had taken good and sensible care of himself, never running for a bus or climbing stairs in a hurry and looked besides far younger than his years. When the end came, it came with shocking suddenness and without attributable cause.

The funeral was private, which, being the man he was he would have wished, and indeed clearly said so in his will. There was no sort of religious ceremony, as he had decided at the age of fifteen to discard conventional religious beliefs and above all to belong to no denomination, dismayed and disgusted even then by the splintering into countless sects or sections of even the simplest teachings of Christianity. 'I suppose I go to bed a Christian and wake up a Christian,' he had once said to her, 'if I require some sort of label.'

Her father had looked upon death as a friendly thing and feared it not at all. Sometimes it seemed to her that he even looked forward to it, troubled only by the knowledge that when it came she would be left alone to deal with such problems as would inevitably come the way of an attractive – though he was glad to think fastidious – young woman.

They had occasional talks about it and quite recently, within the last month, she had questioned him as to the reason for his indifference to death.

'Surely most people are a little apprehensive, to say the least; wouldn't you agree?' she had asked him. 'Why aren't you apprehensive at all?'

'Apprehensive of what? When one comes to the end of a task or a day or a journey, one isn't apprehensive.'

'No, because one's looking forward to another task, another journey. At least the young and the middle-aged are, and I still look on you as middle-aged.'

'Ah, the young! The death of the young is the most hideous of all the evils the world deals out to us. And, cave-men as we still are, we deal out to ourselves and each other when we make war.'

'And yet,' she persisted, wanting to get at his reasons, 'you're happy in your work. I know you are.'

'If I'm happy, it's entirely because of you.'

'Still, I can't understand your being so willing to leave it all. All the beauty there is. I'd even hate to think that I'd never again look up and see a great full moon following me along a London street. To say nothing of the beauty of mountains and lakes and forests.'

'The beauty of nature is infinite. But finality is a beautiful thing too. Perhaps the most beautiful of all. Take, let's say, the very last note of Beethoven's Sonata in C Minor, or the little Sonata in G Major, delightfully played. One's enjoyed the music, but how lovely that final and perfect note is. For a timeless moment, all's well with the world.'

'But Father, aren't you taking an awful lot for granted when you talk about death? How can you be so certain that you may not go on to things you never dreamed of?'

'My dearest girl, I haven't the smallest fear of that. There's consciousness, which remains the mystery of mysteries, and there's death about which I believe we know all there is to know – except that few of us know how to meet it.'

That day of the funeral the last thing to be faced was the quiet sliding away of the coffin, out of sight. But, she thought, how decent its disappearance, how decent its destination! How else, she wondered, could those left behind endure the hateful thought of the slow decay of a loved body after burial? However much one feels a part of the earth when living, it was another matter to choose it as one's final resting place. Now it was good, it was even comforting to know that they were leaving nothing of him behind. Their thoughts and memories need never be drawn back to that place; never.

Just before their departure she saw the urn containing the ashes being put furtively into the back of his car by Mr Beallby. She guessed that he would scatter them in a field adjoining his house in Surrey. Another reason to feel grateful to him.

'I shall be coming to see you quite soon,' he told her as they stood on the steps of the house in South Kensington after Mrs Tronsett, red-eyed, had gone indoors.

'Whenever you like, of course.'

He took out his little diary and turned its pages. She knew very well how much she would be in his thoughts and how much she would look to him for the support and counsel she could rely upon him to give her, whenever needed.

'Next week, shall we say? What about Thursday at five. Would that suit you?'

'Perfectly. I have no engagements at all. I shall have my hands full here.'

'As you probably know very well,' he said, putting the little book back into his pocket again, 'I always think of you as a most unusual young woman, as I used to think of you as a most unusual child. I think it more than ever now, if possible.'

Touched by this, she put an affectionate hand on his arm.

'Is it because I haven't shed tears? You don't know how hard it's been not to. But it was all so *merciful*, Uncle Hugh. All of it. My going into his room with a cup of tea and finding him like that, with his head on his arms. What could have been better for him?'

But he saw now that tears had suddenly flooded those remarkably clear grey eyes and he looked quickly away, giving her time to whisk a handkerchief out of her bag and use it.

'I know. Well, we'll talk again on Thursday. I shall have a good deal to say, so please keep plenty of time for me.'

'Couldn't you stay on and have dinner with us – I mean, with me?'

'I think I ought to get back to Charlotte. I'll warn her that I'll be late.'

'There's a bottle of your favourite "Speaker" in the

house,' she told him. 'Father always kept it on hand, as you know. How lucky for me, now more than ever before, that you were his lawyer as well as his friend.'

'I tend to think of it the other way round,' he said, and gave her a discreetly tender look as he turned away to get back into his car.

She waved him a goodbye and pushed open the front door that Mrs Tronsett had purposely not quite closed. The building – two ugly houses converted into flats – had a small rumbling lift which she very rarely used, preferring to run up and down the two short flights of stairs that led to their door. They had lived there ever since the house where she was born had been sold, soon after her mother's death. She had died at the age of thirty-two of a rare kidney disease, leaving a desolate man already nearing middle-age and a three-year-old daughter. Very soon after that, Mrs Tronsett, lonely and bereaved herself since the death of her farmer husband, came to them and offered to stay for as long as she was wanted. As she went up the stairs, Sibyl knew how much their old friend and helper must be in need of comfort. She would ask her to make tea for them both, and they would drink it together and talk. She passed by the door of her father's room knowing that she could not go into it yet. Tomorrow would be time enough. Today she could not have borne the sight of that empty chair, the desk with a writing-pad still open upon it, the pad on which his head had lain and on which were the last words he had written – 'There is little more I can say on the subject of "phenomenalism" in this short article' – and the empty, empty room where his absence would be a soundless shout of pain; her own pain, not his.

Later on she would get into bed with a book she had borrowed from the London Library a few days before his death and perhaps fall asleep over it and not bother about dinner unless Mrs Tronsett insisted on bringing her a bowl of soup. And so the day would end, and tomorrow she would have to begin learning how to live

without him. She felt herself to be enormously surrounded now by a ring of empty space, with friends and
acquaintances – though not a great many – standing well
back on the far edges of it, ready to come forward at a
word or a gesture, which she might or perhaps might not,
at least for a period of time, feel inclined to give.

Aloneness might quite possibly become too great a
threat to her enjoyment of living but that she would
discover before long. There was plenty of time. Like
most young women of the present day she looked
younger than her age, and might have been taken for no
more than twenty. She supposed she would fall in love
sooner or later, there seemed no reason why she should
be an exception to the general rule, but she doubted very
much that it would be with any of the men she knew,
though there had been more than one to whom she had
been briefly but strongly attracted, even to the point
of an intimacy that she felt to be timely and a part of her
education and which she was prepared to find enjoyable,
and did. But it had stopped there. It was a physical
attraction, not at all a mental one and so was of no
permanent value to her. In fact she was not ready for
anything permanent. Unlike most of today's daughters
she had been quite willing to discuss these matters with
her father, whose understanding had never yet failed
her.

'All I ask of you,' he had said, 'is that you never consider yourself in any way tied to me. When you want to
marry or make any other arrangement that may please
you, I'll find consolation in the thought that you are
happy. Or let us say happier. You are free to leave me at
any time, without compunction or regrets.'

'Of course. I've always known that. But I've no urge at
present to take myself off. You'll have me with you for a
long time yet.'

'You won't even consider George Gawthorne as a
husband?'

'Not even George, though I like him the best of all.'

'So do I. But if you are somewhat half-hearted that settles it.'

'More than somewhat,' she had replied.

It was just after this conversation that she had picked up a large photograph of herself that he always kept on his desk. She had written across a corner of it, 'Your loving Sibyl,' and underneath had added the words, half teasingly, 'Does what is known exist independently of being known?'.

As she put it back into its place she said, 'How silly of me to write that.'

'It wasn't silly at all. The answer being that if nothing in the universe exists independently of being known, you are the great exception to the rule.'

She lightly kissed the top of his head before leaving the room.

She was now taking two weeks' leave from her work at the Victoria and Albert Museum. After graduating from Ockenden School, to which her father, always liberal with his barely adequate income where her good was concerned, had sent her, she went on to Cambridge with a scholarship and there won herself a degree in Litterae Humaniores. She enjoyed her days at the Museum and sometimes if an older and better known speaker failed them she was ready and competent to give one of the afternoon lectures on Medieval Art, which she had made one of her subjects. She hoped that if she were forced to give up their three-bedroomed flat as being too expensive she could find somewhere to live in the same neighbourhood, perhaps even a little basement flat, but all this she would in due course learn from Mr Beallby.

She went to bed early the night of the funeral and had just opened her book, after pleasing Mrs Tronsett by drinking to the last drop the bowl of soup she had brought in to her, when the telephone rang beside the bed. She took up the receiver guessing that it would be her old friends Gerda and Lionel Hardwick wanting to talk to her.

This was so, and in answer to their questions she said the funeral had been just as her father would have wished it to be, and that she was all right and had gone to bed early to rest and read. They were much concerned about her all the same and took turns in trying to persuade her to come to them in Essex for the weekend, but she said she had far too much to do, though she thanked them warmly for their loving sympathy. In two or three weeks, she said, she hoped they'd ask her again.

Then George Gawthorne rang up to ask if he could be of help in any way.

'I thought of coming tomorrow about six if you would be in,' he said, his voice full of concern. 'I can't bear to think of you there all alone.'

'But I'm not alone, dear George. I have Mrs Tronsett, so I'm very lucky. Come later on, if you will. What about Tuesday week at six? I have a great deal of work to do, as you can imagine, though I expect I'll get through it somehow. And thank you for your most understanding letter.'

'All right then, Tuesday week, the sixteenth. I'm putting it in my book now. But you must come out to dinner with me afterwards. Some quiet place.' And before she had time to refuse or argue he said, 'Bless you my darling girl, and sleep well.'

She hung up the telephone quickly, feeling that it was not the moment for endearments. She was not *his* 'darling girl' and she felt it was unlikely that she ever would be.

The next morning as she was reading the papers at about half-past eight, a small breakfast tray on her knees – Mrs Tronsett had insisted on bringing it in to her – Mr Beallby rang up.

'What did you think of the obituaries?' he asked.

'I don't see how they could have been better,' she answered, and she was glad he couldn't see the tears on her cheeks. 'Of the two most important ones I liked Martindale's the best. Within the limits of the space allowed him I thought he said everything that most wanted saying. It moved me so much I . . .'

'I know, I know. I can hear it in your voice. Did you sleep all right last night?'

'Well enough to feel rested this morning. But I want to tell you a curious thing that happened to me. Just at midnight – no, no, I'll tell you when you come on Thursday.'

She rang him up the following morning to tell him that she had agreed to grant interviews to two reporters the following day, one at eleven in the morning, the other at twelve, and had she done right?

When she told him which papers they were representing he said, 'Yes, that's all right and I was expecting it, but would you like someone to be with you when they come? I'm completely tied up myself but I could send Lewis Petersen if that would help.'

She thanked him but said she felt confident she could deal with them on her own. 'I'm sure,' she said, 'that they'll ask me all the right questions.'

'It is much to be hoped,' he replied, but there seemed to her to be a trace of concern in the way he said it.

CHAPTER II

The Tale

On Thursday she looked forward to his coming with impatience. There was much to tell him and much to be learnt from him. She waited for the dry, intelligent, good little man in his black jacket and striped trousers as if he were a lover who had been too long afield. There was a kind of ceremony in the way she put out the glasses; the whisky, the jug of water and for herself some dry sherry, for she felt that a gin-and-something would be inappropriate, hinting as it would of parties, of gaieties, actual or simulated.

She had been dealing every day since the funeral with her father's clothes and small possessions, putting aside some of them to give to his few friends as souvenirs that they might like to have – a little Greek bronze bowl that he used as an ashtray – he only smoked a pipe – for his friend Professor Kindler, a Keats first edition for Edmund Prinsepp and other such reminders for those he had known well and liked. The disposing of his clothes and especially of his ties which she had always bought for him, gave her a sharp and special pain and she was thankful when it was done. She then set to work on his papers, most of which she knew she ought to sort out and set aside for his future biographer. She would have been glad of help there, but felt there was no one she could call upon. Her father had meant to begin the tidying up and sorting out of his papers and letters himself, and she now regretted that she had dissuaded him, hating to see him embark on a task that she felt would be more appropriate at a future time when he had less work to do and was nearer to old age and possibly retirement, though he scoffed at the idea of the latter.

She looked about her at the living-room and saw it

with altered eyes. For years she had accepted it quite uncritically, scarcely aware of its shabbiness. Now it was all too plain that new curtains were badly needed, that a rug much mended by herself was beyond further repair, and that the wall-paper which she had chosen twelve years earlier was badly faded. The windows looked out on houses quite as unlovely as their own, though some had newly painted doors in bright colours which made the fronts look still more drab. Only her father's room – workroom and bedroom combined – looked out on a corner of the unbeautiful square, on a tree or two and some grass much played on by children. These last he both liked to see from his big writing-table in the window and also, in summer when the window was open, to hear.

Their great, their irresistible extravagance had always been going abroad. Looking back she could not remember a single holiday from school or university when the two of them had not gone somewhere together, travelling by boat and train – he had dearly loved trains – and staying at the cheapest and simplest of hotels. Of late the upward leap in prices had dismayed them, but still they went. The urge was too strong for them. The previous year they had abandoned Europe for America, for her father was to lecture at Princeton, Harvard, Amherst and Williams. They had flown over, a new experience for them both – and had returned by boat. An eye-opening trip for her, unlike any other. Her father had been twice before, but these earlier journeys had not been during her holidays, so she had been unable to join him. They had promised themselves to go back again next year; the universities were welcoming, the lectures profitable and they made congenial new friends. It was a heavy sadness to think that there would be no more such journeys.

She heard the bell and went to the front door. Mr Beallby kissed her proffered cheek, put his hat on the hall table and his rolled umbrella into the umbrella stand beside her father's, and followed her into the living-room. After a second's hesitation which was the more noticeable because of the usual briskness and purposefulness of his movements, he sat down in her father's chair as she had hoped he would. That was good. So far no one had sat in it since his death; even the two reporters when they came had avoided it.

She asked him to pour out a drink for himself and filled her own glass with dry sherry.

'First of all,' he said, and she thought how like him to have remembered, 'what was it you started to tell me on the telephone and then changed your mind so suddenly?'

'Oh, that was an odd thing. A very odd thing. I was in two minds about telling you at all, but now I think I would like to, though I couldn't possibly tell anyone else. It was on the night of the funeral. I fell asleep and then, just at midnight – I knew it was, because I looked at my bedside clock – I seemed to hear my father's voice calling to me. I heard "Sibyl! Sibyl!" It seemed to come from a long distance, as if out of a tunnel. But it was perfectly distinct and spoke directly into my ear. And it was absolutely *his* voice.'

He sat looking at her with no more expression on his round, clean-shaven face – only distinguished from many similar faces by a special intelligence and kindness – than if she had told him of some quite ordinary occurrence. He was the same age as her father, but owing to his stocky build and the greater amount of flesh on his bones, looked younger. It was rarely indeed that he showed his feelings, and now, whatever his feelings may have been, he preferred not to disclose them.

After a silence he said, 'Yes, I've heard of that happening before. More than once, in fact, in the same circumstances and more or less in the same way.'

'It made me feel,' she went on, 'that he was very near and was calling out to me as if soon he might not be able to reach me. There was a sort of urgency. I think it was the urgency that I was most conscious of.'

Now it had been told, that startling little experience for

which there seemed to her no possible explanation. The voice had echoed in her head for several days as she went about her work, the tones of it growing fainter, less easy to bring back, and now they had gone, altogether gone. Mr Beallby, who had not been in agreement with many of her father's views, being of a far more conventional way of thinking and never even attempting to read his friend's philosophical works, merely nodded his head. When he spoke again it was on a wholly different matter and she guessed that he did not choose to make further comments on what she had told him.

He then asked, 'Has Professor Kindler rung you up yet to know when it will be convenient for you to see him? He rang me yesterday. I think you know what he wants to see you about.'

'Yes, I do of course. So far I've only had a kind letter of condolence from him, which I've answered. He'll want to discuss father's biography. He's always felt that he should be the one to write it, if he outlived him. Well, I think he should be the one. Do you agree?'

'Entirely. But there is the question of timing, isn't there?'

'There is indeed. Father would have hated any biography of himself to appear until ten years or so after his death.'

'He could begin working on it,' Mr Beallby said.

'I suppose he could, but not until I've had time to go through the papers and diaries. I know he has all father's published works, but it'll be the diaries he'll want to get his hands on, even though they only date from about the time I was born.'

'That is so,' he agreed. 'But before I begin to tell you what I've come especially to tell you, I want to hear how those interviews went.'

'Oh, well enough, I think. Both of the interviewers made things as easy for me as they could. The first, a Mr Lessingford, was sympathetic and intelligent. By "sympathetic" I mean of course "*simpatico*". I wouldn't have welcomed the other sort. He was something of a classical scholar too. I tried to keep myself out of it entirely, but he'd done his home-work and he'd learnt that I'd specialized in Latin and Greek, though I told him it was only my Greek that I took pride in, as anybody can learn Latin. He asked me one question that surprised me, and in a sort of way amused me, it seemed such an unlikely question. He asked if it would be acceptable to me if he made some reference to my father's first marriage. When I told him he'd only been married once, when he was nearing forty and then all too briefly, he seemed a trifle embarrassed and said he couldn't remember how or when he'd got the impression that there'd been an earlier marriage.'

'I see,' said Mr Beallby, and it seemed to her that he saw more in it than she had seen. 'Well, now tell me about the other one.'

'It was a woman the second time, a Miss Hamble, like the river, and she talked rather like one, but we got on all right and she took no notes at all. We just talked.'

'If any others ask you for interviews,' he said, 'I think I would advise you to refuse.'

'I shall,' she agreed.

He drank a little whisky and then asked, 'Tell me about Mrs Tronsett. Does she want to stay on with you?'

'Yes, poor dear. She has nowhere else to go. She's got an older sister in some sort of home, and she dreads it for herself. Her daughter doesn't seem disposed to help her in any way at all. So she looks on this as her home and refuses to let me pay her the sort of wages that are usually paid nowadays. She'll only take money for incidentals, and clothes when she needs them, and of course her food. Shall I be able to keep her with me? I hope so. We're very fond of each other and I would miss her terribly.'

'I see no reason why you shouldn't. There's really nothing for you to worry about. Everything is simple and straightforward. With what you earn – or even perhaps without it – and with what your father has been able to leave you, after death duties are paid of course – you could perfectly well go on living here if that is what you'd like to do. Your father acquired this flat very cheaply twenty-three years ago with a ninety-nine year lease. As time goes on it will become a more and more valuable property. I would strongly advise you to keep it.'

'Oh, thank you!' she said, as if he had made her a handsome gift, and indeed she was deeply pleased to hear such an unequivocal statement of the facts. 'I'd like so much to keep it. It's the only home I've ever known. And now what else have you to tell me? I've been feeling ever since you came that there *was* something else. You seem to me like a man carrying an awkward sort of burden that he'd be glad to get off his back. Am I right?'

She smiled at him as she said it, but it was true. She had noticed, in spite of his intention to be, or appear to be, his usual self, that there was a quite unusual nervousness and uncertainty in his manner, and had been from the first. After she put her question to him he was silent for a few seconds, during which it seemed to her as though he were gathering himself up mentally to perform some task he was far from liking; that he was a little like a horse checking before an unusually high jump, or, it absurdly occurred to her, like a dog warily approaching a dish he fears may be too hot. He had spent most of his life talking confidentially to clients about wills, investments, private problems and disasters, or merely trying to keep them out of waters that were too deep or perhaps too shallow for them. It seemed to her now as if he felt he was in deep waters himself, and was unsure of his ability to get safely to shore. And at that moment she knew without any doubt at all that she was about to hear something of very special import for her. When he had said earlier, 'Before I begin to tell you what I've come to tell you' he wasn't referring to her simple financial affairs, but to something quite different.

Perception is clearer, sharper, more brilliant than knowledge; it has a harder, more revealing light, and she perceived that she was about to learn something not only unforeseen but also perhaps deeply disturbing.

'Well then, what I've really come to talk to you about today,' he began, 'or rather to *tell* you, has nothing whatever to do with the present. It is entirely concerned with the past, with what occurred before you, my dear Sibyl, were even thought of. Over and over again – times without number – I have begged – implored your father to tell you what I am going to tell you now. So you see you were right in your guess.'

She saw his hand move quickly towards his glass, as if he were feeling the need of some re-enforcement, but it was as quickly withdrawn. She waited.

'Alas, I begged and implored in vain. He could never bring himself to do it. I cannot blame him. As you know better than anyone else he was an extremely reticent and sensitive man. Hyper-sensitive. It would have been an ordeal so painful to him that he was truly unable to face it. He *could* not. In short, Sibyl my dear, that young reporter's impression was correct. Your father *was* married before, and you are the only child of his second marriage.'

Now his hand went all the way to his glass and he took a quick drink and put it down. And he put it down with a quite audible emphasis as if to say, 'And that, thanks be to heaven, is at last that.'

He knew of course as well as if it had happened to himself what a shock he had dealt her, for under his formal and commonplace exterior he was a man of delicate intuitions and perceptions. Whatever she might have apprehended from his opening words, she could not possibly have prepared herself for this. The familiar past – her past – was about to be shattered in much the same way as a nicely put-together picture-puzzle can be shattered at the touch of a hand, and this simile, dating from her childhood, was the one that came immediately to her mind.

'Will you please go on?' she said, and only her lips moved. He thought she was keeping her self-control, as he had guessed she would, quite magnificently, but was as tense as if she were performing a difficult balancing feat on a tight-rope.

'I am about to tell you the whole story, from its beginning to its end. It is, I warn you, a tragic story and no one now knows the whole truth about it except myself. There are a few people living who may know most of it, though there are none at all, so far as I know, living in England.

'This first marriage of your father's ended in a disaster that was very nearly the death of him. Your mother's early death was tragic enough, heaven knows, but that was a human tragedy such as may come to any of us. After that earlier horror he did not want to go on living, he longed for oblivion. But he was no coward and by a great effort of will he took up his broken life and made of it what you and I know he made. He had to begin again from the beginning and somehow to put the past – his private past – behind him, to obliterate it so far as he could. He succeeded better than I dared to hope, but speak of it he would not. Even to me he never referred to it unless something forced him to do so.

'Now before I go any further I want to say this, and to say it and stress it with all the emphasis I can. Your father loved you with a total love – as he had loved your dear mother – as indeed he had loved, as you will hear, the girl he first married, until both love and trust were destroyed. He would have told you what I am telling you now if he could. But to bring it all back again, to re-create it and live through once more in the telling what happened on a terrible evening nearly thirty years ago, he could not. That you must understand and accept. Each day that he lived from that time onwards added one more layer of forgetfulness, like earth spread spadeful after painful spadeful on some grave that has to be covered over and forgotten. And thanks to our friendship – and I would call it in a way a curious friendship because no two men could have been more unlike and I had none of his brilliance – I was able to watch over this difficult feat and even, I'm thankful to say, to help him.'

She was listening as if she had one faculty only – that of hearing.

'Well then, my dear child, here is the story, the tragic story. Your father met a young girl when he was in his third year at Oxford, fell in love with her and later married her. When he first saw her she was not yet eighteen. Her name was Angela Kellerman. The Kellerman family came originally from Frankfurt, in the eighteen sixties, I believe. They lived near Abingdon, in Oxfordshire, in a modest house, and the father was in the wine-trade, a member in fact of a quite well-known firm of wine importers. She was their only child, an elder brother having been killed in a flying accident a few years earlier.

'She was an extremely pretty girl – I think one could have called her really beautiful – and she was well aware of her charms and of her effect on young men, undergraduates and others. At the time she and your father met – it was at one of those May-time balls at the university – I had just been articled to a firm of solicitors in the City. As I needn't remind you, the friendship between your father and myself went back to the days when we were at school together, and it deepened but never altered. From time to time in those far-off days he would come up to London and we would dine and go to a play or we'd take a couple of girls out and dance somewhere. Even I danced in those days. My Charlotte was very often one of the four. Then came a night – it is very clearly fixed in my memory – when he brought Angela with him, and that was my first meeting with her though he'd talked of her a great deal. He was then twenty-three and as you know was specializing in Philosophy and

Mathematics. At that time he was one of Bertrand Russell's most ardent disciples, though much later on he diverged from his path for a variety of reasons that he used to try, quite unsuccessfully, to explain to me.

'But young though he was, he was already looked upon as an outstanding scholar, certain to have a brilliant career. Angela, it didn't take me long to discover, possessed a superficial cleverness, or perhaps I should call it, *brightness*. Cleverness, one might say, without real intelligence. Certainly she was highly attractive and there was charm in her vivacity, but I did not take to her, then or ever. In fact I neither liked nor trusted her, though I was careful not to let your father guess what my feelings about her were. He was very happy and now deeply in love, and I wouldn't let slip a word that might damage our friendship.

'As for her, she was of course much attracted by his distinguished looks and flattered by the attentions of someone so highly thought of. Her parents – an uninteresting couple – were no doubt relieved when she told them, some time later, that she was in love with and intended to marry such an eligible young man.

'Your grandfather, as I need hardly tell you, had then been dead for some years, and had settled a useful though modest annuity upon your father. Then your grandmother re-married and went to Canada to live. It was not an easy decision for her to make as it meant leaving her son during his first year at the university. However, he found comfortable lodgings in Oxford and I don't think he missed her too badly when she died of pneumonia in Ottawa. So your father had very little home life indeed, and he longed for a home of his own. It was decided that he and Angela should be married the following spring and that in the meantime she would go to Paris to a sort of young ladies' academy or finishing school with an Irish friend whose name I forget, and in fact don't wish to remember. Now is there anything you would like to ask me at this point?'

She had not moved since he began his story but sat stiffly upright, her eyes fixed unseeingly upon him. It was the far-away past she was seeing, making her own pictures out of what she heard, private pictures thrown upon the highly receptive screen of her imagination. 'No,' she answered. 'I only want you to go on. After the first shock, and it was a very great shock, I'm slowly coming to terms with what I'm hearing. Now I'm even beginning to have the feeling of *déjà vu*.'

He gave her one of his looks of appreciation and affection. He was a part of her life as she, through her father, was a part of his, and they understood each other. She guessed that in one of the infinite ways there are of loving, Mr Beallby loved her, was possibly even in love with her, such lines not being easy to draw. It had never mattered one way or the other, but it no doubt had its private and perhaps cherished place in his life.

'Very well. I'll go on now to the year your father graduated, before he was twenty-five. He had won a First in both his subjects, and you must know how hard he had worked on them. You also know that as soon as he graduated, "*summa cum laude*" as they say in America, he was offered the post of lecturer at his own College. Nothing could have pleased him more. Occasionally, when opportunity offered, he would go to Paris to see Angela, and more than once I joined them there. And what fun it was in those days! One could enjoy all the delights of a foreign city – *the* foreign city – so very cheaply. Also I was lucky enough to be acquainted with a French family who were very kind to me, and I sometimes stayed with them. I'd made friends with their son, a lighthearted somewhat too extrovert young man who thought me too dull and staid for words – later on, alas! he was killed in the war – and he used to insist on taking me, as a part of my education, to night-clubs, some quite respectable, some rather less so. At one of the latter sort I saw one night to my great astonishment Angela and her Irish friend with two men, considerably older than they

were – in their mid-thirties, I would have guessed. As
their table was quite near ours I went of course to speak
to them and was – after a fashion – introduced. I got the
impression that Angela was anything but pleased to see
me. One of the men, my friend told me, was a Comte
So-and-So – I won't mention his name, which is well
known. When I rejoined him at our table I found he
was greatly and genuinely shocked at seeing two such
very young girls in such a place and in such company
unchaperoned – for in those days chaperones – at least
for girls of good family – were not yet things of the past.
Or at any rate, not in France. He took particular pains to
warn me about the Count, who, it appeared, was well
known for his gallantries. When I told him the two girls
were at a certain finishing school he shrugged his shoulders and said it had the reputation of being very lax.

'Not long after, he wrote to me and told me he'd seen
the same two girls in the same night-club with the same
two men, and he urged me to warn my friend, the fiancé
of the very lovely one, of what was going on. But this I
felt I could not do, nor did I place any great importance
on what he said. Permissiveness began, I suppose, in
those between-war years, and I felt that Angela was only
one of the many who wanted to make the most of such
freedom as they could get.

'Then, to your father's great joy, Angela decided to
come home sooner than had been arranged, saying that
she was tired of Paris, tired of the finishing school and so
homesick that she could bear it no longer. She had
changed her mind, she said, about wanting a big
expensive wedding with bridesmaids and all the rest of it.
She thought it would be much better and less costly to be
married quietly, and earlier than had been planned. She
said she felt sure your father would be pleased. Nothing
could have suited him better, of course. If he could have
had his way, they would have gone before a registrar and
been married without fuss or trouble, but this would have
deeply distressed Angela's parents. So they were married

at the local church with only the family and a few friends present. I acted as best man. The young couple then went off to Cabourg in Normandy for a brief honeymoon. On their return they learnt that Angela's mother had found a suitable house for them only about ten miles from Oxford. It turned out to be just what they wanted. Your father's happiness fairly shone out of his eyes. It was a joy to see.

'All went very well at first and I was hopeful that the marriage was not going to be the mistake I had feared it might be. Then, when they were well settled in their new house and I went to dine with them, Angela complained bitterly – though not of course in your father's hearing – of the dullness of the life, the total monotony, in fact, that she now foresaw for herself. I asked her what on earth she'd expected when she married a young don devoted to his work. She told me that she would never meet anybody now but students and other dons, and so far the ones she had met made her want to scream with boredom. I reminded her that she'd looked forward to having time to read and study. Her answer was that there'd be plenty of time for that when she was old.

'I went away saddened and disturbed. She had help in the house – her parents saw to that – and I suppose had time on her hands that she didn't know what to do with. Then, soon after this she took up riding, and this she immensely enjoyed. She met people in the neighbourhood who kept horses and she joined them on their rides, much to your father's relief. In fact he got her to promise that she would never go riding alone.

'Well, then, my dear, one day your father rang me up with jubilation in his voice to tell me that Angela was expecting a baby in the new year. You can imagine my relief and satisfaction. Nothing else, I felt, could make that marriage genuinely successful. It seemed to me the answer to everything. Not that your father had ever even hinted to me that he was anything but entirely happy – his love and loyalty were too complete for that –

but, well, I knew him as no one else did, and I could feel the anxiety beneath the surface.'

At this point Sibyl said, very quietly, 'I've been waiting for this. I felt it was on the cards. I know how difficult all this must be for you, poor Uncle Hugh, but please don't be sorry for me. What I feel now is a sort of numbness, almost a suspension of belief. Are you quite sure you're not inventing it all?'

He responded with a sad little smile and the words, 'How I wish that were true! Well, there is much more, my dear, so be as patient with me as you can. At first I hoped, of course, that this coming event would bring about a change in Angela and perhaps cure her restlessness and dissatisfaction, but my hopes were ill-founded. I went to stay with them not long after and found her nervous, irritable and inclined to be quarrelsome. Also she was anything but pleased by my congratulations and good wishes. Your father bore her moods with sympathy and understanding, and I never admired him more. At one point he went down to the cellar to bring up a bottle of wine and Angela took the opportunity to tell me that the very thought of having a child terrified her. "If he'd let me have an abortion," she said, "I'd have it thankfully. I simply don't feel as if I could go through with it." I remember saying to her that if she needed reassurance surely her doctor could give it to her, whereupon she said that she had no use for their doctor, he was just an old fuddy-duddy who seemed to think that all women should enjoy having babies. What was more, he was urging her to give up riding in the near future. "But I won't give it up until I'm absolutely forced to," she told me. "It's the one thing I enjoy." And I could see that she meant every word of it.

'Well, one day shortly before Christmas, she had an accident. She'd had to give up riding and a friend had lent her a pony and pony-cart so that she could get about. On that day, it appeared, the pony had been frightened by a large dog and had bolted, out of control. The cart went over the root of a tree in a lane and she was thrown out into the brambles. She came home limping and leading the pony, and she was bruised and bleeding. She was put to bed at once by the young woman who acted as daily help, and the doctor was sent for. The result of the accident was a premature birth. Your father's anxiety was terrible and as soon as I heard about it I came and stayed at a nearby inn, just in case I could be of some help and comfort to him. But when the child was born – it was a seven-months child – our worst fears were forgotten. It was a perfectly normal baby boy, though his size was below the average. However, he very soon began to put on weight, and when he tipped the scales at eight and then eight and a half pounds, there was no further cause for worry. Angela seemed for the first time really contented and happy. Even, one might have said, triumphant. The baby was soon baptized and named Felix Carl, after Angela's father.'

It was in Sibyl's mind to ask, 'But wasn't my father consulted?' but was glad she had not because Mr Beallby went on, 'Your father would have liked him to be named Edward or James or Robert, but was overruled. The most important thing was that Angela was delighted with her little son and he soon became the pivot about which her life revolved. I used to think that a less loving and unselfish man than your father might have resented her absorption in the boy, but at first he welcomed it. I say "at first" because soon the spoiling began. His mother could refuse the child nothing and the foolish grandparents behaved as if never before had a young woman given birth to a male child. Nothing was too good for him and nothing your father could do or say could lessen the pampering that went on. Angela's maternal instincts – if she ever really had any – now seemed fully satisfied and she vowed that never again would she go through the horrors of giving birth. But when Felix was four she was pregnant again, though I am sure she did everything she could to prevent it. However, this time, bitterly resentful though she was, all went smoothly. She even gave up riding some months before the expected time of the birth. To your father's immense delight, it was a girl. She was named Felicia.'

He half expected that, at this point, Sibyl would speak, but she did not, nor did the deeply tranced look on her face alter. He therefore went on.

'From the very beginning this second arrival seemed to belong to him and not to the mother, whose affections were entirely concentrated on her son. She wanted as little to do with Felicia as possible and never even pretended to be fond of her. There was a very capable young nursemaid named Ellen in the house at this time – in fact she was cook as well as nursemaid – and between this young girl and your father, Felicia lacked for nothing in the way of affection. I doubt that as she grew older she was even aware of her mother's indifference to her. It was her father – and Ellen – that she loved. She was a most delightful little creature with an enchanting gaiety and sense of fun. It was a joy to see father and daughter together, and they were together at every possible moment.'

At this pause Sibyl spoke. 'So,' she said, and managed a wry little smile, 'I was only second best when I came along, years later.'

His reply was, 'I don't think I need answer that, need I? I'll go straight on. Angela said to me once with that unpleasing frankness of hers – frankness is hardly a virtue, I find, when it pertains to people one heartily dislikes – "I never wanted a daughter. I only like boys. It suits me perfectly to see her father so devoted to her."

'When Felix was old enough to go away to school, Angela used to send him so many presents of food and other things that the headmaster was forced to put a stop to it and threatened that if it continued he would be obliged to insist that the boy be removed to some other school. It wasn't surprising that the relations between husband and wife grew more and more difficult, for in spite of your father's patience and sweet temper there were disagreements, invariably caused by Angela, which were apt to be embarrassing for others who were present, however much your father strove to avoid them. As for the boy, when he came home for the holidays he showed himself to be all too ready to tease and upset his little sister. Perhaps jealousy may have played its part; he must have realized how much closer Felicia was to his father than he was himself. It was a difficult situation and full of pitfalls, though in spite of it all, your father's forebearance and devotion never seemed to falter. Never, right to the end, when Angela left him for ever. I marvelled at it, I still do.

'But in spite of all he tried to do to conciliate her, the situation was growing progressively worse. I rarely went there now, feeling that my presence did little good and perhaps only made things more difficult. By this time, of course, Angela had many friends of her own in the neighbourhood and she refused any longer to meet anyone connected with the university. She was the most entirely selfish human being I have ever known. That did not prevent many people from finding her exceedingly attractive, as indeed she was. Her beauty – though it was never a beauty that had charm for me – increased with maturity. She was undoubtedly very lovely. She liked to dress in bright colours and was always extremely decorative.'

He paused there and finished what was left in his glass. Sybil made a movement to fill it for him, but he held up his hand.

'No, no, my dear, thank you. At any rate, not yet. I must give my whole attention to the real climax of the story, the hideous tragedy that is now to come. I hate to tell you of it, I hate to speak of it, but of course I must.

'Just before Christmas when Felicia was five – nearly six – years old I was persuaded by both Angela and your father to spend a few days with them. I had of course every intention of spending Christmas as usual with

Charlotte, to whom I had been married for half a dozen years, but it was arranged that I should stay with them from December twentieth to the twenty-third. Charlotte would never accept an invitation to go there, she disliked Angela too much, and besides, the spare bedroom was hardly large enough for two.

'Felix of course was already home from school when I arrived and I thought him more than ever arrogant and self-willed. He behaved in fact in a way that made me want to put him across a stool and give him a good birching. I well remember being birched myself at school on two occasions, the first when I fully deserved it, the second time when I thought I didn't, but painful though it was, I resented it not at all. It was probably good for me. I think it was Dr Johnson who approved of birching and said, "The body remembers."

'Now we come to the night of the twenty-third. Angela and your father were going out to dinner with some of Angela's friends and on their way they were to drop me at the railway station so that I could make my own way home. I didn't possess a car in those days. While his parents were upstairs dressing to go out – the children had already had their supper – Felix discovered where some of his Christmas presents were hidden and brought them into the playroom where I was reading to Felicia. I ought to explain that the playroom was on the upper floor of a small annex added on to the house – which was square and Georgian – in Victorian times, and underneath the playroom was your father's study.

'In spite of my remonstrances, Felix began at once to open his presents. The first he picked up was a parcel that greatly intrigued him because on opening it he found inside it another parcel, and inside that still another. I could only have put a stop to this by taking it away from him by force, which I didn't feel inclined to do. The last parcel he came to he found to be a small box lined with velvet and containing a Roman coin. He had been collecting coins for some time and this was a present from his grandparents. At this moment Angela and your father came in ready to go out and well muffled up, for it was a very cold night. Your father at once told Felix to take his presents back where he'd found them, but Angela of course said it didn't matter in the least, she had plenty of things to surprise him with on Christmas day. Your father gave me a look which I can still remember.

'Show me what you found in that little box, darling,' Angela said, or something of the sort, and Felix at once proudly showed the coin to his mother and to me. "It belongs to the Trajan period," he said. "It must date from about 110." He could always surprise me by his intelligence. Then Felicia asked to see it too, whereupon Felix said, most unkindly, even rudely, "You're only a baby, you wouldn't know what it was." Her face puckered up, as if she were about to cry, but her father opened his arms to her and she ran into them to be lifted up and kissed.

'Angela presently said it was time for us to go. My hat and coat and suitcase, I remember, were down in the hall by the front door. She kissed Felix goodnight and your father and I gave goodnight kisses to Felicia, who seemed to have forgotten her hurt feelings, but I noticed that she got no kiss from her mother at all, merely a warning that she must go to bed in fifteen minutes, as soon as Ellen came for her, but Felix was told that he could stay up until nine o'clock, if he wanted to. She also told him that if the room got too cold he had better ask Ellen to put more wood on the fire. It was a big open fireplace with a nursery screen in front of it. You see how vividly I remember it all, every detail, almost every word.'

He passed a hand over his face then in a tired way and Sibyl got to her feet saying, 'It's time I filled up your glass again, and I'll have some more sherry. I don't know what I'm going to hear next, but I'm already dreading it. Yes, dreading it.'

He thanked her when she brought his glass and then took up the story again.

'None of us of course knew this until later, but soon after we had gone Ellen was rung up by a friend in the village and told that her mother had suddenly been taken seriously ill. She was urged to come at once. The poor girl was torn between two duties but she decided that, after all, Felix, who was ten, was quite old enough to be left in charge of the house. So she took Felicia to her own little room and put her to bed, tucking her in for the night. A passageway connected the addition to the main part of the house, and led out from your father's study into the main hall and the main staircase. There was always a bell on the child's bedside table, I remember, which she could ring if she wanted anybody. After a goodnight kiss, Ellen hurried off to the village on her bicycle, hoping to be back within an hour or two, and feeling, poor girl, that she had done what was right and proper.

'Now what follows from here on we know only through Angela, who later wrote me a very long letter. To me, let me repeat, not to your father. It has often puzzled me why she wrote such a detailed account of it all, but I had often in the past been her unwilling confidant, and in her way I suppose she liked me. And there is another reason, and I am sure it is the real one. She didn't want me to think too badly of her son. So she told me, and, I think, quite accurately, what Felix had told her when she asked him for an account of what exactly had happened on that night. This is the gist of it. I have read the letter many times and almost know it by heart. I still have it.

'As soon as Ellen had gone, Felix discovered that his Roman coin was missing. His recollection was that he had put it back on the table beside, or perhaps into, its box while he was saying goodnight to us and being kissed by his mother. He looked for it in the box, on the table, on the floor, even behind the sofa cushions, but couldn't find it anywhere. Then it occurred to him that perhaps Felicia, to pay him back for his rudeness to her and his refusal to let her see it, had hidden it somewhere. He went to her nursery, found her in bed but still awake, and asked her if she knew where his coin was. She said yes, she had hidden it just for fun, so he made her get up and come to the playroom in her nightdress to show him where it was. All this, I think, rang quite true. Delighted by the success of her trick she danced about laughing and saying, "It's a game, it's a game. You look for it and I'll tell you when you're hot or cold." He did look for it, but not finding it began to get cross with her. "You show me where it is or I'll punish you." She cried gleefully, "You're stupid. You can almost see it." Then he lost his temper entirely and said, "All right, then, I'll lock you in. If you don't show me where it is when I come back, I'll give you a good spanking." All this his mother got out of him and later, eager to put most of the blame on Felicia, passed on to me.

'Your father, mistrusting keys in the hands of children, had long ago hidden the playroom key in what he thought a safe place, in a little vase or bowl on a high shelf above the children's books. But Felix had somehow found out where it was. He got up on a chair and brought it down, put it into the outside of the door and locked it. Then for some reason he couldn't explain, he put the key in his pocket. "I don't know *why* I did it," he seems to have said again and again according to his mother's report, "I tell you I don't know *why*. I just did. That's all."

'He then went out to a tool-shed at some distance from the house where he had his own tools and a carpenter's bench and began working on a picture-frame he was making for his mother. He spent so much time there during his holidays that she had an electric heater put in, to allow him to work in comfort. He became entirely absorbed in what he was doing and had no idea at all how much time had passed while he was there, but on opening the door which he'd closed to keep out the cold, he suddenly smelt smoke. Going outside he saw smoke pouring out of the top of the playroom window, which Ellen always kept a little open for ventilation. At the same instant he heard Felicia screaming. He dropped everything, and ran into the little hall of the annex and up the stairs as fast as he could go. Felicia was still screaming and was now beating on the door and calling "Felix! Felix!" He put his hand into his trouser pocket to get the key, but it wasn't there. It simply wasn't there. It had fallen, I suppose, through one of those holes so often to be found in the trouser pockets of young boys, and there was no time to look for it. In a panic, he said, he ran downstairs again and out to the front of the annex where there was a wistaria vine that he had climbed more than once. But this time it broke and he fell, spraining or painfully twisting his ankle. Then he limped into the main part of the house and rang up the fire-brigade. It was the custom of his parents when they went out to dinner to leave the telephone number of the house they were going to beside the telephone, so he rang this number as well, and his father was called to the phone. "Get the ladder!" he cried. "For God's sake get the ladder and break the window." He ran and got one but it must have been the wrong one for it was too short or perhaps he was too short, and by this time flames and smoke were pouring out of the window which had been broken by the heat. Felicia's screams had ceased. Felix said he ran upstairs and threw himself again and again against the locked door, but of course was unable to break the lock.

'Then at last he heard the fire engines coming, their bells clanging, and only a few seconds later your father and Angela arrived. Your father of course raced up to the playroom and just as he got there, the firemen broke down the door. He pushed past them and ran straight into the room, which was an inferno of smoke and flames. His clothes caught almost at once and one of the firemen dragged him out but not before he had seen Felicia's blackened little body lying under the window, burnt beyond recognition. They rolled him in a rug to put out the flames and Angela had the sense to ring for an ambulance, which soon came. He was taken to the hospital in Bamfield, the nearest place. The burns were, thank heaven, superficial, but he had suffered his first heart attack. He longed to die. With all his heart and mind and will he tried to die. But his time was not yet.'

Then Sibyl spoke.

'So the heart attack he had when we were in Switzerland together was the second.'

'That is so, yes.' He leaned his head against the high back of the chair and, for a moment, closed his eyes. Then he seemed ready to go on again, and she knew what an ordeal this was for him.

'You've just told me,' she said, before he could speak again, 'of the death – the dreadful, pitiable death – of a little half-sister I never knew existed until now. How did it happen, that terrible fire? How could it have happened? You must have your own solution. Can you tell me what it is?'

Tired though he was he was not too tired to take note of the fact that she had claimed the child at once as someone pertaining to herself, to her own flesh and being. It passed through his mind that she must always have felt alone, the motherless daughter of a father who wanted and needed no one else, who wanted and needed no intimates. Only he himself was truly close to them both.

'I can only surmise,' he said. 'Your father could never speak of it, but I had to try to make some sort of sense of it, so at least I can surmise. Left alone, wearing only a flimsy nightdress and Felix failing to come back, she must have felt cold. Wood burns down so quickly and it was freezing out-of-doors. She must have decided, I think, to put more wood on the fire herself. Perhaps, very possibly I would think, she picked up a log and fell. She may well have pushed aside the fire-screen first rather than try to lift the log over it. She might easily have stumbled with the weight of it and fallen. Her nightdress being what is correctly called nowadays highly flammable would readily have caught fire. I think she would then have run to the window, screaming for help, and no help came. Then, I imagine, the curtains too would easily have caught fire and the whole room would soon have been in flames. It seems the only possible explanation. The annex was completely destroyed, including of course your father's study immediately below, and everything it contained. But the firemen fought on until the rest of the house was saved.

'While this was taking place, Angela's brain was working to some purpose. She acted with speed and decision and, I suppose I must admit, with some courage, incredibly cruel though it was. In spite of the smoke from the burning annex and the fire-hoses that must have been playing on the main part of the house as well, she managed to salvage as much as she could of her own clothing and some of Felix's and crammed it, together with such valuables as belonged to her and could be snatched up, into two suitcases. Then, helped by Felix who was a strong lad, they got them out to the garage and put them into her own little Morris Minor. Before leaving the house she scribbled a note to Ellen telling her where your father was and urging her to go to see him and learn what had happened. She put it, together with some money, in Ellen's bedroom where Ellen later found it intact. Then the two of them drove off into the night to her parents' home, which must have been about twenty miles away. She had disappeared long before the firemen had finished their work and the fire was completely out. It was these men, of course, who put Felicia's charred little body into a blanket and took it to the police station in Bamfield. It was all they could do.'

For a short time there was a silence that was like a little period of mourning. Then he went on.

'No one in the village seems to have known about the

fire until the next day. The cold kept people indoors, and the house was screened by trees and was some distance away. Ellen, who had had to spend the night with her mother, returned to the house about eight o'clock. It must have been a terrible shock for the poor girl. As soon as she found Angela's note she went straight off to the hospital on her bicycle. She was allowed a minute or so with your father and he managed to tell her that Felicia had died in the fire. She then telephoned to me, barely able to speak for sobbing and that was the first I heard of it all. I hired a car and went at once to see your father. I went the next day and the next and I found it hard to believe he could recover, though they assured me he would. There had not been a word from Angela. The day after Christmas, Ellen, Charlotte and I saw the vicar of Bamfield church and made arrangements for Felicia's burial as soon as possible after the inquest. When the funeral took place only Ellen and Charlotte and I and a few of the village people were the mourners. So that is where the child is buried, in a little grave with a small headstone with just the name "Felicia" on it and the dates of her birth and death. Not one word came from either Angela or the boy, and Angela had taken care to give no hint of her whereabouts – her letter had had a London postmark – or her plans, to me.

'As soon as your father was well enough to travel, Charlotte and I took him to Bournemouth and we spent a fortnight there. It helped him a great deal. Then on coming home he stayed with us – sleeping on a sofa in the living-room – at our flat in Lincoln's Inn. From there he wrote resigning from his professorship and in one way and another cutting himself off entirely from his old life. Charlotte and I saw to the sale of the house and furniture and collected the few personal things that belonged to him. He wanted above everything to leave England, at least for a time, and it wasn't long before he was offered a professorship at Toronto University. He accepted it thankfully, and what a fortunate thing it was that he did, for it was there that he met your dear mother, who had left her home in Berkshire to visit friends. All this you know.

'Well, to go back to that dreadful time I've been so long in telling you about. It won't surprise you to hear, I think, that your father never saw either Angela or Felix again. Never. As soon as it was possible to go abroad – the war had not long been over – she got passports for herself and the boy and went to Paris. Much later she wrote me a second letter obviously composed under the eye of a lawyer whose name and address she gave me, and told me that she was never coming back to live with your father again. He could take what steps he pleased to obtain a separation or a divorce – she hoped it would be a divorce – nor would she ever permit him to see his son. If he attempted to do so she would send the boy abroad out of his reach. Meanwhile she had good friends in Paris who would look after them both, and Felix would be sent to a Lycée. She added that she was financially secure and wanted nothing whatever from your father.'

'Is she still alive?' Sibyl asked, and would have been relieved to hear that she was not.

'Very much so, and I am told greatly admired still for her beauty and elegance. She had gone straight, I suppose, to her old friend the Count, the one who used to escort her to parties and night-clubs, and he took them both under his protection. His wife had died a year or two before, and for some time Angela shared his house in Paris quite openly. He also owns a small château in Provence. As soon as your father could obtain a divorce – and I'm glad to say I was able to help him there, though the time it took seemed interminable – the two were married and she is now the Comtesse de – well, it doesn't matter what.'

'And Felix? Do you know what became of him?'

'He is alive and well and both paints and I believe writes. He signs his paintings Félix Forbain. He has never married, so far as I could learn, but lives with a young Frenchwoman and her daughter, aged about fifteen. The young woman was a widow. The three share an apartment – or it may well be a house – in the Marais district.'

'I suppose,' she said, quickly adding up the years, 'he must be close on forty.'

'He is forty, or very near it.'

'May I ask, Uncle Hugh, how you know as much about them as you do?'

'Certainly. You have a right to know. I sent one of the younger members of the firm – it was Lewis Petersen in fact – to Paris in connection with a will. I asked him while he was there to make inquiries about the Count and his family. This he did, most thoroughly.'

'I see.' There was a pause during which she tried to make these facts her own, a far from easy matter. She then said, in a voice full of wonder, as though she had just learnt of an almost miraculous thing, 'So I have a brother.'

'Only a half-brother, please remember.'

'Still, my one living relative.'

Mr Beallby made no comment.

'But what a terrible, terrible thing,' she went on, as if communing with herself, 'to have to live one's life with such a memory!'

He said dryly, 'By now, supposing that he remembers it at all, and I suppose he must remember, he'll have transmuted it into something quite different. As for his mother, she neither knows nor cares where that poor little child is buried.'

'That may be so, but Felix is the son of my father too. He must be half my father.'

There was some sharpness in his voice as he replied, 'I believe him to be all Angela. Your father never had a selfish thought. Both his wife and his son were entirely selfish.'

The room was darkening now. It faced east, and the

sun, hidden by houses, was getting low. He could no longer see her face clearly, that high-cheekboned, pale-skinned, somewhat Italianate face – or so he had always thought it – with the brown hair brushed smoothly back from the admirable forehead and those large grey eyes with their unusually clear whites. He had never thought her beautiful, nor wanted to; with beauty character might have been lost. In repose there was even a certain youthful severity in outline and contours, but laughter or a smile or even mere amusement or interest dispelled this, giving her, he sometimes thought, a pleasing touch of the *gamine*. And now, feeling the need of seeing that face more clearly, of seeing every expression – as if her new knowledge might already have made some change in her – he got up and switched on the two lamps that were nearest to them and then sat down again, saying, as if in apology:

'You don't mind, do you? You know I always feel at home here.'

'Of course not. I expect I shall be wanting to see your face as clearly as you seem to want to see mine. You must be very tired. I know this has been a great ordeal for you, but will you please explain to me how all these things have remained hidden for so long? How did this total break, this extraordinary hiatus occur in my father's life? It seems a great mystery to me; as if, almost, he were two men. Or as if at one point he had remade himself, as one remakes a dress, so that it's practically a new dress.'

'You put it very well. That is precisely what occurred. Of course his extreme reticence had much to do with it. This he always had, but it was increased by the disaster and his deep need to put all this horror behind him. He dropped out of his old life completely, he deliberately cut himself off from it, he wanted to see no one who was a part of his past – myself excepted. Fortunately I had friends in the newspaper world and I did my best to see that the affair received almost no publicity. You must remember too that your father's renown as a writer on philosophy and mathematics came later on. How that young reporter got wind of a previous marriage I have no idea. But it is because of my belief that some day you were bound to hear of it that I have told you the facts now. I'm sure I did right.'

'I'm quite sure you did, and I'm deeply grateful. But, Uncle Hugh, I've been doing a good deal of thinking during the telling of it. I've been looking into my own mind and I'd like you to do one thing more for me, if you will.'

'Of course I will. You've only to tell me what it is.'

'I am going to ask you to give me Felix's address.'

His reaction was immediate and sudden. With both hands on its arms he pushed himself up out of the deep chair, and the dark, indignant colour of the elderly suffused his face. She stood up and seeing the havoc she had caused, put her hands lightly on his shoulders.

'Dear Uncle Hugh, you're horrified, outraged, and I'm truly, truly sorry, but let me speak, let me explain.'

'You have made your request quite clear,' he told her, unappeased.

'Yes, but listen to me, listen for just a moment. Hear what I have to say. It's this. I'm glad, glad that my father and I only had each other, only needed each other. He was a wonderful companion and friend and teacher, and I've been greatly privileged. I've no regrets; none. But now it's different. I'm alone, alone. I feel there must be something of my father in this man. There couldn't fail to be. Of course I would never get in touch with *her*. She must be utterly detestable. But this Felix is another matter. People change, there's no knowing how much he may have changed in nearly thirty years. Can you blame me for wanting to meet my father's son?'

'Yes,' he said, and looked sternly, almost fiercely into her eyes. 'I think you would be committing a very great folly. Your father would have deeply disapproved.'

'I wonder if he would. He was the most understanding of men, and the most generous.'

'And I am neither?'

'At the moment, no, but you'll come to it.' Her quick affectionate smile somewhat soothed his anger, but he was by no means ready to be softened. He took her hands gently but with firm purpose from his shoulders.

'I've said I would do anything you asked of me, but naturally I never envisaged this. I am profoundly unhappy about it. I suppose I cannot refuse you, but I do beg you to reconsider. If you have any affection for me, if you put any trust in such sagacity as I may have acquired over the years, I beg you to think again.'

'You're talking to me as if I were a stubborn and self-willed client. But Uncle Hugh, dear Uncle Hugh, do please try to understand. I feel so strongly about this that if you refuse to give me the address – but I'm sure you won't – you'll simply put me to the trouble of finding it out for myself.'

He walked away to the window and stood looking at the houses across the way, his bulky figure blotting out most of what remained of the daylight. Then he turned and came back to her.

'I feel you'll be putting yourself in touch with something evil, something it's my duty to protect you from if I can.'

'Well,' she said, 'perhaps it's time. I've lived too sheltered a life. And please remember that I'm nearing twenty-six, and have been about the world quite a bit, and that my father, natural prejudices aside, considered me fairly intelligent. At least he never failed to discuss things with me as if I were.'

'Oh,' he said, sadly, 'of course you can talk me into it, of course you can and you will. I've already said that I am profoundly unhappy about it, but if that carries no weight with you, I'll be forced to do what you ask.' He put a hand into his pocket and drew out his little black diary. 'The address is here. Lewis Petersen gave it to me three years ago, and I've copied it into each one of my diaries ever since. Your father knew I had it, but wished to be told nothing. He said, "You've satisfied your curiosity, Hugh. Please don't refer to it again." I never did.'

He went to the table and on a corner of it, among the empty glasses, he copied out the address on a back page of the little diary, tore it out and gave it to her, saying, 'Here you are. I've never disliked doing anything so much.'

She said, 'Thank you, and please trust me. I've decided to ask the V. and A. to let me take my holiday the second week in June. Then I'll go to Paris. If I get into any difficulties, I'll ring you up. Are you satisfied now?'

'No,' he said.

She put the little page just inside the cover of one of her father's books, which lay on a small table near by. The book was *A Philosophical Journey,* by Professor A. R. Matherson.

'Thank you,' she said, 'and now you must go home to Charlotte. She'll comfort you, and please give her my love.'

They moved to the door together without speaking. She, being the quicker, picked up his hat and umbrella and gave them to him. He took them in silence.

'Thank you, dear Uncle Hugh,' she said, 'and bless you for what you've done for me. My life has been altered, but not before it was time, and a lot of adjustments will have to be made. It's like being born again. I feel as if I'd just been held upside down by the feet and slapped. Quite an experience at my age, and I shan't sleep much tonight. But please, we'll see each other again soon, won't we?'

She leaned towards him as she spoke, proffering her cheek for his usual kiss, but as she did so she saw that his eyes were brimming with tears that he was doing his best to hide. She drew back with a look of affection and pity and opened the door for him. He went out of it without saying one word and she closed it softly after him.

CHAPTER III

The Journey Planned

During the following days she thought now and then of ringing up Mr Beallby – who had begun to seem to her like some monster sulking in its cave, perhaps better left alone – to ask him whether or not she was to regard all that he had told her as confidential, never, for her father's sake, to be spoken of; or whether she might use her own discretion in the matter. She refrained because of the unhappiness of their parting and of the tears she had seen in his eyes. Also because she needed time to adjust herself, quietly and apart, to what he had told her. He would in all probability, she thought, get over his hurt in time, or – and this was at least possible – never entirely forgive her for going against his wishes, and for her totally unexpected brushing aside of his concern for her and all his accumulated sagacity.

Then to her great relief he rang her up himself one evening from his home in Surrey, his not quite suburban little house capably ruled over by Charlotte. So utterly cut off from him had she felt that the call might have come to her from one of the dark places in space.

'Are you getting on all right? Are you all right yourself?'

His voice was just as usual, without any of the anxiety the words conveyed.

'Oh, not too bad. There is still a great deal to be done, but I'm working again at the V. and A., which helps to take my mind off other things.'

'Good. Any new developments? I feel sure there are.'

There were. She had been keeping back some news for him and the words now came with a rush.

'Well, Professor Kindler arrived in a taxi three days ago and took away two suitcases full of father's papers and diaries. He kept the taxi waiting while he asked me questions about the years between father's giving up his professorship at Oxford and the publication of his first book. He said these were years he knew nothing whatever about, except that they were spent mostly in Canada. I simply referred him to you, saying it was all before my time. There was nothing else I could say, was there?'

'Quite so, there was nothing else. I suppose I'll be hearing from him soon. I discussed all this with your father not long ago, but he said that his private life concerned no one, that only his ideas and his writings could be of any interest to a biographer. I remarked that I was afraid it wouldn't, in that case, be a popular biography and he said, I remember, "Heaven forbid that it should be." '

'So you'd prefer that I should say nothing to anyone?'

'Only, I would suggest, to your future husband.'

'Then I shall keep it to myself for a long time. I'm glad you rang me up. I've been worried that you might cut me adrift.'

'My dear girl, whatever folly you may take it into your head to commit, I shall never do that. Are you still bent on going to Paris?'

'Indeed I am.' She took pleasure at this point in asserting her freedom of action.

'What will you do? Write to him that you're coming? He quite possibly doesn't know of your existence unless he reads the English papers pretty thoroughly.'

'No, I thought I'd simply ring him up from the hotel. I want to hear how he takes it, and how his voice sounds. That will tell me a good deal. Voices do.'

'But the person who answers the telephone may be his mistress, or even her young daughter.'

'I'll risk that. In any case I shall want to meet them.'

'I'll make no comment. But we must see each other before you go. Will you dine with Charlotte and me at my club?'

That club, those dinners – easy communication between the three of them would be unlikely.

'Oh, no, Uncle Hugh. You must both come here. I'll give you a nice little dinner – or at least Tronny will. She'll be getting bored with so little to do. While I'm in Paris her older sister is coming to stay with her here.'

'Excellent. Then we'll come with pleasure. I was going to suggest the evening of June 9th.'

'That will suit me perfectly. I'll ask George Gawthorne to come too, to make a fourth.'

'Good. I've heard him highly praised lately by a Q.C. friend of mine. I gather he's doing remarkably well at the Bar.'

Uncle Hugh, at times, she thought, could warm the heart. 'I'm so happy to hear it, though I'm not surprised. Come at seven if you can. It's ages since I've seen Charlotte.'

'May I enquire where you are proposing to stay in Paris?'

'Of course. I've written for a room at the small hotel where father and I sometimes stayed. It's in a rather shabby part of Paris on the edge of the Marais and is called the Petit Cercle. It used to be quite cheap. I hope it still is.'

'It won't be. But don't worry too much about prices. It's quite useless.'

She felt this was sensible, though perhaps beyond her powers.

But he had forgiven her, and her world took on a happier look. For the moment, God was in his heaven, if only, alas! one were able to keep him there. In this more cheerful mood she decided to ask the Hardwicks as well, feeling that a party of six was even better than a party of four. Numbers, on such occasions, had a certain lubricating power, which was much to be desired. She was fond of the Hardwicks, who had very little money but were courageously hospitable. They had long been a part of her life, and she and Gerda had known each other since childhood. Even her father, chary of loving, admitted to loving them. Their sparsely furnished house in Essex was a refuge for many who had met with sorrow or disaster, and they had even adopted an orphan from Vietnam, a little being whom they brought up as lovingly as they did their own two children, a boy and a girl. The house, the visitors, the children, her husband, the garden and the claims of a straggling and struggling village occupied Gerda's entire life. She had no time to read, still less to write, though before her marriage she had published two small books of poems. Lionel was an economist who taught at the University of Essex and now and then joined in BBC discussions, one of them a series that had proved popular called 'Can We Agree?', his earnest, intelligent face one of a circle of other such faces. Sibyl enjoyed staying with them because she was never made to feel a guest but was one of the family and shared the work. Quite recently she had spent a weekend with them and had rejoiced to see two long rows of broad-beans that she had planted in the late autumn, now, judging by the numbers of flowers they bore, soon to produce an almost excessive crop of beans.

As for Charlotte Beallby, she had always been fond of her. She was capable and clever in many unexpected ways, and she, not he, drove the car. She was given to wearing bunchy skirts and shawls and reminded Sibyl of some little character out of Beatrix Potter's books, she could never decide which though it was possibly Mrs Tiggy Winkle. She did not know that she herself was sometimes referred to, by Charlotte, as 'Hugh's lovely blue-stocking', but she did know that Charlotte was the perfect wife for him.

It was a happy little party, the sort of party, Sibyl felt, that her father would have enjoyed, and no one was in a hurry to leave, not even the Hardwicks, who had sixty miles to drive in a battered old Ford (bought second-hand ten years ago), and had left the young daughter of a neighbour in charge of the children. The Beallbys were also driving home but had not so far to go. It was a lovely, moonlit night and Charlotte said that as they hadn't spent a gay evening out for months, she proposed to make the most of it. But George, as Sibyl had known he would, outstayed them all. George, it seemed, always knew exactly what he needed to do and did it. Charlotte having admitted that she hated the smell of cigars, he had refrained from lighting the one he had brought with him until the two had departed, and now sat peacefully smoking and talking as if he had the whole night before him.

'I wish you weren't going to Paris alone,' he presently said. 'There's so much crime about these days, one can't help worrying about the people one loves, particularly an eye-catching young woman like you. I can visualize all sorts of horrid happenings. Can't you take a girl friend with you?'

'I can't, and I wouldn't if I could,' she answered with spirit. 'Your fears are quite absurd. Both you and our dear Hugh Beallby seem to look on me as a helpless Victorian maiden just out of the schoolroom. What makes you imagine I can't take care of myself?'

'Just my total devotion, I suppose.'

'I see you've forgotten the promise I extracted from you the night we dined together.' This had followed his proposal of marriage, made seriously and quietly, and for the first time.

'Yes, all right, I'm not going to "proposition" you again this evening, if I can help it. But my darling Sibyl, you aren't and you never will be a career girl. As for me, merely as a matter of interest and in case I haven't mentioned it before, I want nothing so much as to be happily married, preferably to you, to have a reasonable number of children – which to my mind is two – and to do well in my chosen career. I'll say no more than that, but do please continue to bear it in mind.'

He looked so comfortably settled there, his cigar in one hand and a small glass of her father's brandy in the other, that she decided not to scold him. Surprisingly enough he had never, in the three years she had known him, attempted to make love to her, or even to kiss her taking her home in a taxi as other young men were all too inclined to do. This had its quite clearly calculated effect. He was not nor did he wish to be like other young men – young? He was thirty-four. He wouldn't even wear his hair an inch longer in order to keep in line with present fashion. He was neither fat nor thin, his height was a little above the average. He had a good face for a lawyer, a plain, honest, not too open face – it was full of thoughtful and sensible reservations – and a pair of blue and very observant eyes. In fact they missed little and were by no means lacking in a quick awareness of the humorous side of things. She wondered at his complete self-control, but that was his way, he would rarely act impulsively. This she decided that, on the whole, she very much liked.

'If your plans didn't include me,' she said, 'I would think them wholly admirable. But I do want you to know – ' and she said this with warm feeling – 'how much my father liked you. Far more than any other male of my acquaintance.'

'I loved him,' he said simply. 'I can't tell you how strongly I felt his absence here this evening. I loved him.' Then he asked, 'Are you going to Paris for some special reason? When your trip was spoken of at the dinner table I saw looks being exchanged between you and Hugh Beallby.'

'You see too much.'

'*C'est mon métier.*' He said it with a smile, then slowly and carefully put out his cigar, finished the brandy that remained in his glass, and got to his feet. 'I suppose it's time for me to go. I see I'm not to be taken into your confidence. Perhaps it might be a good thing if I were, but I must respect your reasons. Thank you and Mrs Tronsett for a delicious dinner.'

'I'll tell her what you said. It will please her.'

She too stood up, and he came directly to her so that

they stood face to face, looking at each other. It was plain to her that here was a change in tactics. She was wearing a long dress of a pretty, printed material with long sleeves which ended at the wrists in little frills. Her arms were at her sides and he came nearer and took first one wrist and then the other, and without haste drew her to him. He then raised both wrists to his shoulders and putting his arms around her drew her whole body close to his.

'I've waited a long time,' he said quietly. His embrace was firm and unhurried. So was his kiss, a long kiss during which she was quiescent, neither responding nor drawing away. Then, when he released her she surprised herself by taking his head between her hands and repeating his kiss, as if it were a gift she wanted and needed to make to him.

'Yes,' she told him, stepping back now out of his reach, 'you've waited a long time. It had to come and now I'm very glad it has. I know you better than I did, and I like you better. I even liked the taste of your cigar.' And she smiled as if it had all been in play and was without too much significance. But he was serious, he wanted her to know it had not been play, and he took her hands, put them together and kissed each one.

'I love you very much. Try to love me. More than ever now I hate your going away alone. Shall I drop everything and come with you? I would, you know.'

'No,' she said with firmness. 'Indeed not.'

But even as she spoke with such decision something totally unexpected and new to her took place. For the first time she knew what it was to feel isolated and she suffered a sudden and total lack of her usual self-confidence, a thing she had never before experienced. She felt – even while telling herself that it was only temporary and foolish – that she was like a very inadequately armed man confronted by one who was heavily armed and standing in her path. And there was no one at her back, her unprotected back. It was as though she had glanced over her shoulder and seen no help. True there was Mr Beallby, a good life-line, a kind of safety-rope, but not a filler of gaps, not a sword-wielder, and it was now George who suddenly became this. And in her so unexpectedly lonely and defenceless state she turned to him. Horrid though the moment was, she knew it for a passing thing; she was not really menaced on that narrow path, but a need is a need, however impermanent it may be. She had always trusted herself, but now in this strange, brief interval she felt she could not trust herself, nor endure her feeling of aloneness any longer. So she spoke and did not pause to choose her words.

'George, I must talk to you. Quite suddenly I feel the need to take you into my confidence. There's a matter that is terribly important to me. It's, in a way, the story of my life that I want to tell you. It explains why I am here and how I am here, and on what terms. Here in this queer unaccountable world. Will you stay and listen? Will you?'

'Good God! What a question!'

'Then come and sit with me on this little sofa, under the lamp.' And once there, she went on, with such trouble in her face as he had never before seen there or even pictured to himself.

'I've lately learnt that I exist because of an extra-ordinary and quite horrible event. Now that I know about it, it's with me almost constantly. And it has a nightmare quality.'

He saw how tense she was, and took her hand and held it on his knee, as if she were his child.

'But my dearest girl, so are we all here owing to contingencies and events, probably millions of them, many of them, no doubt at all, extremely horrid. Before you begin, let me tell you this. My own existence here in this world today is due to the fact that my father, aged twenty-seven, missed his train to Scotland because of an accident to his taxi and took the next train which happened to have my mother on it. They sat by chance in the same compartment and she tied up a cut on his hand with her handkerchief. They were married six months later. An agreeable contingency, I admit, but a million to one chance.'

'Yes, I know, of course I know. But mine is an ugly story, ugly, ugly, and I must tell you about it. It comes to me in dreams. Even last night I dreamt about it. I saw two figures, a boy and a woman, struggling with suitcases, making their get-away in the hideous light of a burning house, and in the burning house was the charred body of a little child. And even tonight, in the midst of all the friendly talk, I wasn't able to shake off the dream.' She took her hand back and it joined the other in her lap. 'I can concentrate better like this.'

He would have expected her, knowing her orderly mind, to tell her story in an admirably orderly way, and this she did, only at one point going back to say, 'Oh, I forgot to tell you,' but otherwise proceeding as if she had the whole thing by heart, putting everything in its proper place in relation to time and making the people in it as alive to him as they were to her. She made it so vivid with all its treacheries and cruelties, that he felt he had experienced it himself. When she had finished the telling of it she relaxed as if she had been suddenly unbound, as if cords had been cut. After a moment's silence he said what was so indubitably the right, the kind, the good thing, that tears came to her eyes.

'What an amazing dispensation of Providence that your father should not only have had another daughter but one that belonged almost wholly to him. The Fates took pity on him and gave him back what he had lost.'

She touched her eyes with the handkerchief he quickly took out of his pocket for her, and smiled her thanks for his understanding. Then in a voice that was strange to him because of its uncertainties, she said:

'So you see now, don't you, don't you, why I feel I must go to Paris?'

'I see why you want to go, of course, though I'm not

at all happy about it, nor, I think, would your father have been. Promise me that you'll ring me up or send me a telegram if anything goes wrong.'

'You or Hugh Beallby,' she agreed.

'Well, either or both, so long as you keep in touch. The image you've left with me of those two, the wife and the son, hurrying away from the burning house and its tragic little occupant without even knowing if your father was alive or dead, fills me with a kind of horror, as it does you. How old was that lad?'

'A child still.' (A little on the defensive, he wondered?) 'Only ten, I think.'

'Then we must exonerate him, I suppose. But the mother, the mother! Well, how do you picture him now? He'll be nearing forty, I suppose. Tell me what sort of man you expect to find.'

'I've thought about him a lot, of course,' she answered. 'I picture him as looking like someone you might see any day in the King's Road, or on one of the Paris boulevards, perhaps in the Latin Quarter. Careless in his dress, bearded, I think. But intelligent, surely he must be intelligent. Whether he's likeable or not, remains to be seen, though I'm not very optimistic about it.'

'Let's hope at least that he doesn't resemble that appalling woman, his mother.'

'Somehow I don't think he can be like her at all. He paints, he lives unconventionally. I think he must long ago have gone his own way, and it wouldn't be her way. But of course none of that makes me feel sure I shall find him likeable.'

'Do you know her name?'

'Yes, I got it out of Hugh Beallby with some difficulty. She's the Comtesse de Chantal d'Anteuil. It appears to be a well-known family.'

'So in the end she married her school-girl days admirer. How very strange.'

'Yes, so it would seem. I shall have nothing to do with her, of course.'

'What an extraordinary tale,' he said. 'Now I shall live with it too.' And he got up and began pacing about the room between sofa and fireplace. He went on, 'You're not a philosopher's daughter for nothing, are you? I can see that your father's distrust of memory, as being wholly different and apart from perception, has had its effect on you. You needed to share this with me – how thankful I am that you did! – and you were right to. Now that I share it, it's more than a remembered tale, subject to philosophical doubt. It has body, it has its own truth. We *know*. You and Hugh Beallby and I – we know.'

She gave him a quick little smile of acceptance and gratitude.

'My dear father used to tell me about a Greek philosopher named Cratylus. To avoid making any statement the truth of which couldn't be proved, he ended by saying nothing at all; just wagging his finger. But when I see this man, Felix, I shall *know* him to be my father's son, and then I shall be living in a world of fact. No more doubts, no more dreams.'

'When do you go?'

'On the fourteenth, Sunday. My ticket is bought. Everything is arranged. I go by air, of course.'

It was nearly half-past one when he left. On saying goodnight he gave her the sort of kiss Hugh Beallby might have given her, for fear, as she knew, of prolonging or wanting to prolong his stay beyond reasonable limits, or the limits laid down by propriety, if such a thing existed now, and with him, it seemed, it still did. She closed and locked the front door softly, hoping not to wake Mrs Tronsett, or 'Tronnie' as she had been in the habit of calling her since childhood. She herself was simply 'Sibyl', for having had the care of her since she was three Mrs Tronsett had never yet found the right moment to add 'Miss', though she did sometimes before strangers, if she happened to think of it. She was a sad and lonely woman and such happiness as she now had came from the feeling that she was needed and depended upon by father and daughter. So it now devolved upon Sibyl to keep her feeling loved and wanted, a little duty she was happy to take upon herself, for her gratitude to 'Tronnie' was genuine and deep.

Making herself ready for bed she thought, 'That dear George! So much more there than I ever guessed there was, and so much that I badly needed. A blessed evening. And now, no more dreams. Just sleep.'

Paris the First Day

There is a kind of clever craziness, she thought, about air travel, the whole thing being made fantastic and somehow inhuman by speed. Countries merge with liquid ease, though they were never farther from truly merging than now. She thought of the eighteenth century before the French revolution when everyone with money in their pockets – and some with very little – moved from one part of Europe to another without let or hindrance, all of it as natural as going from London to the country, and thought how much more enjoyable it might have been. How Gibbon must have revelled in his freedom of movement, how happy and at home he was in France, in Switzerland, in Rome which he made his own. And all the clever, busy diarists and diplomats of the time seemed to be on the move. Naples, in spite of its appalling slums, was like a small outpost of London society, as also was Florence. Both she and her father sometimes felt they would have liked to live in the middle of that century. 'I could have written on philosophy,' he said, 'with all the wealth of past knowledge at hand and with such new ideas as I hope I would have had,' and they loved to read memoirs of that period. Burke was one of their great favourites; her father collected every worthwhile book written about him as well as his own writings and they had once tried to follow his movements in Paris so far as they could. Well, that was all far in the past but it often puzzled her in reading those memoirs how easily the people of that lively period seemed to understand each other's languages, almost as readily as they understood their own, making contact with one another as if some lingua franca had existed which had since been lost. Now here she was, one of a crowd – the plane was full –

not speaking to a soul, nor likely to. She was sitting next to a wholly unattractive business man absorbed in reading the *Financial Times* and not even troubling to ask her if she objected to his smoking.

She barely had time to read two chapters of her book and eat a light lunch on a tray when they were told to fasten their seat-belts for landing. Though she had flown only once before, the routine of air travel already seemed perfectly familiar, almost as if she had been born knowing it. Soon they were on their way from the airport by a route which surprised her by its shortness and then she was in the city she loved. No adjustments were necessary, she was in France where she had great possessions; all the places she and her father had delighted in she owned, and was rich with them. No one could take them from her.

But when her taxi dropped her at the Petit Cercle, that inconspicuous little hotel off the Rue du Temple, she felt less at home. Either the people in charge were new or they had forgotten her. There was no one to say, 'Of course, Mademoiselle, we remember you well and your father the professor.' The place had a wholly different atmosphere, a different 'feel', and she was a stranger there. The decor had been changed and not for the better. The bedroom to which she was taken was smaller than any bedroom she could remember occupying before. Probably, she thought, they had all been cut in two, to accommodate people on package tours, though the Marais was hardly the district for package tours. Well, all the same, here she was, but without the father who would probably have said, even before they had unpacked, 'Let's go straight to the Louvre, shall we? There's so little time. Or would you rather go first to the Jeu de Paume?' He liked best to please her, though mostly they wanted the same things.

She started to unpack, then paused to consider. She had been trying not to think of Felix, trying to keep her mind from forming pictures of him, from giving him

CHAPTER IV

flesh and a personality. Why wait? she asked herself. Why not ring him up now, at once? Lewis Petersen, after some difficulties, had found out that he was not in the telephone book under his own name but under his professional name, Félix Forbain, and she quickly found the number. As she dialled it she said aloud, 'I have a brother at the end of this line,' then recalled Hugh Beallby's dry admonition, 'A half-brother, remember.' Well, that would have to do. Why had he never married, she wondered? He might of course ask her the same question but she could reply, 'Give me time.' He on the other hand, had had more than enough time. And the mistress? She hoped to get on well with her, it was important that she should. The young daughter – still, probably, little more than a child – she felt more sure of. She was glad on the whole that there was no wife to present possible difficulties. A mistress, kept no doubt, might have less authority. A wife might conceivably pronounce a de Gaullist 'Non'. So on the whole she was thankful there was no wife who might come between them and deprive her of even half a brother.

She thought, as she waited, 'This may well be a turning point in my life.' Then a woman's voice said 'allo.'

'Is Monsieur Matherson at home?' she asked in French.

'He is in his studio, upstairs. Who is calling, please?'

'He won't know me. I have just arrived from London and would like to speak to him if possible.'

'It is Mademoiselle Hanson, perhaps, to speak about the picture?'

'No, I am not Mademoiselle Hanson. My name is Matherson, Mademoiselle Matherson, the same name as his.'

Surprise and uncertainty silenced the other speaker for a moment.

'*Tiens, c'est curieux.*' Then she said in quite good English, 'I will call him. Wait a few moments, please.'

So she waited, determined to feel no nervousness, to

ignore the fact that her heart was exceeding its usual quiet pace. Then a man's voice came through after an interval of perhaps three minutes, a voice that at once gave her hope and even confidence, and it was good to feel that confidence so soon. It had a certain *timbre* of its own and she thought she would recognize it again wherever she might hear it.

'Hello. Who are you please? I am sorry to have kept you waiting, but my studio is on the top floor.'

'May I ask, first of all,' she began, 'if you happened to read in the *London Times* the news of your father's death?'

'I very rarely look at the English papers.' She could hear the note of caution now. 'I know nothing at all of this. Who are you, please?'

'I am your father's daughter, your half-sister. His only child by his second marriage. My name is Sibyl.'

'Good God! And how old are you?'

Enough of a Frenchman, she thought, to be immediately interested in her age.

'Twenty-six, or very nearly. My father died on the tenth of May. I have only recently learnt of your existence.'

'And I, until this moment, had no knowledge at all of yours. Why should I? It belongs to another life, a life I know nothing about. When did he remarry?'

She gave him the year and month, adding, 'My mother died when I was three. I was brought up by my father, whom I greatly loved. I would like to meet you if you would like to meet me. If not, I will continue my holiday and simply enjoy being in France once more. It's three years since I was here. Too long.'

'*Tiens!* But this is most interesting. How did you find me? I am in the telephone book only under my professional name, Félix Forbain.'

'Do you remember Mr Beallby? He had inquiries made.'

'Of course I remember Mr Beallby. Who could possibly

forget him? He was my father's alter ego. But why do you want to meet me? Surely you would have been told of many unpleasant things.'

'I want to meet you because I loved my father, and I have a hope that you may resemble him, even a little.'

There was the briefest of silences. Then he said, 'That perhaps you can answer when we meet. Naturally I hope we shall meet and soon. I remember him of course quite clearly. He was not very fond of me and with good reason, but that is long ago. I like your voice, which sounds most agreeably in a half-brother's ears. Where are you staying? Shall I call on you?'

'We would have to talk,' she replied, 'in one of those dreary little French hotel sitting-rooms. I am at the Petit Cercle, not far from you. Could we meet some-where else?'

'Yes, yes, I know the Petit Cercle. You could come here, I suppose, but I live with a young woman and her daughter – hers, not mine. My "*petite maîtresse*" is very nice but inclined to be suspicious of people she does not know well. Will you meet me for a drink this afternoon at the bar of the Restaurant Fragonard? It is quite near you, just around the corner from the Place des Vosges. Your concierge will tell you how to find it. And they're open, luckily, on Sundays.'

'I can find it quite easily. What time shall we meet?'

'Six o'clock, if that would suit you.'

'It would, perfectly.'

'Is it to see me that you are in Paris?'

The directness of the question took her by surprise, but she answered truthfully, 'Yes.'

'*Alors. À six heures. Bons baisers, petite soeur.*'

She hung up the receiver with a feeling of enormous relief and thankfulness. The ordeal was over and had gone far better than she could have hoped. And his mother had not once been mentioned.

She unpacked, took up her handbag, locked her door

and went joyfully off to the Jeu de Paume, his voice echoing pleasantly in her ears.

He was there before her, sitting at a table in the window. The restaurant was not large and there were not many people in it but even if there had been, the fact that he was alone, that he looked the right age and was obviously waiting for someone at a table for two would have told her who he was. She received at once a wholly pleasurable little shock of surprise. He was clean-shaven, was wearing a suit of light colour and material and was more or less of the same height and build as her father, who had been five feet eleven inches. She had feared that he might be fat, that good living in Paris would have had its all too likely effect on a man nearing forty, but there was no sign of a paunch. She felt a sudden pride in him, in his presentability, in the fact that he had had the good manners to be there before her, waiting. Happiness, relief, gratification were all present. She went straight to him as he got to his feet and slipping her handbag above her wrist, offered him both her hands. He grasped them warmly, giving her at the same time a look of surprise and pleasure, but he made no attempt even to kiss her cheek. The '*bons baisers*' of their telephone talk was, she was glad to find, figurative. He looked every year of his age and his face was not unattractively but quite deeply lined. They were lines that suggested a sardonic humour capable of being turned against himself. They were not, she felt certain, lines of sadness or ill temper. Here, she thought, was an incisive mind not softened by weakness or sentiment. That might also have described her father. They sat down facing each other.

'You far surpass my expectations, grey-eyed Athene,' were his first smiling words.

'Ah? You read a little Homer when you were a school-boy I see,' was her quick response, and she was glad they had begun in this light and bantering way. 'But how brave of you to form any expectations! I tried not to, but

I did rather fear that you might wear a great beard. I'm so thankful you don't.'

'But surely our mutual father wore a beard?'

'Yes, but he kept his short and neat and well-trimmed.'

'In my opinion,' he said, 'the last thing a painter should do is to try to look like one. As a student I wore a beard, but that is a long time ago. This, my dear half-sister, is a great occasion for me, but first of all and above all I want to express my sympathy at hearing of the death of your father. I say "your" father because he was mine so briefly and so long ago.'

'I loved him very much,' she said quietly. 'I miss him more than I can tell you, and in more ways. He had great knowledge and wisdom, as well as goodness. I had only to say to him, "Tell me," and he would always tell me, and in a way I couldn't easily forget. He . . .'

She faltered and lowered her eyes. Aware of her emotion he touched her wrist with a light finger.

'I understand. I see how close you were, closer than I have ever been to anyone.' Then to give her time to recover herself he changed the subject and asked, 'Where did you go to school? In England?'

The moment of emotion had passed. 'Yes,' she said, 'and then, luckily for me, to Cambridge, where I was very happy and worked very hard. Meanwhile my father wrote his books, chiefly on philosophy, but also on mathematics. They're very well known,' she added with pride, 'and they've been translated into both French and German. During the holidays and until just before his death we travelled together, whenever and wherever we could.'

'I can remember boasting at school,' he told her, 'that my father was *the* professor of philosophy at Oxford. You will have heard from Mr Beallby no doubt that I was an unsatisfactory and boastful boy.'

She answered quickly, dreading that he might say more on that subject, 'Shall we not talk about the past? There's so much I want to know about the present.'

But he was not satisfied. He felt that certain matters had better be got out of the way before going further. 'Put me first of all *au courant* with things I don't at all understand. But here is the waiter at last. What will you drink?'

'A gin and tonic, please.'

'*Tiens*, already I see we have tastes in common. In many ways, as you will learn, I am still an Englishman.' He ordered the drinks and the waiter departed. 'Now, please, if you will be so kind, tell me something that I find very puzzling. You say you only heard of my existence a few weeks ago. How can this be? Surely your father – you were on close and happy terms – must have told you about his first marriage and how it ended.'

'You're quite right, of course, to ask me that. Otherwise too much is incomprehensible. No, the answer is he *never* told me. For the simple reason that he could not. He had suffered too much. It went too deep. He could never speak of it to me or to anyone. Only Hugh Beallby knew, and he told me the whole story *after* my father's death, and then only because he feared I might hear of it in some sudden or distressing way.' And she told him briefly about the years in Canada, and the dichotomy in her father's life.

He leaned his elbows on the table. 'What an extraordinary story! And how very strange, when you heard it for the first time and so recently, it must have seemed to you! I see that you are a young woman of character. I am proud to have such a half-sister. But may we not drop the half? At least, between ourselves?'

'Very well,' she said, after a brief debate with herself that she hoped he had not noticed. 'By all means if you prefer it that way.'

'Why not? After all, there are only a little more than a dozen or so years between us. Now I am quite sure that our good Hugh Beallby will have told you, as a result of his inquiries, that I am not married, that I have never married, and that I live with a young woman and her

daughter, a girl of fifteen. Her daughter, not mine. I
had better tell you all about it. It does me, I think, a little
credit. Not much, but some. If I did a good deed it was
one I couldn't, I felt, avoid doing.'

'But *why* have you never married? You're a very
attractive man, as I'm sure you don't need me to tell
you.'

He answered with amusement and some irony.

'That may, at least partly I suppose, be the answer. All
the same, at the age of twenty-five I was engaged to a
young woman who was a singer. I loved her very much.
She was hurrying to a rehearsal one day and she was hit
by a taxi. She died in the hospital before I could see her.
She wouldn't, I am sure, have made me a very satisfactory
wife. Her career would always have come first, and
rightly, but I loved her. After that – well, there was no
one I really wanted to marry. Then came this unforeseen
happening that I will tell you about, as briefly as I can.
Ah, here are our drinks.' He raised his glass. 'To my
sister, and the happiest of surprises.'

She raised hers. 'To my brother, and our fortunate
meeting.'

'I'll do my very best to make it so.'

When he told her how and why he came to be living as
he was, he told it all very simply and in a manner she
liked. It was almost as if he were speaking about someone
else, some acquaintance perhaps. He was walking through
the gardens of the Luxembourg one afternoon on his way
to the Lycée Montaigne where he intended to leave a note
for someone. He never got as far as that. He saw sitting
on a bench in the Gardens, eyes streaming with tears she
made no effort to wipe away, a neatly dressed young
woman, and sitting close beside her, leaning against her
arm, a child of about seven who was sobbing most piti-
fully. The place chanced to be deserted. It was near where
people came to play boules but that day there was no one,
for there was a slight mist and the wind was cold.

'I had half a mind to pass by,' he said, 'pretending not

to have seen, but I have a certain curiosity and on this occasion it had to be satisfied. I am also, I hope, human.'

The young woman, it appeared, was desperate. He got the story out of her with some difficulty because she was unable to stop crying. She had been married to a fairly well-to-do shopkeeper considerably older than herself, and the child, Annette, was theirs. Four years ago, he died. She mourned him and was lonely. Then, about two years later, she had the misfortune to meet one of those brutes who prey upon lonely women. He took her and the child to live with him and before long, by means of trickery and plain theft he robbed her of everything she possessed and then left her. He simply disappeared. And, worst of all, she was going to have a child by him, in four months' time. 'That,' he said, with a very French gesture of the hands and shoulders, 'was the last straw. For her, and for me too. She had no friends, no money, no hope. She had made up her mind that death was the only answer, both for herself and the little girl. They would jump together hand in hand at night from one of the *quais*. I looked quickly at the child and was told that she was backward and would understand very little that was said. Well then, I persuaded her that they must come home with me, but it wasn't a simple matter, as she was reluctant and suspicious. I lived then in the house I live in now. It has three bedrooms, two living-rooms and a studio. The first and most necessary thing of course was for her to have an abortion, and this was brought about without too much difficulty through my good doctor, though not without considerable expense. As soon as she felt secure I found that she was a companionable and quite charming young woman, though not of course very well educated. The child was gentle and obedient. Lucille proved to be an excellent housekeeper and a good cook. I think you will agree that I might have done much worse for myself.'

'I want very much to meet her. When shall I?'

'Soon. Perhaps even tomorrow.'

'How long ago was it, this encounter in the Gardens?'

'It was eight years ago.'

'I wish I could have known you then,' she said. 'You were over thirty, but probably without a line in your face.'

'I doubt that. I think they came early.'

'But what a brave thing to do! And how amazed she must have been to see you stop and come towards her, with concern in your eyes. Then while she was telling you her story she suddenly made up her mind to trust you. To trust you completely. So she got up and went with you, through the deserted Gardens, holding the little girl by the hand, wondering, probably, what the end of it all would be, and if she were only postponing death for a little while. I can see it all so clearly.'

He smiled at her, moved by her understanding and her feeling for the drama of that day's events.

'I see,' he said, 'that I can talk to you as I have never talked to anyone. Do you know, can you guess what first reassured her and quieted her fears? The sight of the kitchen. It was tidy, and the saucepans were shining. I had a woman who came in daily to clean the house, and sometimes she did a little cooking for me. She has never had to come since that day. Lucille fell in love first of all with the kitchen, with me later. I suppose that I have grown to be very fond of her, even to love her, and in a way that I think you will understand. Or is it that I've simply grown accustomed to her and the child, and to my present way of life?'

'I think perhaps I will know that when I meet her, and when I see you together. When Mr Beallby – yes, of course it was Mr Beallby, who else? – told me you lived with a mistress and her child I tried to picture them as they might be. And I'll tell you something else because I see I can say anything to you – I felt nothing but relief because there was no wife who might perhaps come between us.' He agreed that possibly this might have been so.

'I'd like you to meet Lucille soon. You'll have to overcome her shyness and suspicion and I am quite sure you can and will. Why not tomorrow? But tell me first how long you will be in Paris? When I know that it will be easier to make plans.'

'I'll stay at least a week – perhaps a little more. Afterwards I thought of going to the Dordogne for a while. There are parts of it I'm very fond of and in a way it will be a little journey of piety, because I went there more than once with my father. And while I'm here there are certain things I have promised to do for my museum. Inquiries I must make, and a tapestry I've been asked to look at.'

'But for what museum? This grows more and more interesting.' When she told him where she worked in London he laughed and said, 'My father – ours, I should say – took me there once but I much preferred the one nearly next door – the one where the dinosaurs are.'

'That doesn't surprise me, at the age you were then.'

'Well, we shall have plenty to see and to talk about and I hope also to do, while you're here, so please don't make plans to go away soon. A week is far too short. We must change that. Can you come and lunch with us tomorrow? Lucille will cook a very nice meal. I've told you already, I think, that she has one troublesome fault. She is inclined to be jealous. But you'll soon win her confidence, and I'll make such explanations as seem necessary.'

'Thank you,' she said. 'I shall come with the greatest pleasure.'

'Good. I've taught Lucille to speak English fairly well, and the young daughter, Annette, takes lessons at school, though she doesn't make much progress. In any case, I'm sure you speak excellent French.'

'Good enough.' And she added with a little laugh and not without a touch of pride, 'but my Greek is better.'

'Ancient or modern?'

'Ancient, though I can make myself understood in modern Greek. My father and I went to Greece twice on holidays and were planning to go again. If he hadn't been what he was, I think he would have liked to be an archeologist.'

'Who wouldn't? I would. But I am very happy to be a painter.'

'Portraits?' she asked.

'Rarely. I prefer landscapes, strange ones with a character of their own. And lonely, deserted houses. But you will see for yourself. I imagine that you know the galleries here pretty well?'

'As well as a mere occasional visitor can. I was at the Jeu de Paume before coming to meet you. I walked here, feeling full of eager anticipation and,' she added, 'some fears and dreads, which I'm sure you'll understand.'

'And now?'

'Oh,' she said with frank happiness, 'it's all turned out so much better than I even dared to hope.'

His reply was, 'For me this is a never-to-be-forgotten day. And how much you have packed into it, my child! Let me see if I can tell you. You left your home in London early, you took a coach – or perhaps a taxi – to the airport.'

'A taxi. I am being reckless with my money.'

'Then you waited as we always do till you were called to board the plane. You must have had a light lunch on the plane. You then took a taxi, I feel sure, to your hotel. You then telephoned to me. After that you ran off to the Jeu de Paume and spent perhaps an hour there. You then walked here, you tell me, to meet me. You are a most surprising girl.'

She laughed. 'Well, I have never liked wasting my time.'

'*Ça se voit!* And tomorrow, before you lunch with us?'

'Oh, the Louvre. The Louvre first of all.'

'Don't hurry away to the Dordogne, please! We have

far too much to say to each other.'

'Well, first tell me this. Are you still British, or did you take French nationality?'

'I am French. If my life was to be spent here, it seemed better so.'

With what tact and understanding, she thought, gratefully, he avoided any reference to his mother. Perhaps he never saw her. Perhaps she neglected him after her second marriage and he had ceased to love her. She had been a failure as a wife, possibly as a mother too. Why had she not seen and sewn up that hole in the boy's pocket? Then, she at once thought, I would not be here. She would have been grateful to life for being less inexplicable and also less exorbitant. Yes, that above all. For her to be here, that child had to be burnt to death. And the man who sat opposite – could she think of him, though with pity, as responsible? Better try to put it out of her mind. It was now seven o'clock. He had told her, in answer to her questions, something of his student days, of his struggle to make his way as a painter, which he knew he had to be. He had been very poor at first, then lived on an allowance, he did not say from whom. Slowly his paintings began to sell. Some of them were now being shown at one of the galleries; he would take her there soon. The Miss Hanson, mentioned by Lucille, was coming from England to buy one for a gallery in Manchester. Now, he said, he must go. There was much to explain to Lucille. He drew a little map to show her where his house was. Did she like the Petit Cercle? He knew of a much better hotel quite near. 'I'll go there on my way home and inquire about a room. It's on a busy boulevard but has trees in front. I think you would be happier there, if I can get you a room at the back.'

Then they parted, walking briskly away in opposite directions as if their meeting had been a quite ordinary one, no different from other people's meetings; just a chat over a drink.

CHAPTER V

The Second Day

Twenty Rue Lapique turned out to be an old house in a little terrace of old houses which she guessed to be late eighteenth-century. Like one or two of the others it had had its attractive front carefully re-faced. The neighbourhood was unlovely, almost squalid, though there were a few glossy new buildings not far away, showing what was all too soon to come. The people in the streets were of mixed races, shabby, interesting and varied, and she saw a few bearded Jews wearing their traditional black gowns. She thought, 'If I lived in Paris, I too would like to live here,' but she doubted that she would care to go out after dark alone. Too many places to lurk in, too many decaying and broken-down doorways, but all the same, it fascinated her, and she and her father had explored it with delight.

She rang, and the front door was at once opened by a girl in a school uniform and Sibyl guessed that she had been waiting in the hall for the bell to be rung. She was pale and her fair hair was lank and lifeless; her blue eyes had the blank look of people who do not respond quickly to events either good or bad. She felt instantly sorry for the child and held out her hand. 'You are Annette. I am very glad to see you. My name is Sibyl.'

The girl said without any change of expression, '*Bon jour.*' And then in careful English, 'Please to come in. I will show you.'

The interior of the house could hardly have been simpler. All the walls were white – the hall, a dining-room which opened off it through a pretty archway, and a kitchen at the rear, the door of which had been left wide open, probably by Annette. Sibyl could see that it was a modern, neat, practical kitchen and she caught a glimpse of the gleaming pots and pans which had so reassured Lucille. She followed Annette up the stairs to the floor above and into what was obviously the main living-room, and there she found her host and hostess waiting for her, Felix wearing an open-necked shirt and an old pair of working trousers which showed that he had just come down from his studio. This time he came to her and kissed her cheek, then turned to the small woman who stood beside him.

'Here is my half-sister Sibyl, Lucille,' he said, and there was distinctly a note of pride in his voice. Lucille, with a dutiful air as if she were obeying orders, kissed her on both cheeks, then said, 'You are very welcome here.'

She had on a simple, sleeveless blue linen dress with a very short skirt which showed her pretty legs. Her fair hair was ingeniously arranged in a neat roll on the top of her head. Her eyes were large, round and light blue, like her daughter's, and Sibyl thought they were the sort of eyes to which tears come easily.

'It's so good of you to let me come to lunch today, and on such short notice. I hope it wasn't a great trouble.'

'It was no trouble. There are very good shops quite near.'

There was no warmth in voice or manner, nor had Sibyl expected it. She then said, looking round at the three of them, 'Shall we speak French or English? I do speak French, though of course not as well as I could wish.'

'We will speak English now, and French during lunch,' Felix replied for them all. 'Annette too. It is good practice for her.'

Annette quickly put both hands over her face, as children do, with the fingers outspread, and wailed, 'I speak English very bad. I am not clever.'

'You're quite clever enough,' Felix told her, and put a fatherly hand on her shoulder. 'Now then, I have prepared a gin and tonic for you, Sibyl, and one for myself. Lucille and Annette prefer to drink Dubonnet.' He went to a table where the drinks were, saying, 'I hope you found the house without any trouble,' and Sibyl assured him she had, saying she had only asked her way once. 'I would have been worried if you had been late,' he went on. 'It's not the best *quartier* in Paris for pretty young women alone. When Lucille goes to do her shopping she wears trousers, an old coat, and a cloth cap on her head. It's safer that way. But I love it here, all the same. They wanted to pull down this beautiful little row of old houses, but the owners banded together and put a stop to it – I hope for as long as I may live.'

As they took up their drinks, Lucille, who had clearly been prompted, lifted her glass of Dubonnet and said, 'We welcome you to our home, and hope we shall see you here often.'

Sibyl thanked her, and said, 'I hope so too, and I also hope that you will all come to London one day.'

Lucille shook her head and said sadly, 'No, I think not. When we leave Paris it is only to go where Felix wishes to paint.'

Sibyl caught Felix's eye, and said quickly, 'Please, Felix, tell me which of the pictures I see in this room are yours. I am quite sure they are not all yours.' And she went, glass in hand, to a painting she had caught sight of, a picture of young girls playing some game with a ball. It was painted in flat, bright colours but although the girls were doll-like, it had a certain charm. She looked at it more closely, and then exclaimed, 'But how splendid, Annette! I see your name on it. Were you taught – ?' She hesitated, rather at a loss and then said, 'by your step-father?'

This word conveyed nothing to the child, and Felix, coming to her aid, said in French, 'Shall we say your adopted father?' Annette, overcome with embarrassment, turned away her face. 'But Sibyl has asked you a question,' he said, 'and you must try to answer it.'

Shyly she shook her head. 'No one has taught me.'

'It's quite true,' Felix explained. 'I wanted to teach

her because obviously she has talent, but she did not want to be taught. I think she was right. The painting of innocence has much to be said for it. She's done others, but they are in her bedroom.'

Sibyl couldn't resist making a quick tour of the room and was greatly interested in the four paintings she saw of Felix's. She was much attracted by their highly individual, even idiosyncratic style and subjects. She well knew how painters dreaded the comments they were obliged to listen to out of politeness, so she made none, but merely said with a smile, 'I like them so much that I'll tactfully refrain from saying anything about them.' He gave her a quick little look of approval and said, 'I'd have welcomed *your* comments, but all the same, I thank you.'

They presently went downstairs to an admirable lunch. There was a game paté, tender veal cooked with mushrooms, creamy potatoes served as a soufflé and browned, and new peas. Then followed a variety of cheeses and afterwards fruit. Lucille contributed little to the talk, though Sibyl did her best to draw her into it, and Annette was silent. Sibyl supposed that when they were alone there must be talk in plenty, though perhaps not of the kind in which Felix would find much to interest him. He must have, she guessed, many friends whom he saw outside his home; in fact, he no doubt went out and about a good deal. A far from easy life, but he had chosen it – or had it chosen him? Determinism might have played its unknowable part – or was it, putting aside the insoluble question of determinism altogether, simply a magnanimous and spontaneous human impulse on his part? One could take one's choice.

Lucille was a far from uncommon type, but certainly she had the *métier de femme*, kept the house well and no doubt looked after him with loving assiduity and gratitude. As for Annette, she seemed a good and biddable child with one surprising little talent, even though the painting had obviously been done from a photograph.

She had hoped to win Lucille's liking, but the jealousy and suspicion were undoubtedly there. It had all been too sudden. One day everything was as usual, on the next a half-sister, never before heard of, had appeared among them. Felix's interest in and approval of this newcomer could not be and were not hidden. No, it couldn't be expected to 'work', she told herself; she could only do her best not to be a cause of dissension. She made it clear that her stay in Paris would not be for long and this had a slightly ameliorating effect, but even so, the unease was there. When it was time to say goodbye, her warm thanks seemed to fall on stony ground. Then, to her surprise and slight dismay, Felix announced:

'I'll walk with you to the hotel I told you about and introduce you to the proprietor,' and ignoring her polite protests he followed her out and Lucille closed the door behind them with unmistakable disapproval.

'It isn't going to work,' Sibyl said regretfully.

'I still have hope,' he answered. 'The trouble is, of course, that you're too young and attractive. I felt she doubted the whole story, even as I was telling it, but you'll win her over.'

'She must know, surely, that you don't tell lies.'

'I try not to, but I'm forced to practise small deceptions, of course. Otherwise, my life wouldn't be worth living.'

'Then what are we to do?' she asked sadly. 'I hardly know you yet. I want you to take me to see your pictures, though of course I could go alone. Was it my fault? Was I tactless?'

'No,' he said with weariness in his voice. 'It's an impossible situation, of course. How could it not be? But that child – how can I leave her? Lucille would get over it in time, but Annette might not. Lucille,' he added, with one of his half amused, half sardonic little smiles, 'has two admirers – I'm not suggesting for a moment that they're anything more than admirers. One I don't like at all; the other is a very nice fellow who would treat her well. He lost his wife not long ago, and he lives near by. He's very lonely, and I know he envies me Lucille. In fact, they get on extremely well.'

'I liked her. She's simply not right for you. Now I've said too much. More than I should have said.'

'You've said nothing I haven't known since the beginning.'

'Well,' she said with firmness, 'I've quite made up my mind to leave Paris soon, too soon to make it worthwhile changing hotels. So let's turn around now and walk the other way.' They were at that moment approaching the Boulevard Beaumarchais by way of the amusingly named Rue du Pas de la Mule.

'No, we're nearly there and I want you to see it. I'd take you to the Galerie Soixante-Dix afterwards but I can't very well go dressed like this. We'll go tomorrow afternoon after a lunch at the Fragonard. Then we'll take a taxi to the gallery.'

'But can you make it all right with Lucille? Only by telling her – well, I'll call them untruths.'

'No, I'll tell her the truth. She must be reasonable.'

'Today,' she said, 'I saw for the first time what struck me as a look of my father's. It was when you were speaking to Annette. I long to see it again.' Then she looked at him smiling. 'Perhaps if you wore a beard like his – '

'I would grow one to please you.'

'No, no, I like you better without one. What about me? Do you remember him well enough to see any resemblance between us? I've been told I look more like my mother.'

'If that is so, she must have been lovely.'

'Come, come!' she said lightly. 'That isn't at all a brotherly remark. But I believe she was lovely. My father used to say she was all Celt and that one day I'd be very like her.'

They went into the small, unpretentious hotel and were shown the only room that was soon to be available. It was at the back and looked on to a small courtyard in which was a chestnut tree. She felt at home there. In three days, they said, they would expect her. 'This settles it,' she told Felix. 'I will always come here in future. But, alas, I've booked my room at the Petit Cercle for eight days.'

'Leave that to me, my child,' Felix said. 'In any case, you must be my guest. I've sold five paintings in as many days and the day after tomorrow I will be selling one to a gallery in Manchester, so in the end, England will pay.'

She looked doubtfully at him. 'I'm not really poor, though I must go carefully and think before I spend. But I could never come to Paris if you insisted on playing host.'

'We'll discuss all that another time,' he said. 'Meanwhile I've been making plans.' They were walking now in the direction of the Petit Cercle. 'I think it would please and reassure Lucille if I were to take the three of us and a friend of mine, Henri Dumontelle, if he chances to be free, to dinner and the theatre. Not tomorrow, the day after. There's a play called *Après la Gloire*. I've heard good accounts of it.'

'But what about Annette?'

'We never take her anywhere at night. There's an old "*bonne à tout faire*" we've known for years who comes and stays with her when we go out, and if we're very late, she sleeps on a sofa in Annette's bedroom. She lives near by, so there's no difficulty.'

'It all sounds delightful. I haven't been to a play in Paris for years. But now, having planned this, why are you walking back with me? You must have many things to do.'

'I have a reason. There are things I must say to you, and I think this is a good moment. The noise of the traffic will help me, and I won't have to face those candid grey eyes of yours. You may have noticed that I haven't once mentioned my mother.'

'Naturally I've noticed it, and I'm grateful to you. But if you *want* to speak of her, do. I'd hate to feel there are subjects that must be avoided, and I'm interested in all that concerns you. All, at least, that you feel you want to tell me.'

She looked up at him as she spoke and for the first time had a quick glimpse of deep unhappiness and a weary self-disgust.

'Don't imagine,' he began, 'that I don't despise myself for this. I do, I must, as I'm sure you'll agree. But for many years, soon after I broke away completely from my mother and my two homes – if I can call them that – one in Paris, one in Provence, I've been receiving a generous allowance from my stepfather. He's a very rich man. The family own large estates and have fingers in a good many pies. The title, if you're interested, is merely a Napoleonic one.' Some people pushed between them as they were crossing a street and when they came together again he went on, 'You know the story of course. Our good Hugh Beallby must have told you. How my step-father met my mother when she was at a finishing school here and barely eighteen. My stepfather was one of its trustees. So doubtless there was some slackening of the rules if he wished to entertain certain of the pupils. In fact, he could arrange such things pretty much as he liked, for the headmistress stood in great awe of him. My stepfather's first wife was the sort of woman who was always ailing and complaining, and thought of little but her own health. She must have been a boon to doctors. One can hardly blame my stepfather for straying and he was well known for an amorist. However, what he felt for my mother, who was exceptionally beautiful, must have been more than an infatuation for a young girl. He really fell in love with her, beyond a doubt. If he had not had a wife he would have married her at once, in spite of her youth, and she, I need hardly say, would have broken with your father and married him. With the aid of an Irish friend who went to the same school, the two kept in touch for years by means of letters. Your father, of course, suspected nothing. It's painful for me to tell you this, but I feel I must. When the break came – that tragic and shameful break I won't speak of yet – she hurried to Paris with me as soon as she could and went straight into the arms of her old admirer. The war hadn't long been over then. Can you hear me in the midst of all this racket?'

'Perfectly. Every word.'

'His wife, most conveniently for them, had meanwhile died, so my mother, at last, got what she had always wanted. My stepfather told me the whole story, when I was seventeen. He called it his great romance. He, of course, knew only as much about the break between my mother and our mutual father as she chose to tell him. She is still a beautiful woman, though well into her late fifties. She is the fortunate possessor of a face with a fine bone structure and perfect features. She dresses with elegance and good taste. She is almost never ill. She can be extremely charming when she wants to be. In fact, an ageing Circe. But I am obliged to confess that I do not love or even like her, though I suppose no son should dislike his mother. That fierce, possessive love of hers became unbearable to me, and her hold over me gradually weakened and then vanished, though it took time. I have admitted that I dislike her but I dislike myself equally for having benefited for so many years from her husband's wealth. I'll say more about this later, because I want you to know.'

A determined young woman pushing a pram with a baby in it came between them. When they were together again he went on:

'The truth is that I like the old Count, I always have. He never had a son of his own and I suppose he felt that at last he had a son in me. With all his faults and follies I don't believe there was ever any real vice in him, and I doubt if he ever treated any of his women badly. He's a Catholic and goes regularly to confession. I often think,' he added, with a little ironic laugh, 'how much easier it must be for him now that he's eighty. In the château in Provence there's a private chapel and a priest goes to him there. They live quietly in the country for about four months of the year, seeing only a few neighbours who live in the same way. There is also a villa in Corsica where my mother, who still loves bathing, often goes to stay. Not my stepfather, he refuses to travel now. She usually takes a friend or two with her. I never go. When they're in Paris they entertain from time to time but very formally. Their parties are fantastically dull, and I keep away. They include only people of their own circle. When I go to see the old man we talk quietly and always alone. He's one of my most generous patrons. Wait, we must stop here. It's a very dangerous crossing.'

He presently continued when they were safely on the other side:

'To return to my mother. She was bitterly angry with me after I left the Sorbonne, for refusing to go into the family banking house. She's never forgiven me for it. And of course the fact that I was determined to be a painter and nothing but a painter disappointed and disgusted her still more. You can perhaps imagine the sort of reproaches I had to listen to. "I've given you all these wonderful opportunities and you refuse to benefit by any of them. If you insist on going your own way don't ever expect any love or help from me." '

At this point they were separated once more by people pushing their way between them on the narrow pavement, so when they came together again she took his arm and held if firmly, not wanting to risk losing a word. Then he went on:

'You may be wondering if she ever spoke to me of my father, and of those years during the war. Of the dullness and I suppose the deprivations, when she must have hated the life she was living and pined for the sort of life that she felt, with all her beauty and charm, she deserved to live. Well, oddly enough, she never did speak of them. After we left England I don't think I ever heard her refer to my father once, or to her old life. She simply

began a new life, and never looked back. Or if she did
look back, she kept it to herself.'

'And I,' she said at this point, 'am too young to know
anything about the war except at second-hand. From
books, and talk and what my imagination has supplied
me with. I do know that my father worked at the
Ministry of Information at one period, and I think I
only heard that through someone else. Now it has all
become history. But go on, I didn't mean to interrupt.'

'Well, I myself,' he told her, 'chiefly remember
austerity at school and at home. I remember the bomb-
ings and the slaughter and the sight of uniforms, and
some of the teachers I liked going away, and never coming
back. And hearing stories when I came here, of the
Resistance, and then of course of de Gaulle, de Gaulle,
de Gaulle. Then painting absorbed me, absorbed me
completely. The Algerian troubles seemed close and real,
but not real enough to trouble my mother, or my stepfather. Money has a marvellous power of insulation.
Well, never mind all that. I must finish my story, and go
back to my own life.

'The old man – though he wasn't really old then of
course, he only seemed so to me – was unhappy about
my mother's treatment of me. It's the only time I've ever
heard him criticize her. He made a great fuss, but all the
same I managed to break away and for a time disappeared into a part of Paris and a world of which they
knew nothing. I had refused to accept any help from
either of them, and struggled along in the usual garret
room until they succeeded in tracking me down. As soon
as my stepfather learnt I was only earning enough to live
on by washing dishes in a restaurant and couldn't even
afford to buy paints and canvases, he called me a fool
and said I was merely wasting my time. Besides which I
was depriving him of one of his few remaining pleasures.
Then I gave in and accepted what he offered me. I went
to the best art school in Paris, found a studio and got
down to work. So now, my dear sister, you know my

story, or at least enough of it to despise me as you should. I am what I am thanks chiefly to my mother's far from admirable character. That fact I have had to face and come to some sort of terms with. But the roots of it all, the primary cause of it all, lie in my own disgraceful, unforgivable behaviour as a boy of ten, when I was for the first time in my life put into a position of trust. Well, that is what I have had to live with. Because of it a child died and three lives were entirely altered.'

They had now reached the Petit Cercle and standing by the wall, away from the passers-by, they looked at each other, eyes fixed upon eyes.

'And here am I,' she said, 'owing to the fact that you locked a door and put a key in your pocket.'

They might have met on some desert island, so deeply were they discovering each other.

'It makes one feel,' he said, 'that life is what it is far more through human failure than through human achievement.'

'I think I would agree to that,' she replied.

She was still holding his arm, feeling that there was so much more to be said, but that there was one thing that must be said and said now.

'And bless you, Felix. Bless you! You've made clear to me many things that weren't clear before, and because of you and what you've become, I have more than I ever dreamt of having. Much, much more. And chiefly, above all, the feeling that I'm no longer alone.'

He looked at her with a softened and tender look.

'Then my dear, if the Fates are kind, we shall neither of us be alone again.' And he released his arm and turned and walked quickly away in the direction from which they had come. Back to Lucille and her reproaches? It seemed all too likely. But she felt as she stood for a moment watching him as he pushed his way along the crowded pavement with a quick, impatient stride, that she would never forget the look of relief in his face when he had said what he had to say, what he had never before in his life been able to say to anyone; and that he had been able to say it above all, to her, to the child of his father. As for her, she had got what she had so much needed; a brother, a friend unlike any other friend she would ever have, someone she had found through her own obstinate will, whose life she had now entered and become a part of, however separated they might be in space.

She went to her room and wrote two brief letters, the first to Hugh Beallby, the second to George Gawthorne.

Dear Uncle Hugh:

It still contrives to be the same old Paris and I am more than happy to be here again. The weather, at present, is perfect.

Well, I rang him up before I'd unpacked. Lucille, the little mistress, answered the telephone very nicely, though she was understandably puzzled. Quite quickly things fell into place. Felix and I agreed to meet later at a restaurant near here for a drink and a talk. He is understanding and very intelligent, which is all and more than I dared to hope. His resemblance to my father is elusive and fleeting. I lunched at their house today. Lucille is a splendid cook and takes good care of him. The young daughter is backward and pathetic but is loved and not, I felt, unhappy.

I have seen some of his paintings and liked them, and I expect to see more at an art gallery where they are on show. I am moving to another hotel not far away and you will find the address and telephone number at the bottom of this letter. The Petit Cercle is not what it was, and I shall be glad to leave it.

My love to you and dear Charlotte, and I promise to keep in touch. What else have I to say? Oh yes, an important thing. Felix seems to have no love for and avoids his mother. I'll write more fully later on.

As ever, yours affectionately,

Sibyl

To George she wrote:

Here I am and thoroughly ashamed now of all my doubts and fears. I felt I was going headlong into a sinister unknown and I have a cowardly horror of *evil*. What joy it was to find nothing at all of it here! I like and trust Felix, and his little mistress is as harmless as a milk pudding. I lunched with them and her backward young daughter at their house today. Felix, by the way, found the two of them in the Luxembourg Gardens destitute and contemplating suicide, and took them home to live with him, a generous and apparently irresistible impulse on his part. I can't see in him as much resemblance to my father as I'd hoped to see; just, every now and then, some look in the eyes, but it's not the gentle, thoughtful face my father had. I imagine he looks more like his mother's side of the family.

I'm moving from here to a more congenial hotel in the same quarter. Please note the address at the top of this page, also the telephone number. Now that I've seen more of the Marais I like it even better and it's full of amusing courtyards that one wants to stop and look into, and of course many lovely old buildings. Felix has a pleasant house of five or six rooms and feels very strongly that he belongs here, though he dreads the changes he foresees. I have seen a few of his paintings and I hope to see more of them at an exhibition tomorrow. He is no amateur, but a dedicated painter, and becoming well known.

I think of spending about ten days here and then moving on to the Dordogne and a small hotel we used to stay in, near some old friends.

I've just written to Hugh Beallby and hope I have set his (and now your) fears at rest.

Goodnight, dear, dear George, and bless you for that evening, and for being – well, just what you are.

As always, your affectionate,

Sibyl

CHAPTER VI

The Third Day

At the Fragonard next day neither had to wait for the other but met, pleased by the little coincidence, at the door. The warm, sunny weather had gone for the present, it had been raining delicately and pensively all the morning and before going to their table Felix hung up his raincoat and her wet umbrella went with it.

'It won't last,' he said, 'the clouds were breaking as we came in. I'm very cloud-conscious and even in Paris I like to watch what goes on up there.'

'I know that,' Sibyl told him, 'from what I've seen of your paintings. And I'm a devoted cloud-watcher myself.'

'I'd expect your father's daughter to be observant,' he said as they sat down. 'And did he also teach you to be prompt?'

'Perhaps. But it seems to be something I was born with. To be late for anything offends my conscience and my sense of orderliness. I take no credit for it.'

'It's a virtue such female friends as I have seem not to possess. Tell me, are you hungry?'

'Well, I dearly love good food though I have a modest appetite. You tell me what to have, please, but something light.'

'I suggest sole Veronique. They do it well here. And I'll have a plain grilled sole. We might start with melon, if that's agreeable to you.'

'Perfect. Confronted with these vast menus I feel half-witted. By the way, I've told them at the Petit Cercle that I'm not staying over the weekend, but that of course I'll pay for the extra days.'

'Leave that to me, please. I'll settle it. No,' he held up his hand, 'there's nothing more to be said. Now I have some news for you, and I hope it will be good news. I've got seats for *Après la Gloire* for tomorrow night. It's had excellent reviews, if one can believe in them. We'll dine first at the Grand Vefours because it's a part of old Paris and an attractive place. Lucille and I will call for you in a taxi at seven. The play begins at nine. After that we'll look in at a night-club because Lucille adores night-clubs, and I almost never go to them. So prepare yourself for a late evening.'

'It all sounds the greatest fun. How kind you are to me!' And then she broke off to say, 'There's someone at a table near the window who's longing to attract your attention. A man.'

He turned quickly about and exclaimed:

'How very surprising! It's the friend who's going to join us tomorrow night. He seems to have finished his lunch, but I'll ask him to come and have his coffee with us.'

They met halfway, and a waiter followed with the coffee. With a hand on his friend's shoulder Felix introduced him to Sibyl. 'This is Henri Dumontelle, one of my oldest friends. Henri, this is Mademoiselle Matherson, from London. What a lucky meeting, but what are you doing in my *quartier*? I would have thought you never came here except to lunch with me.'

His friend explained in careful English.

'The Quai d'Orsay sometime treat me like a very small messenger boy. When I am leaving here I go to the Place des Vosges for some papers which are so much confidential that they must not be given to the post. Now you know all.'

He was a solidly built, broad-shouldered man of about thirty-five, Sibyl guessed, with small but very intelligent dark eyes behind large glasses. He was most formally dressed, but she decided he was probably less conventional than his appearance suggested. Something more, perhaps, than the well-trained young diplomat on his careful way up the ladder. He kept looking at her with a frank interest he did not trouble to conceal.

'Did you say Mademoiselle Matherson?' he asked Felix. 'Then perhaps you are cousins.'

Sibyl was prepared for this and, preferring to leave to Felix such explanations as he might think necessary, she answered quickly, 'Probably if you go back far enough all the Mathersons are related.'

'You see you can speak French to her,' Felix told him. 'In fact her French is far better than your somewhat pedantic English.'

'I congratulate you, Mademoiselle,' Dumontelle said, 'your accent is excellent and you speak with assurance.'

'That's very flattering, but I'm often at a loss for the right word and my grammar I know is faulty.'

'Failure to find the right word is common to us all. If one never failed to find the right word one might become a Flaubert.'

'And would you like to be a Flaubert?' she asked him. 'Would he be your first choice?'

'Most certainly. "*Madame Bovary, c'est moi.*" But where did you learn to speak such excellent French?'

'At school, at Cambridge, travelling in France and reading plenty of French books. And talking to French people of course.'

'She speaks excellent Greek too,' said Felix, in a teasing way. 'I stand in the greatest awe of her. And she is the reason for our party tomorrow night. Lucille, by the way, will be the fourth.'

'Good!' Dumontelle said with noticeable heartiness. 'It is too long since I've seen her. And how is Annette?'

'Much the same. I think she improves a little. I hope so.'

'The stresses and strains of modern life are hard on the young,' Dumontelle said sagely, 'and that poor child has suffered too much.' Then he asked Sibyl, 'What are your plans for this afternoon? Something agreeable, I hope.'

'Very. Felix is taking me to see his pictures.'

'Ah!' Dumontelle exclaimed. 'How I wish I could

join you. I haven't been there yet, Felix. Since the opening I have been swamped with work.'

'Don't worry. They'll be there for another week.'

'Soon,' Dumontelle said to Sibyl, 'he will be like
Picasso, his pictures sold before they are painted.'

'Give me another thirty years, if I live so long, which
God forbid,' was Felix's reply, 'then I may also in the
end become a prince of jokers. Now, some suggestions
please, Henri, for Mademoiselle Matherson's enter-
tainment. You are better qualified than I am to produce
ideas.'

'Then first of all,' said Dumontelle with promptness,
'she must come to my sister's birthday party next week.'
And he added, with urgency, 'You will come I hope,
Mademoiselle? Felix will bring you. There should be
some amusing people there, and my sister I think you
would like.'

'How very kind of you! I shall be delighted to come.'
And then she was struck by a moment's doubt. Might
Felix's mother be there too? She would have to inquire
later for she would run no risk of finding herself under
the same roof with her.

She liked Dumontelle and it pleased her to see that he
had a great admiration and liking for Felix. Men's men
friends, she thought, were of far more significance than
their women friends. He lingered on over his coffee, then
looked at his watch and exclaimed:

'I am already late! I must run. Where are you staying,
Mademoiselle? I will have an invitation sent to you.'

'She'll be at the Marie et Hugo,' Felix said. 'You know
where it is. Now off you go, Henri, or those documents
will already be in the post. I'll pay for your lunch, and
you can repay me if you like some other time.'

Dumontelle picked up his despatch case, bowed to Sibyl
and said, 'This has been a very great pleasure. I am
happy that we shall meet tomorrow, and also next week at
my sister's party.' And he hurried off.

'You've made a conquest,' Felix said when he had

gone. 'I've rarely known him to be so forthcoming, something not encouraged at the Quai d'Orsay. Also, if you are interested, he has no wife.'

'So I gathered,' Sibyl replied. 'He told me he lived alone. I liked him and I'm glad we shall see more of him.' Then she laughed and went on, 'I'll tell you something that I'm ashamed of because it's schoolgirlish and absurd. I can never meet a likeable man without marrying him imaginatively. While we were talking I was marrying your Henri and deciding it wouldn't be at all disagreeable. I mean, that it might "do". I've no doubt he has an interesting life, though perhaps too conventional for my taste, and a kindly nature. One could get on with him and even grow fond of him. This is pure nonsense, it's only a game I play. Perhaps a game we all play. What do you think?'

'I'll tell you what I *feel*,' he answered promptly. 'Nothing but jealousy. Even a half-brother has the right to feel jealousy, I suppose. But of course, we all play that game until we grow too old. When I meet an attractive young woman I am probably considering a variety of possibilities. Well, Henri might do very well for you, much though I dislike the idea. Now I will ask you a question that perhaps I ought not to ask, but I want to know the answer. If our circumstances were different, do you feel that I might perhaps, as you so cautiously put it, "do"?'

The words, 'Oh, good heavens, yes!' were out before she could stop them and after that there was nothing for it but laughter. The simple truth was that for the moment she had forgotten that this was her father's son. He was becoming less and less that, more and more simply a person, simply himself and he was a person she immensely liked. Her sort of person. And not only liked but knew it would be all too possible to love. She had not in fact realized just how greatly she did like him until this moment. Hence the laughter, as at an amusing joke, to cover up, to save herself. And she was quick to repeat his words, 'If our circumstances were, as you've said, "different".'

'You could hardly have paid me a greater compliment,' he said, and put his hand for a moment on hers. 'I don't deserve it because I was fishing for it.'

'Well, you caught your fish,' she said, 'and caught me off balance. Now, Felix, I want to ask you something that is important to me. I'm looking forward to Mademoiselle Dumontelle's party, but I wouldn't dream of going if there were even a possibility of your mother's being there too.'

'Well, there isn't,' he said. 'They'll mostly be quite young, and anyway she's in Corsica. And, by the way, both Henri and his sister have suffered the same fate. Both have had divorces. Louise's husband left her for another woman, not, I would think, worth Louise's little finger. As for Henri, his rather too intellectual wife left him for an American physicist, and they're now living in Stanford, California. Henri agreed that she should keep their six-year-old daughter. Is it any wonder that young people form attachments outside marriage? Or avoid marriage altogether? I sometimes wonder if it will outlast our time.'

'That's a pretty cynical outlook,' was her comment. 'I know quite a lot of happily married couples who only dread the thought that death will separate them. Surely you know many like that?'

'I think I could count them on the fingers of one hand,' he answered. 'By the way, divorced women as you probably know, take back their maiden names here in France, so Louise is Madame Dumontelle.'

'Yes,' she said, 'I did know that, but thank you for reminding me.'

They sat talking until half-past two, when he called the waiter and paid their bill and Henri's. But even then they went on talking as they walked, looking out for a taxi, not always easy to find in that part of Paris, and when they eventually found one and were on their way, he took her hand and kissed it.

'My dear friend and sister,' he said, 'marry Henri and live in Paris. I need you.'

She felt it was time now that she told him of such nebulous plans as she had for herself, if plans they could be called. They had only been forming since that recent evening in London. 'Forget the nonsense I talked about Henri,' she said, 'though I like him. But there is someone in London I believe I might like well enough to marry. He is a barrister, and he very much wants to marry me. In spite of what you say about marriage, marry I know I must. I couldn't possibly go on living alone for very long, though I admire and marvel at those who can and do. Even in the short time since my father's death, I've learnt that I need and must have the companionship, the permanent companionship, of an intelligent and affectionate man, whether husband or lover, and I would prefer a husband. Am I asking too much? I want to grow, I want to develop such faculties as I have, and I think I could do that best in marriage. And I don't think I'd feel complete unless I had a child. So now you know.'

But this seemed not to satisfy him. 'How much do you love this man, this barrister? Somehow it doesn't ring quite true. If he's as important as you now say, you would have told me before. Or so I feel. Think well, my dear child. Please, please, I beg of you, do nothing in a hurry. You are still very young. Promise me you will do nothing impulsively.'

'I promise you I won't. I'm not, by nature, a very impulsive person. Now, to change the subject, I want to know Lucille better. I'm fascinated by her story. May I take her out to lunch one day soon?'

'But of course. Why not? I am often out to lunch, and Annette doesn't get home until four on weekdays. A school bus takes her and brings her back, so it can be arranged at any time. It's a kind and charming thought of yours. As you know, you won't find Lucille a very interesting companion.'

'Oh, but I shall, I shall! I look forward to talking with her. To me she's unknown territory.'

'Within a very small compass, as you'll learn.' And then he said with a short laugh that was not without bitterness, 'I suppose I'm more tied to Lucille than if I were married to her. And how could I leave that child now?'

She considered this for a moment and then said:

'As far as Lucille herself is concerned, I hope you'll never feel it's necessary to leave her. You're the sun in her sky. I think too that she makes you reasonably happy. She certainly makes you comfortable! But let's suppose that some time you might have to leave her. Couldn't you set her up in some small business or shop of her own? She strikes me as highly competent and very practical. I hope it won't happen, but if it did, wouldn't that be a possible solution?'

'I've thought of it, of course. And I've thought too of my neighbour, who would gladly marry her tomorrow. But what would become of that poor child? I send her to a special school for children like her, who can probably never be taught to read, or to live a normal life. My neighbour might not think it worthwhile to keep her there. Still, in spite of all these problems, I don't regret that I walked through the Luxembourg Gardens that misty day. It's probably kept me from making a foolish, impulsive and unhappy marriage. Who can tell?'

The taxi came to a stop and they got out. Sibyl was all eagerness to see what was in store for her. As they went into the gallery she saw that it was much like the other galleries she knew, with a large front room with desks in it, and the walls hung with important-looking but probably unsaleable paintings of mixed origin. Beyond this were the exhibition rooms, and these were already crowded. Felix put a programme into her hand, saying as he did so, 'It's a joint exhibition but even without this you won't have any difficulty in deciding which paintings are mine and which are Radinski's. He died quite recently and was so eccentric as to be just a little mad. But all the same – well, you'll see for yourself. Now in you go. I'll keep an eye on you and we'll talk later.'

It was not easy to get what she wanted, a clear and uninterrupted view of his paintings. Heads bobbed between them, and she could only be thankful that few women wore hats. But with patience she managed to study each one. She kept asking herself how she would have described them to her father. Might she have said, she wondered, that though he owed something to the Impressionists, without doubt, he also had a special 'verve' and freedom and a way of seeing that was all his own? This struck her forcibly in a painting of a broken bridge in a wild gully during a freshet, the waters tumbling crazily down and a group of gipsies watching. But the very first one she saw seemed to her to provide the key to most of his work. This was of a deserted house at the edge of a strange wood of twisted and contorted trees. Part of the roof had fallen in and on the sagging steps sat a woman wearing a red apron, her despairing head cradled in her arms. Yet another that struck the same note was of a village street through which an army might just have passed (but he was too young to have seen that!) The broken iron balconies were still bright with geraniums and a broken doll lay on the cobblestones. Death and tragedy were there, and the folly and cruelty of man. Another, however, filled her with a nostalgic pleasure, for it was a sight she had seen herself more than once – olive-pickers at work among olive trees of unguessable age, some of them split apart, writhing and looking like strange creatures from pre-history. She had begged the driver of the car she and her father were in that day – going down, down through those vast olive groves between Delphi and Itea far below – to stop and let them out so that they could look at them more closely. She did a few quick sketches in the sketch-book she always carried with her when travelling. Well, she would tell Felix all that later and she wished he were beside her now. Then she came to the paintings he had done in Spain and was captured by them. She knew he had been painting there the previous year because Lucille had said at lunch,

'In Spain all day he painted. We were in a very small hotel where Annette and I had nothing to do and the food was not good.'

It was one of these, she heard someone say, that had been bought for the Manchester art gallery. They were strong, robust, full of heat and dryness and the sad, harsh beauty of unproductive, unyielding soil, and a great loneliness of sun and sky. She felt suddenly happy, happy because he had done so triumphantly what he had set out to do, and there was pride in her happiness, which was probably a greater happiness than the painter himself could feel for he was bound to know dissatisfaction, the artist's disease.

The next moment she heard his voice behind her and turned eagerly and with a glad smile to speak to him, but it was someone else he was speaking to, a small woman conspicuously odd and standing close beside her. She wore a bright silk turban which might have been the pride of some rich Turk of earlier days, and about her neck were fanciful gold beads, one long string of them ending in a heavy, ornate gold cross. She was quite unlike anyone Sibyl had ever seen before and her face with its wrinkled, painted lips and small sharp nose was grotesquely ugly. She was speaking of one of the Spanish paintings, not the one that had been sold to Manchester but to another that Sibyl longed to own.

'Yes, how lucky I was to have got it,' she was saying to Felix, 'for my rich wine-growers. They'll be delighted with it. Three people I know wanted it, one of them, as you may have heard, the Count himself. He'll be furious with me for getting in ahead of him, but it won't be for the first time. We're always quarrelling about something. He enjoys it.'

She had noticed Sibyl's quick turn towards Felix, her smile, and the fact that she had been on the point of speaking to him, and now said, 'Who is this young lady, Felix? I see you know each other. Introduce us.'

'A friend of mine from England,' Felix replied, and had to lower his head in order to be heard in the chatter about them. 'Sibyl, this is Madame Villet-Rocca who is kind enough to buy a picture of mine now and again for her friends' collections.'

He had avoided calling her Miss Matherson and Sibyl guessed he had a reason. The queer little woman's accent, in spite of her foreign name, was more than faintly Irish. She knew Felix well, she knew his stepfather well, she belonged, in some way, to his youth. Suddenly, as she told Felix later, 'The penny dropped'. This could be, this must be his mother's Irish girlhood friend, the purveyor of secret letters, the friend who had contrived to keep her in touch with her old admirer over the years. She saw that she must go warily and extricate herself from this intolerable meeting as soon as possible.

She said, 'I think you have made a good choice, Madame. It is one of the paintings I like best. Now I must go. Thank you for bringing me, Felix. I've enjoyed it even more than I expected to, and my expectations were very high.'

She turned then and slipped away through the crowd, but not, she hoped, in noticeable haste. Once out of the gallery and on the pavement she drew a deep breath. She was sure she could trust Felix not to give that woman any information about her, least of all her name. He would say she was a Miss Smith or a Miss Jones if he were pressed – whatever came into his head. As for Madame Villet-Rocca herself, or whatever her name was, she was a dangerous little parcel of intrigue and avid curiosity, and had contrived, no doubt, to marry a Frenchman and live in Paris near her best friend. It was to be hoped that their paths would never cross again. She felt as if, after drinking from a fresh, clear spring, she had seen a toad at the bottom of it, and felt a shudder of disgust.

At that moment, appearing from around the corner, came Henri Dumontelle. He seemed very pleased to see her again and said that as he had found, after his errand in the Place des Vosges, that he had ten minutes to spare, he thought he would look in at the exhibition. They talked briefly, then as she caught sight of Madame Villet-Rocca about to come out of the door of the gallery and pause to speak to some acquaintance, she bade Henri a hasty goodbye and hurried off.

She dined alone that night at a small restaurant she had discovered the day before and found it convenient to keep the book she was reading open beside her plate. When she got back to the hotel after dinner – but well before dark – the night porter, whom she had come to dislike, took her up in the lift and said, 'All alone tonight, eh?' She replied, 'As you see.' She then rang up Lucille from her bedroom, after locking her door, and found that she was in, and that she also was alone. Annette was in bed, and Felix, she said, was dining out with a painter friend of his. Sibyl asked if she would lunch with her, the day after their theatre party. 'Then we can discuss the play and many other things. By that time I shall be at the Marie et Hugo, so perhaps you will meet me there. Come at twelve-thirty, and we will lunch near by, perhaps at the Fragonard. There will be just you and myself.'

Lucille was more than pleased, she was much gratified, and seemed to have lost her fears and suspicions. 'That I will like very much,' she said. 'Felix is so clever, when I am with him I am always shy. But not,' she added, 'when we are alone together, of course.'

CHAPTER VII

The Fourth Day

The next morning Felix rang her up very early, soon after eight, in fact. Lucille must already have gone out to do her shopping, she supposed, and she thought with sadness of the dullness of most women's lives, filled too often with too many dull little duties and with such talents as they might possess unused. Felix, it appeared, had not yet begun his morning's work. He spoke urgently, as if expecting opposition.

'I want you to do something for me. I hope you can be ready by half-past nine or even a little earlier because I want to take you to a shop I know. I want to buy a dress for you. It isn't one of the *Grands Couturiers*, I promise you, but a small shop where some of the really well-dressed women I happen to know – they aren't many nowadays – buy their clothes. I want you to have a pretty dress for Louise Dumontelle's party.'

She demurred. 'No, please, I don't like the idea at all. I have a dress that will do well enough.' (It was the dress she had worn in London the night of her little dinner-party, when George Gawthorne had kissed her and she had told him her fears.) But Felix insisted. She *must* have a new dress. A pretty coloured chiffon, full-skirted, gathered in at the waist. He knew exactly what he wanted for her, and so would the shop's owner, clever Madame Ginette. But Sibyl still protested.

'Really this is absurd. I don't need such a dress. I can wear my own.'

'But it's to please me,' he begged her. 'Get ready at once and I'll be there just after nine. And there's something else we must do as well. Something I've been wanting to do ever since you've been here, and the sooner it's done the better. It's something very important to me.'

'Well then, I'll give in about the dress. But I should hate Lucille to know.'

'She won't know unless you tell her. And she already has a new dress, for tomorrow night. She refuses to come to Louise's party. I've never in my life bought a dress for a pretty young woman, and this little expedition will give me great pleasure. Order your breakfast and dress quickly.'

She thought, 'Why not, if it pleases him? It's his own money, not his stepfather's.' And she said, 'I'll be ready.'

In the taxi – he owned a Citroën, he had told her, but only used it for trips into the country – she remarked to him:

'You're really far more of a Frenchman than an Englishman, aren't you? And I'm not suggesting you're any the worse for that. But I think only a Frenchman would have thought of buying me a dress and even coming with me to help me choose it.'

'I shall enjoy myself. Now I must tell you that I've arranged everything with the hotel people and your bill is paid. When you leave the Petit Cercle you need only give a tip or two. I don't like the place, and I shall be glad when you're out of it.'

'I too. Was there ever such a generous half-brother? When may I talk to you about your paintings?'

'Don't worry. There'll be time for that later. I know you liked them, so I am satisfied.'

'Well then, tell me something now that is very important to me.' And she asked him if she had guessed rightly, and if that highly unlikeable little woman she had met at the gallery was in fact his mother's old friend.

'I knew you'd twigged,' he said, and she was much amused to hear from him this bit of school-boy slang left over from his English childhood. 'I guessed it because of the promptness with which you took yourself off. Beallby, I must admit, left very little out. You heard of her through him, obviously. How else could you have heard?'

'I did. Naturally you didn't tell her who I was.'

'Naturally I didn't, my dear. I think I said you were a Miss somebody or other who sometimes came to Paris to buy antiques. She lost interest at once. Her world is the *haute monde* and she lives in it and by it. Years ago she made up her mind to live in France, and finding spinsterhood a drawback, she married a Corsican who probably thought, knowing the sort of people she associated with, that she was very rich. They parted years ago and though she's far from rich she makes a very good living by knowing her way about and helping any wealthy and acquistive friends who need her help and advice. She's an excellent judge of paintings, both ancient and modern, and I don't say this because she happens to have bought some of mine. Would you like me to tell you more of her history?'

'Yes, very much. I want to be well armed against her, though I hope our paths will never cross again.'

'I see no reason why they should. She's a dangerous little gossip and intriguer, but all the same she amuses my mother even now, it seems, just as she did when they first met as young girls. My stepfather puts up with her quite amiably from time to time, and she was clever enough to find a carved wooden sixteenth-century figure of the Virgin Mary which was stolen years ago from his chapel. She's good at tracking things down and she'll go to great trouble. I suspect, too, that she knows some shady characters who are useful to her. That Irish accent is a bit of affectation, but probably pleases American clients. She was born in Surbiton – no harm in that – but it's true all the same that she spent most of her life in Ireland. Her father was in charge of a big estate there that was owned, years ago, by a wealthy English peer. It was in County Waterford, and I imagine the peer was pretty much of an absentee landlord, so Rita's father – their name was Talmidge – had plenty to do. In fact the owner and his wife were so grateful to him that they offered to send his unattractive young daughter to a finishing school in Paris. There she met my mother. She had plenty of wit and daring and was ready for any escapade. She still is. She's looked on as a "character" here, and has made herself useful to many people. She sometimes takes the young daughters of her friends to Italy, to improve their minds. What effect she herself may have on those young minds one hardly likes to think. Her Corsican husband vanished two years after their marriage. So there's her story.'

'Thank you,' Sibyl said. 'I suppose it might be worse. It's unlikely I shall ever see her again, and after all, I shan't be here for much longer.'

He turned and looked at her, and what she saw in that lined, intelligent face deeply disturbed her. If it wasn't a kind of anguish, then she didn't know what the word meant.

'I can't let you go,' he said with great seriousness. 'I can't. Somehow we belong together. If you go away, you'll leave an emptiness I can't bear to contemplate. My sister, my dear little sister if that is what you are, you mustn't go. I need you, I need you!'

She put her hand into his. 'Dearest Felix, don't exaggerate. A week ago – barely a week – you'd never heard of me. We must be sensible about this. There's a great liking between us – call it love if you like, there are so many kinds of love. This is one kind, it's *our* kind, and it's real. I know it's real because I feel it too. But we must *manage* it, we must tame it. And you must help me, and I'll help you.'

'I'll tell you this,' he said, as the taxi made its way along the Rue de Rivoli, 'and I mean every word of it. I'd give my very soul, if I have a soul, if we hadn't the same father. So there it is. Now I've said it. I suppose this must often have happened before, or something like it, but it's never come my way. Byron, yes, we know all about that, but this is different, it's *stranger*, I can almost feel it's unique. Oh, my God! we'll be at Madame Ginette's in another minute, and we'll have to think about a dress.

Promise me that you'll never put it on without remembering me.'

'I can promise you that. But couldn't we go there another day? Do you want, really, to go now, after all we've said?'

'Yes. We'll go now. It's something I want to do.'

The little shop, Madame Ginette herself – 'Never ask her the price of anything,' he had warned her, 'she's entirely to be trusted. You'll know the price when the time comes to pay, and then that's my affair – ' were welcome distractions from that disturbing and revealing exchange of words in the taxi. As they were walking into the shop she was almost physically aware of her father's presence. This had not happened to her before. It was as if he were there to ask her, in his quiet way, 'What am I to think of all this?' Even Hugh Beallby seemed not far away. And what would they have thought if they could have seen her step out of a dressing-room in a chiffon dress of lovely colouring that, it was agreed, was the right dress for her? A dress that was now to be bought for her by the ten-year-old boy who had followed his mother out of the burning house? Buying a dress today for a half-sister who was then merely a part of the unknowable and far-away future. The twist in time fascinated her.

'I could wish that everything were simpler,' she thought as they left the shop, the dress in a neat box under her arm, for she insisted on carrying it back to the hotel herself.

But they hadn't come to the end, that day, of the strange, the bizarre and the unexpected. It took place as their taxi approached the Pont Neuf on the return journey. Felix asked the driver to stop, as soon as he safely could, to let them out. 'We want to walk across the bridge,' Felix told him. 'Meet us on the other side. We'll look out for you.'

Foreign sightseers, wanting one more view of the river; he was used to such as these. After looking cautiously into his mirror, he drew up at the kerb.

'We'll only be a few minutes,' Felix said as they got out. 'Try not to park too far away.'

What in the world has he got into his head now, Sibyl wondered, but decided to ask no questions. The strangeness of their relationship, of the whole situation, was still with her. Even Mr Beallby seemed to be with her still, with his cautions and his warnings. Felix took her arm and they walked until they had reached what appeared to be the middle of the bridge.

'A little ceremony is about to be enacted,' he said. 'I've put it off and put it off for more years than I like to think about. But I'm glad I did, because this is the real, right moment for what I have to do. I wish I could throw away my memories as easily.'

He put his hand into his pocket and took out of it a small, cardboard box. There was something oddly portentous, she thought, in the way he did it, something unusual and unlike him. The box had an elastic band around it and this he removed and threw into the river. Then he took out of the small box – which he likewise threw into the river – a small object. She saw that it was a key, the key of a door, old and tarnished.

'Mr Beallby will no doubt have told you,' he said in a level and expressionless voice, 'about our running away from the burning house and the hideous tragedy in that upstairs room. And the tragedy too of my stricken father, who, I suppose my mother had never really loved. Would he live? Would he die? Was he perhaps already dead? We didn't know. I doubt if she even cared then. The two of them had been dining out with friends and came back to that horror, and the fire engines, and my guilt. I had locked Felicia, my little sister, in the playroom in a fit of temper, then I lost the key, this key you see here, and when the playroom was ablaze I couldn't open the door. I tried to get in at the window, but fell. So it was all as bad as it could possibly be. My mother – I was her treasure, her darling – packed two suitcases quickly and we hurried out to the garage to put them into her little car. I was behind her, half carrying half dragging the heaviest suitcase when I saw this, the key I had lost, shining in the light from the burning house. I don't know what made me stop and pick it up, but I did and here it is. No one but myself has seen it. And now you have. God knows why I kept it. A kind of self-inflicted punishment, perhaps. It's been hidden away all these years. I've taken it out and looked at it endless times and put it back again.'

She too looked at it lying in the palm of his hand and felt chiefly an overwhelming pity. 'Throw it away,' she said, gently. 'Now.'

He gave his hand a little toss and the key fell into the Seine making, possibly, a tiny splash that could not be heard. Then they turned quickly away and she wondered whether it was life or death they turned away from. It could have been either. Or both. They walked away to the far side of the bridge and found the taxi, thanks to the driver's shout, parked in a line of cars. They drove back to her hotel and said, as they parted, 'A demain.' They could have said no more at that moment.

She dined that night with one of her father's few friends in Paris, the only one she knew well enough to get in touch with. He was a lecturer at the Sorbonne, stout, grey-bearded and with a suitably middle-aged wife. It might have been a dullish dinner except that they talked about her father for whom the professor, Dr Duplesse, had a great admiration. They were kind people and she felt she was doing what her father would have liked her to do, but she was glad when they took her back to the Petit Cercle – the wife driving – for she was mentally and physically tired out.

She wanted to be alone to think about Felix and that strange little ceremony on the bridge. What other man would have kept that key, would have known it so deeply for what it was, that small, physical object that might now, it could be argued, have had no real existence? She could imagine her father saying in his often light and humorous way, 'Far-fetched though the hypothesis may be, it is at least arguable that the object with which your thoughts are at this moment occupied, does not and never did exist.' The subject of sense-data would probably have come into it. She loved to follow his arguments as far as she was able and could often follow him all the way. (It was like wandering, she used to think, upon some other planet.) 'Unless a thing has the ability to exist unperceived, it is not to be counted as a physical object.' That key, that key! She couldn't get it out of her thoughts. She wondered while half asleep if it wouldn't be a wise move and one that would have gratified her father if she were to give up her work at the museum and devote herself to philosophy, but a few minutes later she fell fully asleep and the idea, if she had given it serious thought next morning, would have made little sense. She had to find her own way (not his) through the labyrinth of living. It was, after all, the human task.

CHAPTER VIII

The Fifth Day

It was a day she meant to make the most of; she had shopping to do as she wanted to take home presents for Mrs Tronsett and the Hardwick family. After this she spent a half hour at an exhibition of Modern Art at the Petit Palais but found no pictures there that she thought could compare with Felix's. She had a light lunch at a heavy price, visited Notre-Dame for old times' sake, then the Sainte-Chapelle for the same reason and went home by taxi. Her driver seemed pleased to chat with a foreigner and told her about the students' riots of a few years before and said he hoped he would never see their like again. He showed her a scar on his face from a thrown bottle.

Back at the hotel once more she did some work on an abridged translation she was making for young scholars, of Plato's *Timaeus,* a labour of love but of necessity too, for if Greek were too long neglected it took its revenge and made itself doubly difficult, and she didn't want this to happen. So she had with her a small, worn copy of *The Timaeus,* a good Greek-English dictionary and her own half-finished manuscript. Enough to travel with.

She looked forward to the evening greatly, above all because it would be spent with Felix. She hoped at the same time that it would result in easier relations with Lucille. She thought Felix's management of his domestic life admirable, but didn't doubt that the presence of Annette, problem child though she was, helped to draw the two together and keep them so.

They called for her in a taxi at seven. Lucille followed Felix into the lobby of the hotel with a childlike air of wanting to be seen and admired and found Sibyl waiting there with her usual promptness.

'How charming you look!' Sibyl exclaimed, with an admiration she sincerely felt. As the evening was very warm, Lucille had put on no wrap. She was wearing a very becoming black evening dress trimmed with lace, which showed off to their best advantage her smooth, plump neck and prettily-rounded arms. Her fine, shining golden-blonde hair was gathered up on the top of her head and decorated with a black rosette. The prospect of a gay evening and the knowledge that she was looking her best quite took away her shyness and she was pleased by Sibyl's compliment.

'But you too!' she cried. 'You look beautiful!'

'Well, at least,' Sibyl answered, 'neither you nor anyone else here has seen this dress before. It's an old friend.' She felt at once that the reserve, the suspicion, the awkwardness of their first meeting had entirely gone. She was accepted, even, she felt, trusted. Felix said they mustn't linger or they would be late. Dinner at the Grand Vefours must not be eaten in a hurry.

Henri was waiting for them at the restaurant, and both men, in the unavoidable present-day fashion, wore business suits. Looking about her as they went in to dinner, Sibyl remarked, 'One of the words I most despise is the word "*ambience*", but undoubtedly this place has it!'

The dinner was excellent, the wine chosen by Felix was, they all agreed, perfect, Sibyl remarking – for it was a wine she knew – that she had learnt something about wines from her father, and that he would have greatly approved of this one. Which caused Henri to say:

'Tell me something about your father. You speak of him in the past tense. I had hoped he was alive and well in London.'

'No, alas,' she answered. 'He died quite recently and this is the first time I've been abroad without him.'

After a suitable expression of sympathy he said, 'Let me see if I can guess what he was. I think a writer. Perhaps of history?'

She gave a quick glance at Felix. How much did his good friend Henri know? Were they now on awkward ground, or didn't it matter? This should have been discussed between them earlier. 'Well, you're quite right,' she said. 'He was a writer, but he wrote on philosophy and mathematics. Your father, I suppose, was a diplomat like yourself.'

'Not at all. He was a manufacturer.' And he added with one of his gay smiles, 'Of bicycles, if you please. Bicycles in their thousands. I myself would ride a bicycle in Paris if it were not so dangerous. And perhaps it would look odd if I chained it every day to the railings at the Quai d'Orsay.'

'I love bicycles too,' Sibyl said. 'I've never owned a car or even driven one.'

'I,' cried Lucille, emboldened by the wine and her enjoyment, 'would like to drive a fast, fast car, something very beautiful and expensive. Not like Felix's old Citroën. But he won't even let me drive that.'

'I value your life too highly, my dear,' Felix answered. 'You have many skills, but I doubt very much that you would ever make a safe driver.' She pouted at him reproachfully.

They took care that the talk did not become the sort of talk from which Lucille would feel herself excluded and consequently hurt, and Sibyl thought the men showed admirable tact. She wondered while they talked how much Henri knew about his friend's earlier life. Probably very little beyond the fact that he had been born in England and that his mother, after divorcing her English husband, had married into a rich, well-known French family. But he had a quick intelligence and if he had happened also to know – and why should he not? – that Felix's father was at one time a professor of philosophy at Oxford, might he not now be wondering a little? He knew both Felix's professional name and the name he was born with, so he must assume that they were in some way related, though they had not said so. Well, she would leave all that to Felix, who could tell Henri as much or as little as he liked. And what harm could there be in his knowing that they were half-brother and half-sister? However, Felix's reticences were his own affair and were probably caused by his unwillingness to speak about the past. Certainly Mr Beallby would have approved, if he could have approved of anything that concerned Felix.

The play turned out to be a disappointment – his favourite critic, Felix complained, had let him down – and only Lucille found it amusing. She laughed unrestrainedly at all its artificial and clumsily-contrived situations while the others tried not to comment on its ineptitudes because of her enjoyment. So they put a good face on it and pretended to find it entertaining.

Sibyl said quietly in Felix's ear, 'I've seen far worse in London if that's any comfort to you.'

In one of the intervals she remarked to Henri, taking care not to be overheard by Lucille, 'It's hard to pretend it's anything but a bad play, though the audience seem to be loving it. I suppose the general taste has changed more than some of us realize. But I don't much care. There's rarely a time in London when I can't see a well-produced Shakespeare play, and sometimes a good modern one comes along to give us hope.'

'Like most Frenchmen, at least of my acquaintance,' Henri told her, 'I'd much rather see a play by Molière – say the *Bourgeois Gentilhomme* or the *École des Femmes* than a Shakespeare play. I have to admit I find him too hard to understand. I don't think he translates well into French, and my English is too poor to enjoy him in the original. So there, I fear, we part company, though I hope, humbly, to be forgiven.'

She answered, smiling at him, 'I could forgive you far worse things than that, Henri,' but she thought with amusement of her having told Felix at lunch after Henri had left them, that as a husband she felt he might "do". Well, he wouldn't do. There were some things it would be necessary to have in common and in her opinion Shakespeare would be one of them.

At the night-club, later, Henri cast off such gravity as he had so far retained and danced with enthusiasm and a surprising lightness and agility, twirling Sibyl about by the hand and then closing with her again, going through all the newest dance-motions with arms and shoulders and showing great *expertise*. She laughed as she thought she had not laughed for a very long time and took pleasure in her own gaiety. Felix did not dance at all, had never been a dancer, though years ago, he said, he used to go to riotous students-balls, usually in fancy dress.

'Then,' he said, 'I could forget myself. Here I would feel I was putting on an act, and badly.'

Henri danced with Lucille as often as he danced with Sibyl and later looked his fill with an endearing openness and enjoyment at some almost naked and very lovely girls. His gaiety made the evening perfect for Lucille, who was clearly in her own particular sort of heaven. She had not drunk much wine at dinner but the champagne at the night-club was wholly to her taste.

When Lucille and Henri were once again on the dance-floor, Sibyl said to Felix, 'When will it be time to go? You gave up most of a morning to me yesterday, you mustn't lose another morning so soon.'

'We'll go at half-past two,' he said, looking at his wristwatch. 'Lucille would stay of course till they put out the lights. Henri can take a taxi for himself to his apartment, and we'll drop Lucille at our house first and then I'll take you back to the Petit Cercle. I suggest that on Sunday we drive into the country and have a picnic somewhere, in the forest of Fontainebleau perhaps – Annette loves going there – and you could have supper with us afterwards at the house. Then on Monday night we go to Louise Dumontelle's party, and on Tuesday night – '

'Stop, stop, Felix! On Tuesday I must go. I must, I must.'

'No, no. Henri wants to give a little dinner-party for you on Tuesday night. He's told me who he's asking to meet you. Don't, please, make plans to go yet. I can't bear the thought of it.'

'Felix,' she said with sadness, 'isn't it wiser not to prolong this? There'll be other meetings, I hope, in other places. We'll get used to each other. We'll slip into a truly brotherly and sisterly relationship. We must. It would mean so much to me.' He quickly picked up her hand and kissed it, but made no comment.

It was raining when they left and they had to wait a long time for taxis. When they dropped Lucille she was far too bemused with champagne and with the joys of the evening to protest, and also admitted to feeling slightly sick. Then the two of them drove on to the hotel. By this time it was well after three. The hotel door was locked and Felix had to ring the bell several times before the night porter came slowly and opened it. He was a big, heavily-built man with a bloated face that was now full of resentment and ill temper. Sibyl had disliked him from the first. He looked from one to the other with what could only be called an ugly leer, then let loose upon them a volley of abuse mixed with every filthy expression at his command. It was so completely unexpected that for an instant Felix stared at him as if he could scarcely believe what he heard. Then, with a powerful blow of his fist he caught him on the chin and knocked him flat. He went crashing to the floor like a felled tree. The noise brought a frightened little clerk wearing a hastily-donned dressing-gown from a room at the back of the lobby.

'That fellow,' Felix said, holding his right fist in his other hand, 'has insulted this young lady, and I have dealt with him in the only possible way. I will see the manager tomorrow morning before nine. This is a most disgraceful affair and that animal must be got rid of.' Then he turned to Sibyl. 'Will you take me to your room? I must wash my hands, I think the right one is bleeding a little.'

The clerk, stammering apologies and looking frightened, gave Sibyl her key from behind the desk and took them up in the lift. When they were in her room Felix went into the bathroom and gave his hands a thorough washing. The one that had struck the blow was bleeding between the knuckles and she quickly took from her travelling-case a small bottle of iodine and a roll of bandages.

'I'm so sorry! I'm so sorry!' she said as she put on the bandage. 'But what a splendid blow you dealt him! Thank goodness I'll be out of here tomorrow. What a disaster for you though. I doubt if you'll be able to use a brush for days.'

'That doesn't matter. I only hope you didn't understand anything he said, the ugly brute. He must have been sitting there drinking for hours. Now listen to me, my child. I'll call for you tomorrow before nine o'clock, so be packed up and ready.' He looked about him. 'What a poor little room they've given you! Hardly big enough to squeeze two small beds into. But all the same, how I would love not to have to leave it and go home!'

Here was a new Felix. She was not slow to feel the change in him. She answered in a voice that was cool and incisive:

'That I'm afraid you must do at once, my dear Felix. It's terribly late.'

'I know, I know. But how I hate to say goodnight! Oh, my darling, must we say goodnight?' He took her quickly into his arms before she could answer what he knew she would and must answer, and held her to him as if he meant never to let her go. 'What heaven it would be if I could stay! Just stay and stay and never be separated from you again. You must know that I love you, as I've never loved in all my life. Does it matter so much – the accidental fact that we had the same father – *if* we had the same father? I doubt it more and more. I don't believe it, and I don't want to believe it. I could live even here with you and be happy. "Infinite riches in a little room!" Oh, let me stay even for an hour, or two hours. Let me stay!'

He had passed, it seemed, the limits of the bearable, and kissed her with an abandonment and passion that in her thinking about him she imagined he was not likely ever to feel again. This was an entirely new Felix, a young man in the first ecstasies of love, loving as if there were neither past nor future, nothing but this moment and this hunger for more and more and more. She was utterly taken by surprise by these wild kisses, these soiling kisses that could only bring shame and remorse to them both. But were they nothing more than that? She found herself responding in spite of this shame to the very edge of a danger that she had not even imagined, but if danger it was, it only beckoned them on, demanding that they forget everything in this compelling joy.

But it was she, not he, who was still not too far lost to recover the will to resist, and she pushed him from her with all her strength, breathing like an exhausted runner, her eyes pleading with him to help her, to fight against this menace to all their future happiness, their mutual trust and respect. The imploring look in those wide grey eyes brought back his self-control and his pity. For he loved her and knew that he loved her too deeply to demand from her anything she was not willing and happy to give, and there were those age-long inhibitions that he could only fight against if she willed it too, though some deep-down disbelief in their brother-sister relationship had come up to the surface and made itself felt. It was as if he *knew* something he did not know he knew until those wild moments that seemed to have unchained so much.

She crouched down on one of the beds, her hands over her face, her smooth brown hair disordered now and falling over both face and hands. She was like his painting of the despairing woman on the broken steps of the deserted house. He sat down beside her and took her gently into his arms.

'Don't cry, my darling, my poor darling. I'm altogether

to blame, and yet who could blame me for loving you? Think of me what you like, but never forget and never doubt that I love you completely. Lift up your head and look at me, and say you forgive me.'

She raised her head, throwing back her hair and letting him see her streaming eyes and wet cheeks.

'Forgive you? We have to forgive ourselves, as well as each other. Oh, my darling Felix, it was all so happy before, and now it's in ruins! Between us, we've killed something rare and lovely.'

There was a knocking on the wall; they had disturbed some sleeper in the next room.

'We can't talk here, and there's so much I want to say.'

'No, we can't talk here. It's impossible. And you must go. You must go.'

'Yes, I'll go. But remember, I'll be here at nine, to take you to your new hotel.' He took out his handkerchief and gently touched her wet cheeks. 'Try to sleep, my darling. And forgive me. And lock your door as soon as I've gone.'

He went to the door, only pausing to say, 'At nine, remember,' and to take a quick farewell look at the little room, as if he wanted to imprint it and its meagre contents on his mind for ever. She got up the moment the door was closed behind him, and locked and bolted it. Then she undressed quickly, and got into bed, trying not to think, trying not to believe that this was the end of all their happiness together, not even troubling to pick up from the floor and hang up the dress that she wanted never to wear or even to see again. For the first time in her life she felt she had reached, if not the heart and centre of it, at least something quite near enough to total despair.

CHAPTER IX

The Sixth Day

He kept his word, as she had known he would, and was there before nine next morning. (Had he slept at all, she wondered. She had slept for a bare two hours.) He rang through to her room to say he was coming up himself for her suitcase. She said it was quite ready and a moment later he was at the door that she held open for him.

They stood looking at each other as if searching for some change that both dreaded to find, but they had recovered from the emotions of the night before and each appeared to the other to be showing signs of too little sleep, but otherwise just as usual. They went to the lift, he carrying her big suitcase, she with her small travelling-case and handbag. He said as they were carried down:

'That night porter, I almost regret to say, has recovered but of course he will be sent away. I suppose I might have killed him but drunken men are in less danger of serious injury than sober ones. By the way, no tipping. I have done what's necessary and there's a taxi waiting.'

It was the old Felix. What had happened the night before might never have taken place and whatever their feelings they made a show of being back on their old footing. She took his hand and looked at it. The bandage had not been changed. She said, 'Please ask Lucille to put on a fresh one for you.'

'Don't worry about it,' he said. 'It's nothing.'

The taxi took them to the modest little hotel in the Boulevard Beaumarchais, on the edge of the Marais, and a porter took the suitcase and showed them up to her bedroom on the second floor. It was at the back of the hotel and overlooked a small courtyard in which was a young chestnut tree. It was the room which she had been shown earlier and it seemed to welcome her back. She felt at home in it and said gratefully, 'I'll be quite happy here, and now I'll unpack. Will that injured hand interfere with your painting?'

'No, no. I can use a brush perfectly well. Remember we're calling for you with a picnic lunch at ten tomorrow and when we get home you're staying to supper. But what will you do all day today?'

'You forget that Lucille is lunching with me. She's meeting me here. After lunch I'll go to the Carnavalet, which I love, and then later I'll probably go to the Soubise Palace where I've never been, to see Joan of Arc's one surviving letter. Perhaps Lucille will go with me.'

'I doubt that. She has no love for museums.'

'Well, we'll see. And tonight, as arranged, I'm dining with Henri. He's calling for me at eight.'

'Yes, I'm glad of that. He rang me up early this morning before he was dressed to tell me about a letter he'd had from his ex-wife. I'm afraid he's faced with something of a problem and it wouldn't surprise me if he told you about it.'

'Oh, poor Henri! I'm sorry he's in difficulties. I like him so much, and I think I'd like to stay on one more day and go to that dinner-party he spoke of. Then on Wednesday, dearest Felix, I must leave Paris – and you. Wisdom and caution tell me I must.' And she turned away her head. 'I must go, I must!'

'No, no!' he cried. 'That's out of the question. What on earth would you do alone in the Dordogne? You must stay here. You like this little hotel, and I intend to pay your expenses. Stay at least another week, and then we'll see. In a very few days – perhaps even tomorrow – I may have news for you.'

She turned to face him, and gave him a doubting, questioning look. 'What sort of news?'

'Something that will concern us both – very deeply.'

'You'd rather I didn't ask what it is?'

'Yes.' A brief silence followed during which they stood side by side, their arms touching. Both looked out of the window, though there was little more to see than the small tree and beyond and above it the roofs of some very old houses.

'Felix,' she said, 'tell me please how much your friends know about us? Henri, first of all, and his sister whom I'll be meeting on Monday night. Do they know what our relationship is?'

'Not from me. I've told no one. They suppose us to be first or second cousins, I imagine, as we have the same name. Does it matter if they go on thinking so?'

'I suppose not, though I'd much rather they knew the facts. Why don't you want them to know what our real relationship is? I'm proud of it. Why shouldn't they know? Why keep it from your friends? Lucille knows.'

'Why? Because I don't like speaking of it. It brings back too much that I want to forget, and they'd no doubt ask questions. And there are other reasons too. As for Lucille, I've told her to say nothing to anyone.'

She protested with a slight impatience, 'But Felix, dearest Felix, they need only know that your father married again in middle age, and that I am your half-sister by his second marriage. What harm could that do, to us or anyone?'

'Because, if you want a straight answer, I am totally unable to believe it myself.'

There was reproach and incomprehension in her face as she looked into his eyes. She answered, 'Only because you prefer not to believe it, my dear brother, for reasons we both know all too well. There can be no other possible answer.'

His reply came without hestitation. He had made up his mind to answer her in the only way that was now possible for him.

'The reason, my darling Sibyl, is this. From the first moment when you came into the Fragonard and held out both your hands to me I fell in love with you.

Spontaneously, naturally and unthinkingly in love. And this in spite of the fact that you had already told me who and what you were. At first I made a great effort to play the part you expected me to play and treat you like a sister, but it very soon became totally unreal to me – a pointless sort of game. I'm afraid it's as simple as that.'

'Simple!' she cried out in dismayed and startled disbelief. 'You call it simple? It's a tragedy! And I was so proud, so tremendously proud of the fact that you were my father's son. You, *you*, and what you've become. And now you want to deprive me of all that!'

He put both hands on her shoulders and looked her full in the face with his probing, honest and now deeply in earnest dark eyes, and she guessed, even before he spoke, that though he was not unwilling to accept the old inhibitions that had kept them apart the night before, he was now refusing to accept the fact that they applied to *them*. His next words made this quite plain.

'Listen to me, my dearest girl. In spite of all the facts as we know them, or think we know them, I'm convinced that some piece of the puzzle is missing. Every drop of blood in my body seems to tell me that I am *not* your father's son, though how this can be I don't yet know. Your father himself might have expressed it like this: "I am trying to fashion a new concept." And that is exactly what I am trying to do. So trust me for a little longer, for heaven's sake, trust me.'

But she was bewildered and could only demand of him with incredulity:

'Do you imagine you're an adopted child? That's impossible. Hugh Beallby would have told me.'

'No, it's not that at all.'

This refusal on his part to accept what was to her a simple and cherished fact presented new and unexpected problems. She felt rejected and confused. She asked him, with a slight acerbity in her voice, 'Why at this moment of all moments are you using words my father might have used? I thought you had never read a line of his.'

'I bought his last book. I was reading it for two hours last night when I couldn't sleep, lying on the sofa in my studio. It was so quiet that the whole of Paris might have been slumbering, and only I left awake. And I came to a number of conclusions.'

She once again gave him a troubled and puzzled look, then took his hands from her shoulders and turned abruptly away from him. She went with quick and resolute steps to her suitcase which lay open upon a folding stool. For the first time she felt at odds with this suddenly incalculable being whom she had come to love above all others. To love and to need.

'Goodbye then, Felix, for the present. I think I'd better not listen to your conclusions, as I've no faith in them. If I'm spending some days here, and I suppose I must, I'll get on with my unpacking.'

He made no protest but watched her as she pulled out of the suitcase the dress she had been wearing the night before, which lay neatly folded on the top. Then, as if the action in some way expressed what she was feeling, he saw her toss it to the floor. He went forward and picked it up, laying it gently on one of the beds.

'Don't throw away that nice dress, please. Well, if that's the way it is, I'll say goodbye. I may have some news for you very soon.'

He opened the door and went out, closing it quietly behind him. What a lot can be expressed, she thought, by the mere closing of a door. Another man after her curt dismissal might have closed it sharply, or with a bang. She went on with her unpacking, thinking, 'Am I quite mad to be doing this? I ought to be getting ready to go back to London.' But that she knew well enough she could not do. So close had they been, so great was their mutual understanding that she could only marvel at the sudden complete division between her mind and his, the division he had given her the first hint of in the taxi when he was taking her to buy her a dress. What on earth was he thinking of doing now? What could the news be that he said he might have for her soon? Was it conceivable that he might be going to see his lawyer with some idea of changing his name to Forbain? With the further idea, perhaps, that they might go and live abroad somewhere, pretending to be husband and wife? But surely he would never ask her to be a party to such a humiliating charade. And then there were those astonishing words that she could not accept and which deeply troubled her, 'Every drop of blood in my body tells me that I am not your father's son.' Now, instead of mere wishful thinking, it seemed to have taken on the strength of a conviction, and one which, knowing what she knew of the past, seemed to her wholly unrealistic and even absurd.

If indeed, as he so frankly and emphatically said, he had fallen in love with her, the sooner she went home the better, rather than stay and see the situation worsen. The loss of all she had hoped for would be a bitter one, but she had to begin facing it now. And as she took her things out of her suitcase and began putting them away in drawers and cupboards she kept asking herself, '*A quoi bon? A quoi bon?*' and there was no answer.

But for the fact that her bedroom was at the back of the hotel for greater quiet, she might have been able to look out at the boulevard and see Felix standing for a moment undecided on the pavement, bareheaded in the sun and hands deep in the pockets of his jacket. He was looking up and down the street. There was not a taxi in sight. He then began walking quickly away, looking back over his shoulder from time to time in case a taxi might come up behind him and pass him by before he could stop it; but none came. Then, after walking for some minutes he saw one on the far side of the street, an empty one keeping close to the pavement and moving in a fairly leisurely way. He gave a great shout but was not heard. He was too impatient to risk losing what he so badly wanted, and after a quick look up and down the boulevard he decided to chance it. No one would be likely to run him down if they could avoid it, so he darted across in rapid zig-zags – not without a good deal of horn-blowing, screaming of brakes and some curses – ran after the taxi and got into it as quickly as he could. Once inside he told the driver where he wanted to go, and asked him to hurry, though he knew perfectly well that he would probably be nearly half an hour too early for the appointment he had made that morning before setting out for the Petit Cercle.

Early or late, she would be there, and as the taxi turned down the shabby little Rue Lafosse and headed in the general direction of the Parc Monceau and the Rue de Courcelles, he felt he could relax. She would be there; he hadn't known her for nearly twenty-eight years without being sure of that. She rarely went out or was even ready to be seen before midday, and his urgent request that he be allowed to come early, before eleven in fact, had been granted sleepily and not without surprise, but it had been granted. It wasn't that she didn't want to see him, she always wanted to see him and was sometimes a little bitter because she saw him so rarely, but she was an enemy of early rising.

Rita Villet-Rocca was not a rich woman. She lived by her wits but they enabled her to live well. She had two great interests which gave her a foothold in two worlds – the art world, and to a more limited extent and quite unconnected with financial gain, the literary world. In short, paintings and Proust. She had become a Proustian at an early age – soon after she had made up her mind to live permanently in Paris and as near as possible to some area of it connected with Proust himself, preferably the Parc Monceau district. She had no intention whatever of returning to Ireland and in fact never saw her parents again after her twenty-fifth year.

Felix gave the taxi driver a generous tip and thanked him for combining speed with safety. Then he took himself up to the third floor of Rita's apartment-house with a prayer in his heart. If she couldn't – or wouldn't – help him, no one else could or would. He was not in any conventional sense a religious man, and he now wished he could call upon some higher power with a hope that he might not call in vain. Religious feeling, he believed, from its very earliest beginnings, came from the knowledge that man is incapable of controlling his destiny, therefore a Controller is sought for. But what kind of Controller, he asked himself with ironic amusement, could conceivably be concerned or be persuaded to concern himself with the question of whether or not Rita Villet-Rocca knew certain facts it would or might be of enormous benefit to him to possess, and be at the same time willing to reveal them. In short, the question which of two men was his father.

While he was reading *Journey into Philosophy* in the early hours of the morning he had come to the conclusion that he could not be the son of the man he remembered from his boyhood days and the author of that book. He recognized a powerful intellect at work, but one wholly at variance with his own type of mind. He was far too intelligent not to admire its clarity, its honesty and its dedication to the pursuit of knowledge and truth. He had studied philosophy for a short time and having heard Bertrand Russell so often spoken of in his early youth began with his *Outline of Philosophy*, then later on was persuaded by one of the professors he had known at the Sorbonne, to try Wittgenstein. But he found that the light they shed upon the world was too cold and too coldly logical a light for him and he decided to go no further with it. The universe with all its mysteries (even after Newton had performed his marvels) he was content should remain mysterious, one that he could happily and worshipfully move about in, while philosophy, it seemed to him, was like some fearsome old woman wielding an enormous broom, capable of sweeping away too much, capable of leaving the house not only clean but cleaned out, with not so much as a silvery cobweb left behind.

Sibyl had admitted to him in her honest and truthful

fashion that she was unable to discover any outward similarities between him and his father. He had tried to comfort her by saying, 'Why bother to look for them? I happen to look more like my mother. I have her straight nose and more or less the same facial bone-structure. I can see the resemblance all too well. Let's hope it ends there.'

Rita Villet-Rocca's elderly companion-housekeeper opened the door to him. She gave a little cry of surprise and dismay at seeing him. 'But Monsieur Félix, you are half an hour too early. Madame has just finished her *petit déjeuner*. She cannot possibly see you now. She is not dressed.'

'I know, Simone, I know, but please ask her from me to put on any sort of *déshabille* that pleases her, no matter what. Tell her I have something very important to talk to her about.'

She gave him a doubtful and almost disapproving look and went off to give his message. Meanwhile he went into what Rita called her boudoir, but which others usually called her study.

It was a charming room, the walls covered with dark green brocade but hung with many pictures, none of them large, but all of interest and value. She hardly ever made a bad bargain. She sold them when the right moment came, and bought others. There was a small Picasso which the painter himself had given her; a head of a woman whose features were not at all where one would have expected to find them. He went to look at it more closely and decided that if she wanted to sell it, the moment was *now*. There were many others, larger paintings, of less interest to him, in her drawing-room, but the gems, from the point of view of value, were here.

The only books in the room were Proust's. She had everything he had ever published – some of them in foreign editions – and all the best books that had been written about him. They were in low bookcases, below the pictures. He took out one and put it back again, and just as he was beginning to feel impatient, the door opened and in she came.

She looked very much, he thought, her usual self, and not at all as if she had dressed in a great hurry. The little, pointed, inquiring nose was well powdered, the wrinkled lips well rouged, her dyed, red-brown hair neatly dressed. And she was wearing a housegown of vivid green silk which fairly ballooned about her small figure. She raised both arms and gave him a perfumed kiss on each cheek.

'Darling Felix! Don't worry at all about being early. I would get up and dress in the middle of the night for you.'

'You look superb,' he told her. 'And bless you, Rita, for letting me come. I knew I could rely on your kindness.'

'*That* you can always do, my dearest boy, but I am simply longing to hear why you have come to me so early in the morning and in such a great hurry. Sit with me here on the little settee. There is room for us both, and I like to be near you.'

She gathered up and drew aside some of the spreading green silk, and he sat down. No sooner had he done so that she began at once, in a voice shrill with indignation:

'That mother of yours, my dear! That mother! Do you know, would you even *believe* that I have not had one single word from her since before she went to Corsica? *I*, if you please, her closest and best friend. Is she alive? Is she ill? Is she dead? Is she having some *affaire* she doesn't want me to know about? Even at her age, that is still possible.'

He laughed at her, with real amusement. 'My dear Rita, what a lot of nonsense you talk. You know very well that we never write to each other, and if she had been ill, Constant would have told me. As for the other, that's absurd, and you don't believe it for one moment.'

They had known each other for a long time and they never troubled to hide what they felt. In his boyhood, if they chanced to be at the château together, he had been fond of playing quite rough tricks on her and she would either shriek with laughter or call him every rude name she could think of in a mixture of French and Irish-English. The Irish accent was still faintly there and she hoped to keep it, but over the years her French had become fluent and grammatical. He, being wholly bi-lingual, spoke each language with scarcely a trace of the other.

'Well, say what you like, I don't know what to think. This has never happened between us before. She has not, if you please, said one word to me about going to stay with her in Corsica this year. I assure you, my dear, I am very, very deeply hurt. What have I done to make her angry with me? What can I possibly have done? Must I humiliate myself for her?'

Her indignation, her deeply injured feelings were something that he could never have hoped for. The day bloomed like a rose beyond the walls and windows, his heart beat as if it knew that he was poised at an instant in time when his whole life might be changed, and infinitely for the better, indeed for the very best that could be. It seemed that the Controller had taken charge for once with benevolent intent and was being of the greatest assistance to him without once being asked.

'My dear Rita,' he managed to say in a soothing tone, 'Why trouble your head about such trifling matters? My mother no doubt has a list as long as my arm of people she feels she ought to invite to Corsica. Your turn will come later. Probably the water is still too cold for bathing.'

'No, no,' she insisted, 'you're quite wrong. She has never before in all the years during which we've been the closest of friends, treated me like this. I deeply resent it. When I think of all the things I have done for her – they're countless my dear, they're endless – and now to treat me like an old discarded glove! It's beyond belief. One word, a telephone call, a mere postcard – that would have made all the difference.'

'Well, Rita,' he said, 'I really don't know what to suggest. I could write to Constant and ask him if he knows of a reason for this if you would like me to. Or you could write to him.'

'No, no!' she cried again. 'That's out of the question. Constant, as we both know, thinks she's perfect. Well, there it is. I have told you and that has been a small relief. Now I have news for you. Last night I was at a big dinner-party and Raoul Sachs was there. He informed me that he had just sold the last of your paintings. He said he had tried to telephone to you, but you were out, and he didn't want to give the news to Lucille. So now, at least, I am the bearer of good tidings.'

He took her claw of a hand and kissed it.

'I'm delighted to hear it, of course. And did you, by any chance, play some part in bringing about the sale?'

'Not at all. Not in the very least. I tried to persuade my rich Dutch friends to buy it, but they were too late. It was bought by an American named Ollendorf. A New Yorker. Very wealthy indeed, and a big collector of modern paintings. We will bear him in mind for the future.'

'What an extraordinary woman you are, Rita,' he said, and was sincere in saying it. 'You hear of everything, you know everything. You are fantastic.'

'All that, my dear, is my business in life. And now tell me what it is you have come to me about.'

'Well, my dear Rita, if you feel so inclined, and perhaps you may not, you could do me one more kindness; this time, a very great and very important one. So important that it could change my whole life. That's why I have come to you at this hour and in such a hurry.'

She cried out, 'Good heavens, Felix! What a preamble! And so unnecessary. Ask what you like of me. If it's within my power to do it, I'll do it. You've never asked anything of me before, in all the years I've known you, so you are quite unique among my friends.'

'Good, then I shall be unique no longer. I want you, if you will, to cast your memory back to about the time I was born and tell me, if you can, one single extremely important fact. I suspect you are the only person who could or would tell me, and if you can't, I shall have to remain ignorant. It is simply this. Whose son am I? The son of Professor Matherson or the son of Constant? It is absolutely vital to me to know the truth.'

She gave one of her shrill little cries, almost a small scream, and as he fully expected, did not answer him at once, wanting to relish, for a little, the feeling of immense importance, immense power that his question had given her.

'At last! At last! My dear, how often I've wondered if you would ever ask me this, and marvelled that you never did! I used to say to your mother, in no uncertain terms, that it was her plain duty to tell you, but she wouldn't listen. No. No, she knew best, she knew best. The truth was never, *never* to be told. You were hers, and only hers. She talked almost as if it was a miraculous birth. Well, fortunately for her, I am the most discreet of women and not one word of this has ever passed my lips. Not a single word. The answer to your question, my dear, is this. You are *not* Professor Matherson's son, you are the son of your so-called stepfather, Constant.'

For a moment he found it quite impossible to speak. He had to grasp fully this tremendous knowledge and control the wild thankfulness that was overflowing his heart, almost to the point of tears of gladness. At that instant of utter happiness and relief he saw not a single flaw in it, not a single difficulty, nothing that might have to be carefully and cautiously handled. It was quite simply the most colossal piece of good fortune that had ever or probably would ever come his way. He put his arm across the back of the little settee, pulled Rita to him and kissed her cheek, unable to utter one word. She waited, watching him, feeling like a benevolent goddess, with power over human lives. Then he asked, very quietly.

'Does Constant know?'

'He? He knows nothing of it. Simply and absolutely nothing. Why? Because your *dear* mother felt that she could never trust him not to give her secret away. And of course she was right in this. He would have told everyone, from sheer pride, or at any rate he would have told his closest and most trusted friends, and they in their turn would have told it to their closest and most trusted friends. No. No, your mother would never have risked that. She cared too much for *les convenances*. She couldn't bear that all Paris should know that she had had her son, in whom she took such pride, by a man who was not her husband. Her lover, in fact. Consider, my dear Felix, the kind of world your mother and Constant inhabit. It has changed little since the middle of the last century. Can't you imagine how the story would have spread? How people would have whispered to each other, "That good-looking son of hers is illegitimate." And don't forget, also, that in the first place her marriage to her young Oxford don *had* to be saved. It was of the utmost importance. Perhaps if she had gone to her fiancé at once, as soon as she went hurrying home, and told him *why* she had come hurrying home, he might and I daresay would have found it possible to forgive her. But instead she lied and deceived him, deceived him year after year. Few men, I think, could have forgiven that. And I was near at hand, luckily for her, to help her out of her troubles without his ever knowing the truth.'

Felix nodded his head, understanding much, seeing the whole of his past in a new light, and waited for her to go on.

'I suppose,' she then said, 'that you know something of her friendship with Constant when she and I were at Mademoiselle Tessier's together?'

'Yes, I do. When I was seventeen he decided to tell me

about what he called his "great romance", but I can
assure you that there was no mention of a child.'

'There couldn't have been, because he knew nothing
whatever about it. But I see I had better tell you the story
as briefly as I can from the beginning. Constant was one
of the school's trustees, and when she gave evening
parties Mademoiselle Tessier usually invited him. He
didn't often come, but one night he did, and he was
introduced to your mother. It was love at first sight. He
was infatuated, but absolutely infatuated, my dear. Soon
he was asking "La Tesse", as we called her, if he could
take your mother out to dine and dance and she agreed on
the condition that I went also and that he would invite a
suitable young man to make a fourth. It was always the
same one, a boring young man who cared for nothing but
horse-racing. However, I knew I could expect nothing
better.

'Well, Constant was well known to be something of a
roué, but to him, young girls were sacrosanct, and he
never made the slightest attempt to seduce your mother.
So she, knowing he had a wife who wasn't expected to
live very long, decided that she had better do the seducing
herself. She told me what she intended and I begged her
not to make herself cheap. "Cheap!" she cried. "I mean
to do just the opposite. I mean to make myself the dearest
thing in his life." "And what about your engagement to
your young professor?" I asked. "Oh, that," she said.
"I'd break that off at once if only Constant's wife would
have the goodness to die." She lived, by the way, another
nine years!

'So your mother told "La Tesse" that she wanted to
spend a weekend in Versailles with friends of her parents,
and got her consent. Instead she went to some *auberge*
deep in the country with Constant. I warned her about
what might happen, but she said, "Constant will know
how to take care of me." Well, whatever he did or didn't
do, it wasn't good enough. A few weeks later she
came to me crying and almost in hysterics and said that

the worst had happened. She was quite certain she was going to have a baby. If I couldn't help her she would kill herself. She'd been reading *Anna Karenina* and talked about throwing herself under a train in the metro! I told her not to be silly but to write at once to her fiancé and say she was sick and tired of Paris and the finishing school and only wanted to come back to England and have a home of her own with him. She had all the beauty, but luckily for her *I* had all the brains. Also I knew a girl who'd got herself into exactly the same fix and she told me how she'd got safely out of it.

'I didn't go to the wedding. I didn't want to go, but I did pay a visit to the young couple as soon as I left the finishing school, and I went primed with all the information I could get.

'First of all, I told her, she must contrive an accident when the right time came, and the accident must appear to be the cause of a premature birth. Riding, which she loved, was now out of the question, so she borrowed a pony and a pony-cart and drove herself about in it. My suggestion, of course. Well, my dear, she went out alone one day and quite deliberately threw herself out of the cart and into a tangle of brambles. It was a brave thing to do and she did it well. Luckily no bones were broken. She limped home, leading the pony, and said he'd run away and she'd been thrown out. She was put straight to bed and the doctor sent for, and what we'd been praying for took place. She showed great courage throughout. Of course it might have endangered your life, but luckily for us all it did not. So you, my dear, made your entry into the world some time before you were expected. At least by the doctor, and your supposed father. You were a small baby but perfectly healthy. I had begged your mother to eat as little as possible during the last four months, and she followed my instructions. That was no hardship, she was always the smallest of eaters. That beautiful face and figure were far more important to her than food.

'During the war it was difficult for the two lovers to keep in touch, but we managed to get letters across from time to time – "opened by censor" of course – and I was able to inform Constant that his beloved Angela had had her first child. If I got a letter from Constant, I enclosed it in one of mine and sent it to your mother. The professor disliked me so much that my handwriting on a letter was of no interest to him. It was not a pretty part I played and I was ashamed of it even then. I still am. But my devotion to your mother was very great. I was also extremely fond of your father, our dear Constant, and glad to do what I could. Throughout the war, as no doubt you know, he stayed in Provence and was of great help – he and his valet, Bertrand – in the Resistance. Their lives were very often in danger.'

'Yes, he has told me a good deal about that,' Felix said. 'Well, you have made it all wonderfully clear to me, and the remarkable part you played in it. How can I ever thank you enough, Rita? You have changed my life, and immeasurably for the better.' And he got up and began pacing about the room, unable to sit still any longer. She made no move but sat there, it occurred to him, like a basilisk with inflated crest and watchful eyes. But she had something more to say, and say at once.

'So now,' she remarked, giving him a sharp look out of those black eyes,' you can marry that charming girl you must have imagined to be your half-sister, and be happy ever after. And also, we shall all hope, be rid of Lucille.'

He wheeled about to confront her, complete, incredulous astonishment in his face. Her quick grasp of the whole situation had utterly amazed him. 'Rita! Are you some sort of witch? Are you some female devil masquerading as a woman? What can you possibly know about this girl? How *can* you know?'

'Well, my dear,' she said in her usual conversational manner as if she were talking for the sake of talking, 'surely you remember that on the day we met at your exhibition, this very week in fact, you introduced me – in a somewhat guarded fashion – to a pretty young English girl who seemed to know you rather well. She left, very quickly I thought, and I had to leave soon after. As I went out I saw Henri Dumontelle coming in. He and your charming friend met at the entrance and had a brief talk before she hurried away. I said to Henri, "Who is that pretty girl you were speaking to? I think she is a friend of Felix's." He said "Yes, I met her with him at lunch today." Well, my dear, you know my incurable curiosity, and though I could see he was pressed for time I asked him what her name was. He said she was a Miss Matherson, and that he thought you were perhaps cousins. Well, I had never heard of any Matherson cousins in your family and neither had your mother, whom I asked later. As I think you know, I take two papers and two only – *The London Times*, and *Le Monde*. I saw in *The Times* not long ago that our Professor Matherson had died. I read the obituary notice – a most flattering one – and learnt that he was a widower and had left a daughter. I was seeing your mother that very day, and I showed her the notice. She was, as you might expect, not greatly interested. I asked her if I should show it to you and she replied, a little sharply I thought, "I see no point in it whatever after all this time." So I never did show it to you. And there you are, my dear.'

He resumed his pacing, but his face had darkened. What had seemed clear and simple – or comparatively so – was simple no longer. He was beginning to see the difficulties ahead.

'Paris is too small,' he complained. 'It is important that no one should know about this.'

'I can assure you,' she said with some asperity, 'that no one will hear about it from me. But I am delighted to know that you will soon be leaving that common little *bourgeoise* Lucille and will be happy at last, as you well deserve to be.'

He decided to let this pass. Argument with Rita was unprofitable.

'I can see many problems ahead,' he said, and ran his fingers through his hair.

'I am quite sure you can,' she answered. 'Well, my dear, I have done what you asked. I have betrayed your mother's confidence, but only to you, and you had a perfect right to know. I hope all turns out for the best. Will you tell Constant?'

'And make endless trouble between him and my mother? Not for the whole world.' Then he had a new and disturbing thought. 'Rita, it might be useful for me to get some sort of proof of my birth, the sort, let's say, that would satisfy a lawyer. How, for heaven's sake, can I?'

Her black eyes had an amused sparkle in them.

'I really cannot imagine, my dear, unless I go down to the château and purloin your mother's diaries.'

He cried, 'Rita! God forbid!'

'She kept them from her seventeenth birthday until her twenty-first, when she got bored with them. I suppose not enough was happening. They are in one of those books that lock with a little key and usually cover five years. When I was at the château some months ago we had an argument about a date. We were in her bedroom, and she opened a drawer and took out the book, which of course I had seen many times before. The little key she wisely kept in another drawer in an old writing-desk of hers. She was quite right about the date, by the way. So there in her bedroom is the only proof that exists that you are Constant's son. She wrote down every detail of the whole affair.'

'Well,' he said, pausing in front of her, 'I can hardly suggest that you purloin them, my dear Rita. But I really am bothered to know how best to proceed. Never mind, illumination will doubtless come, and we won't discuss it any more.now. For what you have done for me I shall be eternally grateful.'

Then he was suddenly and unexpectedly overcome by the comic, the even absurd side of it all, and burst out laughing. 'Has the perfectly ridiculous aspect of all this struck you as it has me? It's like something out of a bad Victorian novel. It's too grotesquely funny for words. You know what I mean – the mix-up about the birth, the trickery, the lost heir, the secret, hidden for years, that brings two lovers together. It could have been written by – oh, what's her name? – I mean Ouida, don't I, or someone like her? So I am not the son of a humble professor, but the son of a wealthy French Count. The whole thing is a nonsense. And so, at last, thanks to an old friend of the family, I am able to marry the damsel of my choice.'

Rita was quite plainly not amused. She got up briskly. 'You won't think it quite so funny, my dear, when you come up against some of the difficulties that I can foresee.'

'Well then, for pity's sake let me have my laugh now.' But his laughter had stopped and his face was serious again. 'Yes, it will take some thinking out, but such problems as there are will be for me to solve, and solve them I will. I feel a new man, and that perhaps is just what I am. I feel – and am – re-born. And let me say once again that I shall be for ever – or for as long as I may live – deeply grateful to you.'

'Then you may thank me with a kiss,' she said, and he bent his head and kissed her cheek. 'And never forget,' she added, 'that you're my favourite man. Come to me again if I can help in any way. And now, my dear, I must run. Will you let yourself out?'

'Of course.' He watched her hurry off down the long corridor to her bedroom, her green skirts ballooning about her as she went. Then he left the apartment, ran like a youth of eighteen down the three flights of stairs and out into the street. 'We're free!' he was telling himself, still almost unable to credit the glorious fact. 'Free, free! Free to love each other to the end of our days.

What does anything else matter?' What were a few minor problems compared with the facts, the tremendous facts that were now his? He had never before questioned his paternity. Why indeed should he have done so? Such a thought had never entered his head until the appearance of Sibyl on the scene. It began then by his wishing, from the first moment of meeting her, that he was not her father's son. From that point onwards he began to wonder if it could just possibly *not* be true that he *was* her father's son. He remembered then very clearly indeed how, when he was seventeen years old, Constant had told him about his 'great romance'. And so gradually, only within the last two days, it had appeared possible, just barely possible, that there had been a good deal more in that romance than Constant had chosen to tell him.

His mother, whatever her faults, had never lacked courage, and much was at stake. She must have made up her mind to bind her lover to her in what she believed to be the most effective way. The results were not exactly what she had hoped for but luckily for her she had close at hand a tough, hard-headed, clever, cynical school-friend to take charge of things, and take charge she most successfully did.

He thought he would never have believed for one moment that he could owe his future happiness to Rita Villet-Rocca. In fact, it was more than likely that he owed her his life, even, possibly, his mother's life. Left to herself she might have sought an abortion at the hands of an unskilled or dishonest practitioner. Well, there it all was, he knew the facts now and saw that he would indeed have to 'fashion a new concept' for himself. This presented few difficulties for him. He was fond of old Constant, they had many things in common. His feelings about him would be little altered by the fact that he chanced to be his father and not his stepfather, and for Constant himself there would be no change at all.

One of the things he had always liked best about the old man was his love for his native place, his beloved

Provence and its history. This he had studied deeply, as far back as pre-Greek and pre-Roman times, including the two terrible wars he had himself lived through and taken part in, as well as many earlier and even, if possible, bloodier and more savage ones. The final chapter still to be written would describe the Resistance, with all its trials and dangers. He worked slowly, for his hands were stiffened by arthritis, writing down carefully and patiently all that he could learn from earliest recorded times to the near-present, and worrying his head not at all as to whether or not he would ever find a publisher. Felix sometimes went into his library while he was working – he was always welcome – and putting a hand on his shoulder would ask, 'How is it going today, old Visigoth?' Sometimes he called him 'The Grimaldi' for the old man enjoyed a little teasing. He was very often lonely. 'She is off again,' he would say, 'to visit some friends at Versailles.' And more recently, 'I miss your mother badly, although I'm happy at the same time that she's enjoying Corsica. I miss seeing her flitting about the house, like some gorgeous bird.'

It was Constant who had first aroused his interest in painting and had taken him to see the pictures in the fine museums of Provence. Among contemporary painters they had agreed that they liked Cézanne the best. It was Constant too who had often taken him, while he was still at school, to the Louvre. He owed him much. It was thanks to Constant that he had been taught to ride, and to ride well; he had sent him into the surrounding hills and woods and valleys with Bertrand, the game-keeper, (Bertrand later, in advancing years, to become valet and confidential servant. He was still there, older than his employer and an indispensable part of the household.)

As he had always detested, since his boyhood, the formal, unlovable house at Passy and the people who frequented it, Felix had cut himself off, little by little, from his mother's world. When, much later, he took Lucille and Annette to live with him, she was – or appeared to be – ready and willing to cut such weak cords of affection as still remained between them. The old man deeply regretted this break and had done his best, in times past, to mend it, but had long since given up trying.

As he walked towards home it occurred to him that much of the guilt he had felt at accepting money from his mother's husband might now be lessened, thanks to this new knowledge. He felt to some extent vindicated. It was as if he had received partial absolution, though it was only from himself to the self he had now become, that he received it. A burden was lightened.

Tired with walking, tired with thinking, he presently hailed a passing taxi and was driven the rest of the way home. He found on the hall table a note from Lucille saying that she had left a cold lunch for him in the larder. He decided that lunch was the last thing he needed, sleep the first. At about five-thirty a picture he had painted the year before of a weird, lonely and rocky landscape not far from Les Baux was to be called for, paid for and taken away – after a chat and a friendly drink – by a friend of Henri's who had seen and was determined to have it. He had given it a few finishing touches and it was now ready and waiting. It was a joyful thought that he might one day take Sibyl to the same place and paint another.

For the sake of his immediate peace of mind he tried not to think, at this moment of near-exhaustion, mixed though it was with elation, of what he called in his own private thoughts, Problems One and Two. Some solution would have to be found, and it must be a fair and a merciful one. Beyond that his tired brain would not go.

He went up to his studio and lay down on the couch where he had been lying not so many hours before – reading, thinking and trying unsuccessfully to sleep – pulled a light rug over himself and was asleep in seconds. He slept till after four and the first thing his waking eyes rested upon was the picture on its easel, waiting to be taken away.

'At least,' he said, and spoke the words aloud, 'I have a name of my own to give her now. Forbain.'

CHAPTER X

The Seventh Day

Lucille was late in arriving at the hotel in the Boulevard Beaumarchais. There was a corner just beside the entrance with a few chairs in it where people could wait, and there Sibyl sat waiting. Lucille apologized breathlessly when she arrived and explained that Annette had not been feeling well enough to go to school, so rather than leave her alone she had taken her to the old *bonne* who lived near by, and this had delayed her.

'Annette has one of her migraines,' she explained. 'They come quite often. Poor child, she is not very strong. I hope she will be better tomorrow.'

Sibyl said she very much hoped so too or she would miss the picnic, and then told Lucille that as they were lunching at the Fragonard, they had better hurry in case they should lose their table.

'Oh,' cried Lucille, 'please not the Fragonard! It is where Felix always takes his friends. May we go to the Café Huet instead? It is a place I like very much and where I feel at home.'

Sibyl agreed at once and rang the restaurant and cancelled the table. She was not at all sorry; the Fragonard, she felt, belonged to Felix and herself, for it was there they had first met. She took Lucille's arm and they walked quickly towards the Place des Vosges along the Rue du Pas de la Mule, passed by the Fragonard itself and presently came to the Café Huet. It was easy to understand Lucille's preference for it. It was a sort of bar-restaurant and a group of people had already gathered about the bar and were eating sandwiches together and drinking beer. There were some tables covered with the usual checked tablecloths and at one of these they sat down and were waited on by the bartender's agreeable wife.

Lucille said the hors d'oeuvres there were very good, and soon these in considerable variety were on the table. She was now on entirely happy and friendly terms with Sibyl, to whom it was soon evident that her guest's intention was to make her her confidante. She only hoped that her French would suffice for the demands she foresaw would be made upon it. Lucille was neatly and simply dressed, as always, and her pretty blonde hair was gathered up into its usual roll on the top of her head. She began by saying that she had got up very early, in spite of the lateness of the hour when she went to bed – (yes, she said, she had quite recovered, she had been foolish in drinking so much champagne) – and she had been busy preparing for the picnic tomorrow. She didn't know what time Felix had returned, he had gone straight to his studio for fear of disturbing her, and had slept there. He was always, she said, very thoughtful in those ways. Except on such occasions as last night they always slept, she artlessly said, in a large double bed.

'I will tell you,' she went on, 'how this came about. When we first lived in Felix's house, Annette and I shared a room. Then I went away to the hospital and had an abortion – I suppose you know that I had to have an abortion?'

Sibyl nodded. 'Yes, Felix told me.'

'Well, when I came back to the house again, I once more shared a room with Annette. Then one night – I think it was two months later – I woke up hearing, or perhaps thinking I heard, noises downstairs. There had been robberies in our district, and I was afraid there were robbers in the house. So I got up and knocked on Felix's door. He also got up, and when I told him about the noises we went downstairs together and searched all the rooms, but we found no one. When we came upstairs again I said, "Felix, I feel nervous and it is a very cold

night. Do you think I might come in and share your bed?"
He said, "Sooner or later this was bound to happen." So
ever since then, Felix and I have slept together, like
husband and wife.'

'Yes,' Sibyl said, 'I assumed that you did. It seems very
natural. But why are you telling me all this, Lucille?'

The hors d'oeuvres had been cleared away, and they
now waited for an 'Omelette portugaise'. Lucille's reply
was not slow in coming.

'Because I need your help. Will you please help me,
Sibyl? I like you so much and I feel you are my friend.
Also you are Felix's sister, or half-sister. It is almost the
same thing. It is like this. I want Felix to marry me. For
nearly eight years now we have lived together, like a
married couple, but we are not married yet, and I think
it is time. Will you please try to persuade him to make me
une femme honnête?'

There was only one way to deal with this difficult
situation, Sibyl thought, and that was with complete
honesty and candour. Marriage between those two could
only lead to disaster. It was so foolish an idea that she
marvelled that Lucille had given it serious thought.
Sensible and practical as she was, she should have known
better.

'Are you hoping,' she asked, 'that I will say what you
want to hear, or do you want my honest opinion?'

'But naturally, I want your honest opinion.'

'Well then, I think it would be a very great folly for you
and Felix to marry. Felix free and Felix tied would be two
quite different men. He is happy with you and he has
been happy all this time because he knows that you are
both free to make a change if either of you wants it. For
instance, if you should meet some nice man who would
like to make you his wife and give you his name, you are
free to accept him. Why change such a happy and convenient situation? If he had wanted to marry you, he
would have done so long ago. And he has been so

wonderfully good to you, Lucille, and to Annette. Why try to change anything? Especially as he does not want it changed.'

'It is true, he does not want it changed,' Lucille sadly admitted. 'He has said so. But I thought, "Sibyl has great influence over him." I thought perhaps he might listen to you.'

'I wouldn't dream of interfering in any way. I would feel I had no right to interfere. Why not consult Henri? He is a good friend and I am sure would give you honest advice.'

'I have spoken to Henri. He says I am very foolish to try to persuade Felix to marry me. He says that everything would go wrong if we married.'

'Then you have three opinions – mine, Henri's and Felix's, and all are against it. Be happy with things as they are. Don't you realize how wonderfully lucky you have been?'

'Yes, but if he marries someone else, what would become of Annette and me? We would be back on the streets again.'

'That's nonsense, Lucille. Felix would never allow that to happen. He has told me something about your unhappy life, but all that is behind you. You must try to forget it. You are very clever in many ways. There are a hundred things you could do, if ever you were left alone.'

'But I remember the past too well,' Lucille said, and tears came into those large, pale blue eyes. She removed the tears with a paper handkerchief. 'It was too terrible ever to be forgotten. Shall I tell you about the last days of that life, which is now like a nightmare? I had found out, of course,' she hurried on, 'that the man I lived with was a liar and a thief, and I was much afraid, both for Annette and myself. I worked in a shop, and the pay was not good. I took Annette with me each day because she could not go to school. The man always left the rooms we occupied every morning about ten – (he said they were his rooms and I had furnished them with my own furniture) – and he only came back in the evening in time for a meal. He would never tell me what he did. One day Annette had a bad migraine and I had to leave her at home. When I got back from the shop I found her lying on the bare floor, crying, crying. She said the man had gone out, and then had come back again with another man. They had a large van outside, and they took away all my furniture – the beds, the tables, chairs, kitchen things, everything, even curtains – so there was nothing left. We slept on the floor, and it was very cold. The next day a soldier came, in uniform. He said he was the man's brother and he had no right to bring us to those rooms, they were *his* rooms. He said he did not like to turn us out but he must have them as he was soon to get married. He said his brother was bad, and a thief. So we left, and we had nowhere to go, and I was going to have his child. Annette and I walked many miles together looking for a room, but we found nothing that we could afford. You see, that man had stolen all my savings. I had hidden them, but he had found the hiding-place. He said he would kill me if I told the police. I had nothing but what I had earned at the shop that week, and Annette and I slept on benches every night, so that we could pay something for food. When that was gone I had nothing, not a sou. So we went to the Luxembourg Gardens and sat there and I made up my mind what we would do. We were both crying. People looked at us and passed by. Then Felix came. He came and sat down on the bench beside Annette and me and asked what the trouble was. I told him everything, even that in a few months I would have that man's baby. So he said, "Come with me." And we went to his beautiful house, I had never been in such a house. And the kitchen – !'

'Yes,' Sibyl said. 'I can well imagine what you felt.' She took Lucille's hand in hers and said, 'Whatever changes may come, and I think none will come, Felix will see that nothing like that will ever happen to you again, you and Annette. I can promise you that.' But Lucille was not comforted.

'If he marries Madame Dumontelle, Henri's sister, he will never want to see me again.'

'What makes you think he will do such a thing?' Sibyl asked, her surprise mingled with some indignation.

'She loves him very much. I have seen them together and I know. Ever since she divorced her husband she has wanted to marry Felix. And she is very rich.'

'But do you imagine for one moment that Felix would marry for money?'

'Not only for that. He admires her too. That is one reason why I will not go on Monday night. I cannot bear to see her with her big dark eyes always fixed on him. She only asked me because it was polite and because she knows very well I will not come.'

'I think you're imagining things, Lucille. I don't think Felix is particularly interested in her, except as Henri's sister. For one thing, he would never want to live the sort of life she lives.'

'Well, you will see. And you will see why I am so troubled and worried. No one, but no one in the world, could love Felix more than I do. I would gladly die for him. But I cannot bear it if he marries someone else. So I beg you to say to him, "Marry Lucille. You will never regret it. She has only one wish – to make you comfortable and happy." '

This discussion, Sibyl thought, was getting out of hand.

'My dear Lucille, Felix's life is his own. I cannot make him do anything he does not wish to do. He knows his own mind. Now please let us talk of something else. Will you come with me after lunch to the Musée Carnavalet? I can assure you, it is very interesting and you would like it.'

But Lucille said no, she had shopping to do, and after that she had to go and fetch Annette from the old *bonne*, Marie. So they said goodbye at the door of the Café Huet.

Lucille kissed her on both cheeks, thanked her for the lunch, and said:

'You are very kind to me. I am most grateful. Forgive me for anything I have said that you do not like.'

And then, as tears started once more to her eyes, she turned and hurried away, and her pretty shapely little legs in their short skirt went twinkling away down the street.

'Poor child,' Sibyl said to herself. 'Poor child! Poor Felix! It is hard to know who to be sorriest for.'

She walked back, after her visits to the museums, through the Place des Vosges and having more time now to stop and look about her was distressed by the changes she saw in the most beautiful and oldest of Paris squares; changes that were chiefly the result of time and neglect, though some work was in progress here and there. More than a hundred elms had died of elm disease and were waiting to be cut down. Fortunately the chestnuts still flourished, and children were playing under their green shade. She walked through the arcades and the signs of decay depressed her. Years before, when she was eighteen, she had been there with her father and it had then seemed in the height of its beauty. Time, she thought, time! Change and decay! Her father had of course his theories about time and they often discussed it, and she, thanks to him, had arrived at theories that satisfied her. There was no such thing. It was an illusion. Time had no duration. Duration was the property of matter. Her father had told her a French epigram that delighted her, one that she could never forget:

'*Le temps ne s'en va pas, mais nous, nous en allons.*'

Yes indeed, 'Nous en allons,' and with what hateful inevitability! She now longed for 'time' to discuss these things with Felix. So far there had been none and she wondered with sadness if such opportunities would ever come or if the dangers and difficulties of their situation would divide them for ever. Only 'time' would tell. Whatever her feelings about its unreality, its non-existence in fact, it was a concept one could not do without. The parting from Felix which seemed to her bound to come would almost certainly come soon. She decided as she walked back to the hotel that it would be wise to choose a day, book a seat for herself on the plane and then slip away without his knowledge, leaving only a letter behind.

She had had a hasty note the day before from Hugh Beallby to say he would be ringing her up at her new hotel at six that evening, Saturday, and if she was not in at that time he would ring again later. He said he missed her mere presence in London, no matter how seldom they saw each other. He had telephoned Mrs Tronsett, and her sister was still with her. Both were well. He was 'Devotedly hers, H.B'.

She went back to the hotel, had a cup of tea and rested. At six exactly the call came.

'How are you, my dear? How I wish you were here so that I might worry about you less.'

'But you mustn't worry, Uncle Hugh. I am perfectly well and enjoying every moment of Paris. I didn't know how much I loved it.'

'But I feel you're getting involved in things you don't want me to know about. Deeply involved. Am I right?'

(Wicked, clever old dear, she thought! He knows everything and what he doesn't know he suspects!)

'Involved in what? In Paris, yes, and the people I've met here. Pleasantly and happily involved. Felix I see most frequently, and I wouldn't want it otherwise. I am dining with an old friend of his, Henri Dumontelle, tonight. I took Felix's *petite maîtresse* Lucille to lunch with me today. I suspect I am growing quite fond of her.'

'What are you doing tomorrow, Sunday? Something in the country I hope, if the weather is what it is here.'

'Yes, we're driving out to Fontainebleau for a picnic, all four of us, Felix, Lucille, her daughter Annette and I, in Felix's car. When we get home, I will have supper with them. What else can I tell you?'

'Anything. Anything. I am all ears.'

'Well, Monday night Henri's sister, a handsome divorcée, is giving a party, and I even have a new dress for it. Does that interest you?'

'Naturally it does, and I hope to see you in it one day. Do you like Felix as much as you did at first, or have I no right to ask that?'

'You've the right to ask anything. I use my discretion in answering. But the answer is yes, I like him even better.' And then she added, 'Oh, and Uncle Hugh, I've given up all idea of going to the Dordogne. I'll perhaps stay here for another week – I like this hotel – and then come straight home. I'll let you know precisely when.'

'Thank you, my dear. By the way, George Gawthorne and I are both involved in a case of considerable complexity and importance. Two great companies are at war with each other. George acts as counsel for one, and I am and have long been solicitor for the other. I fear it may drag on for some time. Meanwhile very little indeed goes well here. The news is nearly all discouraging – though of course we are all too British to be really discouraged – but as you no doubt read the English papers you will know as much as I know.'

'I doubt that, though I read *The Times* every morning. Things here in France are going better, it seems, than they have for a long time. In fact, better and better, and there is a feeling of optimism in the air. They look on us as poor neighbours, and are not, perhaps, as sorry as they should be. I ask myself, "Have they already forgotten the war and what we did in it?" The answer, I fear, is yes, they have. How human human beings are! But I mustn't go on chatting like this, it must be costing you a lot of money.'

'Money, my dear? What's that? There is one thing more I must say, which is that Charlotte is well and sends you her devoted love, as I do.'

'And please give her mine, and my love to you, dear

Uncle Hugh, and my ever-grateful thanks, and please, please don't worry, just ring me up again when you are in the mood.'

She thought as she hung up, 'How lucky I am to have an Uncle Hugh! Particularly when soon, if things develop as I fear they will and must, I shall not even have half a brother.'

Henri arrived in a small, speedy-looking car, one of the 'roadster' type. He said he had another, more dignified car, but felt that this one was *plus intime*.

'Where are we going?' she asked as she settled herself down beside him. 'To the Bois, I suppose.'

'How did you guess it?'

'Well, in this weather it seemed the most likely place.'

'You are quite right. It is a restaurant in the Bois where the asparagus and the *fraises des bois* are perfect, so I hope your appetite is good.'

'I'm being wonderfully spoilt here,' she said. 'It has never happened to me before, in the whole of my life. I've travelled a great deal with my father but we travelled like pilgrims, spending very little. Not of course in a group like pilgrims, always alone, just he and I.'

'You speak of "the whole of your life". You are, I suppose, perhaps twenty-five?'

'Getting on for twenty-six.'

'A child still. And how lucky I am to be taking such a charming girl to dinner tonight. But for this I might have been contemplating suicide.'

'That, of course, is nonsense, but Felix did tell me that something very worrying had happened.'

'He did not exaggerate. I am in a most impossible situation. Tell me this. Are you going to marry Felix? Or should I not ask? It is quite obvious to me that he is in love with you.'

'You should not ask, but as you have asked, I'll answer. No, Felix and I are not going to marry.'

'Then would you please marry me quickly instead? If

you agree, we will take the first steps tomorrow. No, tomorrow is Sunday. Monday, then. From tonight I will call you my fiancée, and you must call me yours.'

'Henri, have you gone a little mad? I have known you a very short time, but you seemed to me perfectly sane.'

'No, I am not quite mad, but very soon you will understand. Perhaps you would never love me as I am quite sure I could love you, but you could try, and in eight years I could promise to make you an ambassadress.'

'I think you really have gone a little mad. And you're driving much too fast. You nearly ran over that poor woman. She was terrified.'

'She had no right to try to cross there.'

'If it would have a quieting effect on you, you had better tell me – but calmly please – what has happened to you.'

'I will tell you soon, but now I must keep my mind on the best way to get there, avoiding the worst of the traffic.'

'Then we had better stop talking.'

'No, no, I must talk. You see, it is my ex-wife. She has left her husband and she is coming back to me, bringing, of course, our little girl, Andrea. I am afraid that she will force me to re-marry her, as I have been so foolish as not to marry someone else in the meantime.'

'She can't force you to re-marry her, surely.'

'She can. I fear she may. Her will is stronger than mine. And of course there is Andrea.'

'When does she get here?'

'She is flying here tomorrow. She will stay, thank God, with her mother for the present.'

'She might have given you a little more warning.'

'That is not her way. She is a woman of impulses. It was an impulse that drove her into the arms of her American. I have nothing against him, I found him *sympathique*, but she had known him less than a month.'

'And what has happened now?'

'I know no more than you do, except that she does not

like California and wants to come back to Paris and marry me again. Do you wonder I am not myself tonight?'

'No, but I think you are more worried than you need to be. You'll have plenty of time to think things over.'

'Again, that is not her way. She has already obtained a divorce, she tells me, in Las Vegas.'

'Already? My poor Henri! How quickly things can happen in America!'

'It is not a good thing for a diplomat – and I take my career seriously – to be twice married to the same woman.'

'I agree. It's most unfortunate.'

'If only I could say to her, "It's too late, I have already married someone else." Or even, "I am about to marry someone else." '

'Well, it won't be me, my dear Henri. You must know dozens of charming girls.'

'I do, but I dread making another mistake. You are so intelligent, so reasonable, you have so much understanding. I would feel safe with you. Also your face greatly pleases me.'

'Well, I don't feel safe with you. You're driving much too fast again. Fortunately I have strong nerves. But seriously, Henri, why decide anything in a hurry? "Play it cool." Do you know that bit of American *argot*?'

'Yes, but I am most wretched. I have very much enjoyed being a bachelor for three years. The only comfort for me is that I may now watch Andrea grow up.'

'But couldn't you have her with you for half the year, and let her mother have her for the other half?'

'That would never satisfy her. No, I am in for a bad time. In the the end she will succeed in making a *pantin* of me, as she did before.'

'*Pantin?* I don't know that word.'

'It is what you would call a monkey on a stick. And she will pull the strings.'

'What does Felix think about it?'

'He refuses, he absolutely refuses to offer any advice at all. He says it is for me alone to decide. And of course he is right.'

His sorrows occupied them until they arrived at the restaurant. He had to blow off steam. Soon, she felt sure, he would be his reasonable, sensible self again. They were given a table in the gardens, under the trees, and rhododendrons and gay bedding plants were all in bloom about them. Drinks were brought, and two martinis induced in Henri a more optimistic state of mind. Dinner was served while the sun, low in the sky, still had heat in it and birds still sang. There was all the sadness of a perfect day nearing its close, and she was grateful to Henri for bringing her there and a little ashamed of her longing for Felix to be there in his place. But even in his distressed state there was something pleasingly humorous and lovable about her host, and more than a little of the comedian. She understood Felix's fondness for him. Felix! If she could only get him out of her thoughts for a while, could at least stop turning their predicament over and over in her mind with a maddening repetitiveness. A sort of dialogue went on between them even while she and Henri were talking together. She longed to be talking about Felix, but this was impossible, there was too much that had to be avoided. Then, at last, she found a topic that although it concerned Felix, she could at least speak about without indiscretion.

'So far Felix has told me very little about his step-father's château in Provence,' she said. 'Tell me what it's like. Is it all turrets and steep roofs and small windows like so many one has seen?'

'Not at all. On the contrary it has great charm and was built in a good period – the early eighteenth century. I would say it was a château of the Renaissance, almost classical in design. I will try to describe it. You approach it down a long avenue of orange trees – the kind we call *bigarade* . . .'

'Yes, I know. Seville oranges.'

'Exactly. Once there was an avenue of fine *tilleuls* – I believe you call them "lime trees" for some reason – or is it "lindens"? Anyway, some of them were blown down in a terrible storm, so all of them had to go. But the avenue of orange trees is very pretty. The rooms in the château are full of old French country furniture – none of that boring Louis Quinze stuff that fills the house at Passy. I wish you could see the place. There are pillars beside the entrance, and an architrave – I think that is the right word – or should I say pediment? – above it. All rather Greek in style. And a double, curved, wrought-iron staircase of great elegance leads up to the front door. Have I made all this clear to you?'

'Perfectly. So long as you avoid modern French slang, I can always follow you. It sounds a most lovely place, but alas! I shall never see it.'

He returned then to a subject she hoped he had forgotten; 'But why do you say with such determination that you will never marry Felix? Is it because you are cousins? Surely there is no harm in that.'

'I can't discuss it, Henri. If Felix chooses to tell you, he can, but I cannot.'

'All the same,' he persisted, 'it would make an excellent marriage. He is half English, at least his background was English. He is *cérébral* like you, and although I do not pretend to be a connoisseur of art I think he is a first-rate painter. You could have a good life together. But I promise to say no more. I hope I have not already said too much.'

'No, no. I couldn't possibly be angry with you.'

'Then may I perhaps say just a little more? His stepfather you would like. I find him interesting and he has charm. I cannot say the same for Felix's mother. I myself dislike her very much. She is what one might call a professional beauty. Even in her sixties – probably her late sixties, she is avid for admiration and attention. I only go there with Felix when I am sure she is away. He rarely sees her now. All the same, she would be a terrible mother-in-law. Terrible.'

'Well, there's no danger that she'll ever be mine.'

'And yet the old man adores her,' he said.

'I think,' she told him, but with a smile, 'that we've talked enough about Felix and his affairs. Now let us talk about France, Henri, and about world affairs. Do you look into the future with any confidence?'

This subject occupied them for some time, though she found Henri rather too much of the cautious diplomat for her taste. At one point he said with a short laugh:

'Looking about us, and seeing other fortunate people enjoying themselves as we are, it is hard not to be just a little hopeful that the worst will not happen, but I am not, on the whole, an optimist. The first to disappear will be, of course, the rich – people like me. I never wanted or planned to be rich. Is it my fault that my grandfather as a young man learnt to make bicycles in a shed in a back street of Rouen? He was hard-working and clever. He married my grandmother who had a little money, not much, but it went into the business. He bought the shop and it grew still bigger. What harm was there in that? He paid good wages, he was a good employer and he made good bicycles – the best. So must I feel ashamed that I inherited it in my turn? It goes on. It is in good hands. Wages have more than trebled. But I am afraid I can foresee an end to all that, though someone will have to go on making bicycles. But you, what do you think? That one day we shall all be like Russians?'

'Not quite, because we are not Russians.'

'Neither were the Poles and the Czechs and others, but they have to live like Russians.'

'I'm afraid every discussion of this sort ends on a note of gloom,' she said. 'My father hoped to die while England was still the country he knew and loved, but he feared I would have to live on into a very different world.'

'So your father was not an optimist. Was he unhappy?'

'No, because we had our own private happiness and he loved his work.'

'I love my work,' Henri said, 'and Felix loves his work. Perhaps those are the things we can still hope for – work and of course private happiness, as you have said, though I can foresee little of that for myself. Speaking of happiness, I would be glad if Felix could get those two, Lucille and Annette, off his back.'

'Felix again!' she thought. 'All the same,' she answered, 'he doesn't regret what he did, and if he had to live that part of his life over again he would do the same.'

'You think so?'

'I am sure of it.'

'To me,' Henri said, 'he is a romantic figure and unlike anyone else I know. I sometimes feel there was some terrible disaster in his boyhood. Something he will never speak of.'

'Perhaps,' she said, and was surprised by Henri's perception.

'I see you know and prefer to say nothing.'

Suddenly to everyone's surprise the last red rays of the sun that had been colouring the tree-trunks vanished and rain came pattering down. Then all was activity. Both diners and tables had to be moved indoors, and there was much laughter and confusion, though in the end it proved to be no more than a heavy shower. By the time they were ready to leave there was a serene afterglow in the sky and a delicate, barely perceptible new moon. And in the midst of all this beauty they heard, as they were nearly at the end of the Champs Elysées, a hideous crash. Even above the noise of the traffic it seemed to split the air, to tear the evening apart. As they neared the place Henri slowed down and tried to keep as far as he could from the spot where the accident had occurred. People were already gathering round, cars had stopped, the two cars that were involved were locked together and hideously crumpled, and gendarmes were hurrying to the scene. As they passed they saw, thrown out upon the road like a discarded toy, the body of a very young blonde girl, blood pouring from a wound in her head and her long fair hair already becoming soaked in it. It was a sight that sickened them both, Sibyl perhaps more than Henri. Ought they not to stop, she asked him? He most decisively said no. They had not seen the accident occur. They would merely be in the way. If they stopped, their names would be taken by the police and they could tell them nothing whatever. He drove slowly on. Sibyl knew that he was right and yet felt a sort of guilt, as if they were evading something that should have and indeed did concern them, though they could have done nothing at all.

'I hope that poor girl doesn't live,' she said sadly. 'I hope it's all over and done with for her and that she'll enter that lovely world of sleep and nothingness that I look forward to some day for myself.'

'I was brought up a Catholic,' Henri said, and she thought he said it almost sadly as if he wished that he too might hope for nothingness. 'I am sorry,' he said, 'that you had to see that. In all the years I have been driving in Paris that is only the third probably fatal accident that I have seen. I hope you will forget it soon.'

But she knew she would not forget it soon. She thought that she would never forget any part of those few, packed, memorable days in Paris, which would include the evil words and looks of the drunken porter at the Petit Cercle and Felix's blow, his sudden and obsessive love for her, her own anguished love for him, or the dead or dying girl in her pretty dress, her fair hair soaking up the blood. It would be and would remain a part of all the rest.

When Henri took her to the door of her hotel, she thanked him and gave him an affectionate kiss.

'And dear Henri,' she said, 'don't worry too much about the future. I mean your own, personal future. There's nothing much we can do about the other, no more than we can do about what we've just seen. But may I say that I'm not at all surprised that your ex-wife wants to come back to you? The wonder is that she ever left you.'

Then up to her room and back again to thoughts of Felix. Could Hugh Beallby, she wondered, remembering his tears as he left her with Felix's address in her possession, could that dear good man and dear good friend somehow have dreaded the possibility of this entanglement? Surely he could not have foreseen that she would fall passionately, hopelessly in love with a hitherto undreamed of son of her father's, a son heard of for the first time through him on that very day. No, it was a sleight-of-hand trick of fate's, born out of Felix's own tragedy of all those years ago. She thought then of the key dropped into the Seine and put her head in her hands in puzzlement and near-desperation. Into the well-ordered, intelligently planned progress of her life, broken only by the death of the father she had so deeply loved, had come something so hopeless, so potentially mischievous that she could make so sense of it at all. At that moment she could almost have envied that dead or dying girl in the road, lying so still and so far beyond the reach of such a tyrannous and all-consuming passion as had overtaken herself.

CHAPTER XI

The Eighth Day

They called for her promptly at ten. Felix's car was a big and commodious one, by no means new. He said that in fact it was nine years old.

'Cars are like dogs,' he remarked. 'To learn their real ages as we know our own, you should multiply their years by seven. But I don't want a new car, I am fond of this one.'

'I think it's a beautiful car,' Sibyl said, liking it because it was his. 'How long does it take to get to Fontainebleau? I've quite forgotten what the distance is.'

'If the traffic is only reasonably bad, about an hour and a half, driving as I like to drive.'

'He will never go fast,' Lucille complained. 'He drives like an old gentleman.'

It was a hot day. Lucille and Annette wore cotton dresses, as did Sibyl. Felix wore an open-necked shirt and a pair of trousers that looked as if they had been washed and pressed many times. Lucille, Sibyl thought, looked after him well, as well as any wife could. So far as creature comforts went, he had nothing to complain of.

'Do you want to see the Palais?' he asked her.

She said no, she had seen it twice with her father, the second time because he had left a walking-stick there that he valued. It had been given to him by Hugh Beallby and they had found it again on a seat, where he had left it.

'Good,' Felix said. 'Then we can spend the day in the woods. One needs to get the air of Paris out of one's lungs, though I think the air here is cleaner and better than in most cities.'

Annette, who was sitting beside him in the front, asked

if they might picnic where they had picnicked the last time.

'Yes, I'm fond of the place too. I remember that you liked the rocks there.' And he said to Sibyl, 'Some of the rocks in the forest are very peculiar. They seem hollow, and if one jumps on them as Annette likes to do, or hits them with a stick, they give out a queer hollow sound. Some day I must ask a geologist for the reason. And,' he added, 'I have brought my paints. There may be time to do a sketch. Tell us how you enjoyed your dinner with Henri last night.'

She said it had been delightful, especially dining in the garden before the rain came, and Henri had been a charming host. She made no reference to his problem in case Lucille had not been told, as she most probably had not, or to that tragic scene in the Champs Elysées.

'I like Henri the best of all Felix's friends,' Lucille now said. 'He is clever and kind and so gay. He is not as clever as Felix, but he is more gay.'

'He is gay to please you,' Felix said. 'But it is true that he has a great capacity for gaiety. When we were many years younger we used to ride in the woods and hills around the château. It's in a lovely part of Provence. We carried sandwiches and were always accompanied by the gamekeeper Bertrand – the Count insisted on it – and as we rode through the *maquis* Henri used to sing at the top of his voice, mostly music-hall songs, the only songs he knew. Sometimes I had to beg him to stop so that I could hear the birds.'

'Is Bertrand still alive?' Lucille asked. She then added to Sibyl, 'You see I know nothing about the château, except what Felix has told me. I have never been invited to go there.'

Felix ignored this and merely answered:

'Bertrand is very much alive, and a little older than the Count. But he is no longer the gamekeeper, he is valet and a sort of confidential servant. Also, from time to time, watchman. There are some fine pictures in the château including many quite valuable old drawings. Not long ago half a dozen of the drawings disappeared and have not been found, and Bertrand was very upset about it, much more so, I think, than the Count himself.'

When they reached the forest, Felix followed a track he seemed to know well, and soon they were in what Sibyl felt was the very heart of the woods. There was complete silence there, not even the chirp of a bird. Lucille spread some blankets on a mossy bit of ground and partly covered one of them with a white cloth. She then busied herself putting out plates and knives and forks. Annette ran about joyously, amusing herself by making the rocks give out their hollow sounds and once disappearing among the trees so that they shouted to her to come back. She returned triumphantly holding up a few wild flowers for them to see. She ran to her mother, who was sitting down, and put one in the roll of hair on top of her head. Then she put one into a buttonhole in Felix's shirt and, with a little curtsy, held one out to Sibyl who thanked her with a kiss. Felix caught her dress as she was about to disappear again, and pulled her to him.

'Tell me,' he said, 'what it was that I taught you the last time we were here, something I wanted you to remember, something that took place at the Palace?'

She leaned against him with a puzzled childish look, and he took her hands. 'Don't tell me you've already forgotten? It had to do with a famous man. Who was it?'

'Napoleon,' she said, her face clearing, and she looked up at him in triumph.

'Yes, but what about him? What did you learn that day that you promised not to forget?'

'He was going away,' she said with a thoughtful frown.

'And,' he reminded her, 'there were a lot of soldiers.'

'Yes!' she cried, 'yes! And flags. And they were saying goodbye. He was going to an island.'

'Yes. And tell me the name of the island.'

After a moment she cried out, 'L'isle d'Elbe.'

'Good girl. And the date? You learnt it carefully.'

'April,' she said. 'April 20th.'

'And the year?'

But she couldn't recall the year, so he told her again, and made her say 1814, 1814, half a dozen times.

He said to Sibyl, smiling, 'A date some of us like to remember, and others like to forget. But you see, she is getting on.'

'He teaches her something almost every day,' Lucille said with pride.

Sibyl had been thinking during the drive, as she had thought on first waking and at sleepless moments during the night, about what Felix had said to her while she was unpacking in her new bedroom the morning before. What was it that he had had in his mind? What was he preparing – mentally preparing – to do? There had been no time to speak of it since. What could he possibly imagine that he and she could look forward to? There was no future for them together. And yet she felt there was some change in him; there was a different look in his eyes when they met hers, the look of someone with a secret that he longed to share but was unable to speak of and barely able to contain. But what? She must, she must have a few minutes alone with him. Would he be able to bring it about? She was not long in doubt.

'As you're comfortably settled on your rug, and busy,' he said to Lucille, 'I'll take Sibyl and show her our favourite view down into the valley. It isn't far, Sibyl. Would you like to come?'

'I'd love it,' she said, quickly getting up from a log on which she had perched herself. 'Unless, of course, I can help Lucille.'

'No, no, please go with Felix,' Lucille answered. 'Annette can help me if I need help, but really, there is nothing to do.' She showed no sign of displeasure. The brother-sister relationship had given her complete confidence. 'We will have lunch about half-past twelve,' she said, 'so there is plenty of time.'

The two walked away together and when they were out of sight of the others Felix took her hand and they walked side by side along a scarcely visible track, through a pleasant undergrowth of ferns and grasses. Neither spoke. 'It may be the last time we are ever alone together in this way,' she was thinking. 'I love him far too much and too hopelessly. It is just not possible to go on. Not possible for either of us. It is total defeat.' And then the thought came to her that perhaps when they were old, they might look back and recognize it as total victory.

His grasp on her hand was firm, and its firmness seemed to her brotherly, and gave her comfort. There would be, she hoped, no vacillating, no temporizing. What had to come would come. He had reached, she was sure, the same conclusion she herself had, for no other was possible. The ideas he had lately been so unaccountably putting forward he must now know to be as untenable as she knew them to be.

The woods were opening up, more light came in and quite suddenly they opened up completely and there, beyond and somewhat below them, lay the valley with clumps of woodland, meadows and far hills all washed in hazy summer blue, the shadows a so much deeper, almost cobalt blue, that she cried out at the beauty of it.

'Yes,' he said, 'it's lovely. This is the very place I longed to bring you to.' And he turned to face her, and instead of seeing in his look any hint of the sadness of coming renunciation she saw instead a deep excitement and exhilaration. Still holding her hand he pulled her quickly to him and took her in a tight embrace.

'It's all right, my darling. Don't protest, there's no need. I've got the most wonderful, glorious news for you. We're free, we're absolutely and entirely free. Free to love each other like any other lovers. Listen. There isn't a drop of blood in either of us that need separate us. I'm no more your half-brother than Henri is. I've got the truth at last. And the almost incredible truth is that I'm old

Constant's son. And now I'll give you the first honest kiss that I've been able to give you.'

Before she could speak the kiss silenced any words she could have spoken. She still doubted, she more than doubted, but resist she could not. And then she threw away all doubts, all caution for the total joy of complete and willing abandonment. All that they had kept in check – barring that brief emotional breakdown at the Petit Cercle – was now released. While those kisses lasted she was beyond thought, and only his tight hold kept her upright. Then they sank down, still in each other's arms, upon a smooth stone which, whether hollow or not, supported them, but there they continued to hold each other in a close embrace.

'My darling, my darling girl, we're free, do you understand? We're absolutely *free*. We'll marry as soon as we possibly can, and begin to live.'

She was now able to speak and cried out, 'But tell me, tell me! How can you possibly know? What can have happened? Explain, explain!'

He explained. He told her the facts, as Rita Villet-Rocca had told them to him, but for the present, kept back the name of his informant. So recently had Sibyl heard the story of her father's past from Hugh Beallby that she could follow its happenings as Felix now related them to her all the way. She marvelled that Hugh Beallby, as trusting, it seemed, as her father, had been so astonishingly 'taken in', for he had been there, close at hand, supporting and comforting her father through that worrying time, as completely deceived as her father had been. She could well picture Angela's triumph, her relief and thankfulness at having 'brought it off' so successfully. 'I've fooled them all,' she must have said to herself as she no doubt watched that tiny child being lifted up – and with what relief and joy – in his 'father's' arms. And she marvelled that Angela had had the courage and the astonishing cleverness to carry it through. And when she said this to Felix she could see that he regretted, for her sake, the answer he was obliged to give her.

'This may distress you, my darling, but you'll have to know. The whole thing was cleverly stage-managed, as we might say, by Rita Villet-Rocca. I'm sorry to have to tell you this but I must. I know she played a despicable part – she's ashamed of it herself – in getting letters passed year after year between Constant and my mother. Perhaps Constant may be forgiven – he believed my mother was unhappily married and had a sad life that she would have escaped from if she could. Well, Rita is a clever little schemer, but there's this to be said. Without her help, my mother – though she talked wildly of suicide – would certainly have had an abortion. She would have faked an illness and gone into hiding, and something pretty horrible might have happened to her. Besides which, I most certainly would not have been here.'

'Then I'll gladly thank heaven for her and bless her! All I regret is that my poor father was so deceived.'

'Yes, but take comfort from this. My memory of – well, let's say the last three years of that time – is astonishingly good and I'm *sure* that your father never stopped loving her – right up to that terrible night. Yes, in spite of everything, he went on loving and forgiving her. If you could weigh happiness and unhappiness in a delicate balance, I'm sure that in his case – though certainly not in hers – the happiness would have outweighed the other. And don't forget – I only wish to heaven that I could! – that he had Felicia.'

She quickly took his face between her hands and kissed him. 'Don't, don't,' she begged, 'speak of that ever again. Or at least, not in that way.'

They looked into each other's eyes, and the strangeness of the whole past, and of their meeting and of their loving, struck them with a total realization.

'What made you come?' he cried out. 'What on earth put it into your head to come? What gave you the determination and the courage to come here and seek me out?

You were alone and lonely, I know. You wanted a brother. Will you be satisfied with what you've got instead?'

'I needn't answer that.'

He pulled her to her feet and for a moment they clung together without a word being spoken, and then he said, 'We must go back.'

'Yes,' she agreed, 'but there's still so much to say. How amazing it is that my dear, watchful, astute Hugh Beallby was completely taken in. *If* he was,' she added with a first faint element of doubt growing in her mind.

'If he wasn't,' he said, 'it would make the task I see before me a whole lot easier.'

'You mean the task of convincing him that you are who and what you are?'

'Exactly that.'

'My poor darling,' she said, 'what proof have we?'

'None whatever.'

'Possibly, just possibly,' she said, 'he may have had his suspicions. How did he treat you when he knew you as a boy? Was he affectionate and friendly?'

'Not at all affectionate, barely friendly. He thought me arrogant and spoilt and he was right. I was.'

She said, thinking back, remembering the story as Hugh Beallby had told it to her, 'I wonder if he didn't suspect the truth when you were born. I wonder if he quite believed in the story of the accident. He knew that your mother and the Count used to go about together in Paris when she was at the finishing school. He told me how she had come hurrying back to England insisting – and of course my father would have been delighted – on being married much earlier than they'd planned. Hugh Beallby may well have guessed what had happened. If he did, that would, as you said, make matters very much simpler for us.'

They were nearing the picnic place now but still were well out of sight and hearing of the others. They slackened their pace, and Felix said, 'All the same, I'm not sure we want him to play a greater part in our affairs than is absolutely necessary. It's the business of lawyers to look for difficulties and to cast doubts.'

'We can hardly expect any help from your mother,' she remarked with a sad little laugh.

'Well, proofs of my birth do exist, but they will hardly be of the sort that could give us help,' he said, and when he told her about his mother's diaries and where they were to be found, she cried out:

'Oh, never that! Never, never that! As far as we're concerned such proofs simply don't exist.'

'I agree entirely. Enough has been soiled for us already. Well, we'll go on our way with clear consciences, and I doubt if Hugh Beallby would even attempt to interfere. Will you mind being Madame Félix Forbain? Will you mind giving up your London life? Will you mind living in France?'

'My darling, nothing matters to me but the glorious fact that we can live together, so head over heels am I in love. But oh! I'm so sorry for those two, I'm so sorry!'

'Problems One and Two. Yes, and we're almost in sight of them. I think there may be a way of bringing about a considerable amount of happiness for Problem One, but as for the other, I think, my dearest, that we may have her with us permanently. I see no other future for the child at all, and she's very devoted to me. The man who I'm quite certain would like to marry Lucille is coming to supper with us tonight. I hadn't a chance to tell you before. He has let it be known quite plainly that if for any reason I decide that Lucille and I must part, he would like to marry her, but he wouldn't want Annette.'

She took this hurdle with ease and without a second's hesitation. 'But of course we would keep her with us. I could grow very fond of her and possibly I could help her.'

They joined the others and sat talking until it was time for lunch, a time dictated by Annette's appetite. After lunch they moved on to another part of the woods and came to a group of oddly formed trees and rocks that

Felix said he had noticed before because of a certain quality of fantasy in their arrangement, and the way the wind-blown trees clung to the rocks as if with talons, adding, 'I believe I am the only painter in France who has never painted a picture in the forest of Fontaine-bleau. Now is my chance.'

He set up his light easel and Sibyl watched, silent and absorbed, at a little distance. Then Lucille brought a rug and they sat together while she listened to Lucille's chatter which was mostly about Felix. She felt like a murderess in the presence of the victim she has marked down for killing. Presently she took a sketchbook and pencil out of her bag and did a sketch of Lucille and one of Annette who found it difficult to sit still. She then did one of Felix standing with an easy and unconscious grace she thought all his own at his easel. Lucille took the sketchbook from her and ran to show the drawings to Felix, who looked at them and shouted back to Sibyl, 'Bravo!' and then went on with his work, absorbed and happy.

Their visitor, the man who came to supper, was named Ferdinand Bloch. Felix had told her that he was a successful auctioneer, much in demand and fairly well-to-do. He was quite frank about his distaste for living alone, and kept casting admiring – and envious – glances at Lucille. With this admirer near at hand she was stimulated into a quite unusual gaiety and, Sibyl could see, 'played up' to him in order to produce some sign of jealousy in Felix. But this was too much to hope for, and the decent, quiet little man went home after supper with a long and affectionate hand-clasp from his hostess, but not much else, to encourage him. Nevertheless, Sibyl felt, the situation was at least hopeful. Monsieur Bloch lived not far away in a commodious apartment, had no children, and was clearly a very lonely widower indeed. There could be far worse fates for Lucille, she thought, than to be married to him, and become what she so longed to become, *une femme honnête*.

When he had gone, the other three drove her back to the hotel. She had just taken off her dress when the telephone rang. It was George Gawthorne speaking from London.

'I've been ringing you up at intervals since nine o'clock. When are you coming home? You seem to have been away an age. How are you, my child? Is everything going as you had hoped?'

'Everything is going very well indeed, I'm happy to say, but it's good to hear from you all the same. Uncle Hugh tells me that you're both extremely busy, which doesn't surprise me, but is it something special?'

'Well, I'm counsel for the defence in the biggest and most important case that has yet come my way. Hugh Beallby is solicitor for the other side, so when we occasionally meet we talk chiefly about you. But busy though I am, I have time enough to worry about you.'

'But don't worry, please, dear George. Forget the fears and dreads I had that night. I'm well and happy, happier than I could possibly have imagined. Today I've been on a picnic to the forest of Fontainebleau. It was an altogether perfect day. How long will this case of yours go on? I suppose it's hard to say.'

'Impossible to say, but I'm inclined to think it will last another week at least. Otherwise I'd be strongly tempted to fly over and bring – or try to bring – you back. I hear you've given up the idea of going to the Dordogne.'

'Yes. I'll stay here until I'm ready to go home, but I can't set any date for that at the moment. When I can, I promise to ring you up, or Uncle Hugh, or both.'

After they had said goodnight and hung up she thought what an odd thing it was that the two men to whom she was closest in London, were both lawyers, and she thought too how deeply interested they would be if they could have been told at this point, about the whole odd situation, quite apart from their affection for herself. Well, some day Hugh Beallby would doubtless hear it all – or as much as she might choose to tell him. At this moment she was in a state of what might accurately be described as euphoric bliss. The extraordinary news that Felix had given her occupied her mind to the exclusion of almost everything else. She was entirely convinced now of its truth and the one thing to mar her happiness was the thought of her father who had been so pitilessly deceived. Nevertheless she could at least feel thankful that he had never known, or even suspected, the truth. He had been spared that.

The way was now open for Felix and herself, though it was by no means devoid of difficulties. But for the fact that Hugh Beallby was so completely occupied by that case, she would have rung him up, if Felix agreed, and asked him to fly over at once to hear of these remarkable developments and to meet the man Felix had now become, that same Felix who was at present merely an abhorred name to him. Would he understand, could he be made to understand how all these changes had come about? Or would old memories and old prejudices make a fresh approach impossible? No, she told herself, nothing would prove impossible for a man of Hugh Beallby's intelligence and quick perceptions. He too would have to 'fashion a new concept', but she believed she could rely on his affection for her to achieve it. If not, she would have to go on her way without him.

She hoped that she might have the good fortune never to come face to face with Angela, who, thanks to Madame Villet-Rocca's careful reading of *The Times* already knew of her existence, though not – as the two old friends were now out of touch – of her presence in Paris. Long might this state of affairs continue, at least until she and Felix knew what their next step would be, and had made their plans.

As she lay in her hotel bed, the room faintly illuminated, thanks to thin curtains, by the lights of Paris, she wondered if Felix would be preparing to sleep in his studio, on the couch-bed, or whether he would sleep in his own bed as usual with Lucille. She thought he would

almost certainly be in his studio. He would now have to
pave the way, in as decent and kindly a manner as he
could, for their coming separation, and she thought
that knowing him as she intuitively did he would begin
tonight.

She was right, and he was upstairs in his studio. He
had left Lucille in tears, begging him to tell her if he were
angry with her for her 'little folly' that evening with
Ferdinand Bloch. It was only in play she assured him. It
was not at all serious. Would he please forgive her? He
told her, with a kiss on the cheek and a pat on the
shoulder, that he was not in the least angry with her, on
the contrary he was proud of her for the good lunch and
excellent supper she had given them. It had been a long
day, she must be tired and she must go to bed and have a
good night's sleep. He himself might pay a bill or two
and then go to bed in his studio. She looked at him
sorrowfully and not without suspicion, but did as she was
told.

He lay thinking of Sibyl and marvelling that out of the
past, out of the tragedy of the past, this astonishing
happiness had come. He owed his existence – and at this
moment he would not have changed it for any other on
earth – to a schoolgirl's love affair with a distinguished
rake, and his very birth had been accidental and problematical. He had no name other than the one he had
invented for himself, no hope of inheritance and no
money but what he could earn, for he had made up his
mind that he would never again take money from Constant; and in the result he was happier than he had ever
been in his life. He had suffered much boredom from
living with a woman of little intelligence (though he felt
affection for her and much gratitude), and he could
now look forward to a life with a companion of whom
he could never tire. Small affairs with this woman and
that had brought little satisfaction. Sexual satisfaction
was not enough, he was capable of much loving and
needed to love and since the death of his young singer

he had made do without embarking upon any permanent relationship other than the odd and fortuitous one embarked on eight years before with Lucille. It was deliberate, he had gone into it with open eyes. Embroilments with women who had been all too willing to attach themselves to him he had succeeded in avoiding for they were apt to be irksome and time-wasting. It had had to suffice that he had made two people happy, and thanks to a profession that he would not have changed for any other in the world, the years had slipped by.

So much had the day's events occupied his mind that he had to stop and think what arrangements he had made for tomorrow. Then he remembered that in the evening he was expected to take Sibyl to Louise Dumontelle's birthday party. This engagement he now regarded with distaste. There would be far better ways of spending their first evening as lovers than a crowded social occasion, and Louise knew 'everybody'. He would concoct a story and ring her up in the morning. What the story would be he did not yet know, but he would make it as convincing as he could. Social fibs in no way troubled his conscience, and this one was imperative.

He would take Sibyl away somewhere for a day and a night. He was as certain of her ready consent as he was that tomorrow's sun would be on its predictable orbit. She had said that she had never been to Rambouillet, so he would take her there. He knew, thanks to Henri, of a quiet, unpretentious hotel – it was a remodelled country house or small château – not many miles away from Rambouillet itself, and he thought it would do very well. It would not be luxurious but both of them would prefer that it should not be.

As for Louise, he would tell her that he had to leave Paris on an important errand that could not be put off to another day. If she asked him about his 'cousin' Miss Matherson he need only say that as he was unable to bring her to the party himself she would probably prefer to make plans of her own and he would hope to bring her on another occasion. He would remember to wish her the happiest of birthdays.

'It won't be with you not there,' she would probably say, and that might well be true enough.

His mind made up, he went to his not very comfortable couch-bed and set his striking clock for eight o'clock in the morning, the earliest moment when he felt he could get in touch with Sibyl.

CHAPTER XII

The Ninth Day

It was soon after eight when he rang her up, just as she was about to begin her breakfast of coffee and croissants. He said they could now talk quite freely as Lucille had already left the house with Annette. The school bus had broken down, and Annette had to be at her school at eight-thirty. 'Paris,' he said, 'keeps earlier hours than London. Lucille will then do her shopping, which she enjoys as she talks to everyone, and after that she has an appointment with her hairdresser, so she won't be back much before lunchtime. Now I have a question of some importance to put to you. Would you be very much disappointed if we didn't go to Louise Dumontelle's birthday party tonight?'

'Not in the very least, except that I was looking forward to wearing my beautiful new dress. To tell you the truth, I was rather dreading that party. Anyway, I feel you have something else in mind. Am I right?'

'Perfectly right. I'll work all the morning, leave a note for Lucille saying I won't be back until some time tomorrow afternoon, pack a small bag, go to my bank, and pick you up in the Citroën just before one. We'll lunch somewhere en route and then drive towards Rambouillet where you tell me you've never been. We'll put up at a quiet hotel I know of not far away from the château and visit it tomorrow. Today's no good as it's Monday, and nothing is open. How does this strike you?'

'It sounds to me like an elopement. There's nothing on earth I'd rather do.'

'Yes, it is a little elopement. You needn't bring much with you. An extra dress if you like, and enough things for one night. I wish we could stay away longer, but there'll be time for that later. I must see my lawyer on Wednesday. His name, by the way, is Paul-Etienne Tizard, and I want you to meet him soon. So fill in the morning in any way that pleases you, and I'll be there with the car before one. Meanwhile, of course, I'll make apologies for both of us to Louise.'

'Oh, Felix!' was all she could find to say. 'What bliss! What absolute bliss!'

'And remember to leave word at the hotel that you'll be away for the night.'

She spent two happy hours at the Louvre, confining herself to Ingres and Delacroix, but chiefly Delacroix; then it was time to return and to pack a bag. She felt now that her whole life belonged to Felix; he occupied the place in it that her father had occupied, but, of course, plus, plus, plus! She was about to build a wholly new life for herself, and she would build it about this man who had so lately become the pivot of all her hopes and joys – so lately that they had a thousand things to learn about each other, though each already recognized in the other that 'other self' that each had needed. Their coming together, which she had willed and brought about, seemed now to have been wholly taken over and conducted by some benevolent Providence which had cunningly substituted a lover, which she had not been seeking, for the brother she had sought – a being she had dreamed up out of her sadness and loneliness. What a blessing it was, she thought, that one could not always control one's destiny! The unknown, the unexpected, the un-looked for takes over. And in this instance, with what immense benevolence! From here, other, less happy thoughts began crowding into her mind.

As she walked back to the hotel she was thinking that if it were true, as it indubitably was, that the general aim of philosophy and science was to achieve understanding of the universe, she wished with all her heart and mind that they would get on faster with it. She and Felix did not so much part company there as to look upon the whole problem as a fruitful subject of discussion and argument. It seemed to her that in today's world – about which everybody had a right to his or her opinions – good was diminishing, evil increasing. That, she believed, was a self-evident truth. How reverse this frightening process? (Religion seeming to be powerless). It was her belief and had been her father's, that the process might have gradually been reversed but for the dropping of the atom bomb. Then the world – or that part of it that bore the responsibility – had taken the wrong turning, the irreversible turn into darkness and evil.

It was done to save life? But how many millions of future lives might it not have condemned to destruction? The scientists in their legitimate pursuit of knowledge had discovered – as they were bound sooner or later to discover – the nature and content of the atom, but why, oh why had they not agreed to keep the knowledge to themselves? They had come upon the most terrifying secret of the universe, and its public exposure was the ultimate indecency. Now it was in the hands alike of the wise, the foolish and the murderous. *Why* did they? Why? Why?

'We have learned the answers, all the answers.

It is the question that we do not know.'

When she was an inquiring fifteen she wanted to hear about what had happened when the bombs were dropped, most of all what happened to the people they fell upon. She asked her father, and he told her as factually and plainly as seemed right to him.

'Be as happy as you can,' he had said at the end of it. '*Make* as much happiness as you can and spread it as far as you can, for it's my belief that "the night cometh".'

'But father,' she had asked, 'couldn't all that power be used for good instead of evil?'

'It could, but it won't be,' he had answered. 'We inhabit a world, unfortunately, in which the craving of human beings for power over other human beings is greater than all other cravings. Well, enough of that, my

child. Let's make up our minds where we want to go
for the summer holidays. To Italy, or to France?'

Now she was unspeakably grateful for her own and for
Felix's happiness. He especially deserved his, for he had
spent a great part of his life in trying to rid himself of his
feelings of guilt. He refused to make excuses for himself
on the grounds of youth. This, she thought, had very
nearly become an obsession with him.

'In some ways,' he had said to her only the day before,
'I was almost an adult, the top of most of my classes –
never maths – and old enough to be put in charge of the
house. And I locked that child in. After the disaster, I
went with my mother. I was her mindless chattel. I was
old enough to have known better. Unfortunately for me,
I *did* know better.'

But gradually, she felt sure, he would cure himself of
all this. (He could and did forget it completely, he told
her, when he was painting.) Their coming together
which still seemed to them a little miracle, would in
time complete the cure. As for Lucille, if she, poor little
woman, had to be the only sufferer because of this, let her
remember the eight years of happiness that she owed to
him.

They had a light lunch on the outskirts of Versailles, after
which for old times' sake, they had a quick look at
Versailles itself, so pompous, so absurdly grandiose and
yet in its own unlovable fashion, so splendid, and lately
brought, by a man of genius, to its full beauty. Then
they went on their way, and he presently made a little
detour to let her see a shabby old mansion, set well back
from the street, which had obviously been at some time a
place of considerable consequence. It had been the home,
he told her, of Constant's mother. He refrained from
calling her his grandmother which would have seemed to
him a little absurd. It had now fallen into near decay, and
washing hung from its windows. It was in one of those
villages, so often to be found in France, where not a

human being was to be seen. It seemed closed, shuttered, without life. In front of the house Sibyl could see the outlines of what had once been a knot-garden.

'She was said to be very beautiful,' Felix told her, 'and after her marriage became very much a *grande dame*. But she had many vicissitudes. Seven children were born to her, and only two, my father and a delicate daughter who married and died in childbirth, survived.'

'I'm far more grateful for modern medicine and modern sanitation than for anything else in this time of ours,' Sibyl remarked, and then added, 'and of course, for electricity and well-lighted streets.'

After that they went on their unhurried way towards Rambouillet, turning off the direct road that led to it in order to reach the hotel where they were to stay. It had been a large, ugly country house, built at an ugly period, and it had recently been remodelled and modernized.

'Have you stayed here before?' she asked with a quick, teasing look at him, and he replied, 'Never, but Henri has and that's how I knew about it.'

He put the car away while she waited for him on the steps and when he came back they 'checked in' and were taken up a wide and quite handsome staircase to the floor above. There they were shown into what was probably the best bedroom, which looked on to parklike grounds. It was a large uncluttered room with no gilt mirrors, no gilt furniture and the simplest of curtains and covers. There was a double bed in it of moderate size, and, as Sibyl had expected, no dressing-table, without which no English bedroom would have been complete. But the absence of this useful piece of furniture was something she had grown accustomed to on her travels. Instead there was that familiar long shelf in the bathroom – if one was lucky enough to have a private bathroom – with a long mirror over it and underneath it one, or in this case, two handbasins. There Felix would shave in the morning and she would clean her face with cold cream and wipe it off again preparatory to putting on such make-up as she chose to use. Felix protested that she needed none.

'That pale-skinned, Leonardo-like face of yours needs no make-up,' he told her, 'and those grey eyes are adornment enough.'

She said, 'Just a touch of red on the lips then, if you'll permit that, and I trust you will.'

Tooth-brushing, they agreed, like some other functions, was to be done in private. They presently interested themselves, like two children, in the contents of each other's light travelling-cases, and then put everything tidily away.

The sun was lowering in the clear, pale sky. It was after five, and the time had come, both felt, for the casting-off of such few garments as they were wearing on that warm day, clothes that were now to be put aside, clothes that merely separated them from each other. He rid himself of his own in seconds and she now saw for the first time and in broad daylight, his admirable body that moved with such youthful ease; his torso, as smooth, as muscular – and as hairless, she noted with approval – as a Greek statue's, and, she remarked, not at all unlike one. As for her she had always, since she had reached puberty – (having no mother it was Mrs Tronsett who had explained to her this change in her life) – been well satisfied with her own pretty, shapely body, so easy to dress and now so easily undressed by him. It too was done in seconds, but not too quickly for such an eager pair of lovers. The double bed awaited them, and the rest of that day and the whole long night – dinner was not even contemplated – would be theirs.

There was nothing at all of uncertainty, nothing problematical – he knew her brief history of former lovers – about the coming together physically of such a pair. They were in a close, dreamlike little world of their own, belonging nowhere but there and to no one but themselves and each other. During the drive from Versailles they had had the opportunity of finding out that their conceptions of time – possibly derived in each case from her father – were similar. Time was always and perpetually Now, or so they felt it to be, and this particular Now was supreme for them both. The day, faithful to its duties, darkened slowly, lingeringly, and the trees outside their windows were motionless, as if they stood there giving them their silent blessings through the whole of that still, summer night.

They would have liked to spend another day and another night there, so delightfully cut off from the world had they felt. The other hotel guests were mostly quiet, provincial families and when the two lovers were visible at all, paid them no attention. Felix said he had never felt more agreeably anonymous. But they had made up their minds to visit Rambouillet, however briefly, and on getting back to Paris Felix had before him the hateful task of telling Lucille, in the kindest way he could, that the time had come for them to part. Having done so – and the whole miserable business was all too easy for him to visualize – he could hardly expect her to cook a dinner for him. Henri's carefully planned party for that evening had been, to their great relief, cancelled. His ex-wife's sudden return was now known to all his friends, and the long journey had quite badly upset his little Andrea. So the two lovers decided to dine late – after Felix's unpleasing task was done – and then, as he expressed it, he would soft-foot it upstairs to his studio and try to get some sleep.

They presently turned off to Rambouillet, and Sibyl, who had studied her guide-book to some purpose, already knew it for what it was: the setting for many a renowned 'Salonnière,' a rendezvous for countless lovers, a stage for wits, a school for beautiful speech and the perfecting of the French language, a setting for Mademoiselle de Scudéry and well known to her adoring mother; much visited by royalty and later by presidents, and as long ago as 1547 the scene of the death of the aged but still fiery François Premier. The forests surrounding it had been greatly valued as a hunting place for the kings and their *entourages*, and the echoes of the hunting-horns, so hateful to the beasts, so lovely and evocative to human ears, still seemed to echo in them. It was a place, she felt, without equivalent in England or even in the past history of England, and it was a matter of great regret to her that her father had never seen it.

But she was to treasure it now because it was on this day that she and Felix had been there so happily together; two who such a short time ago had been captives and in such an unexpected way had been given their freedom, though they still felt, with fast-waning power, the chains that had so lately bound them. If they no longer exclaimed in wonder, 'We're free!' they were still aware of past doubts and dangers, as swimmers, who only a few minutes before had been in danger from the sea, know that it is still there after they have safely reached the shore.

But the break with Lucille must not be postponed a moment longer than need be. Lucille had devoted herself to him without stint, she had been an agreeable and fond little mistress, though Felix would have preferred never to have embarked with her on this relationship. And after he dropped Sibyl at the hotel, she watched his departing car with sadness and pity in her heart, knowing there was nothing she could do to help.

He came back in a taxi about half-past eight, and she was waiting for him downstairs. She got in beside him without a word, and put her hand gently on his knee. They went to a small restaurant off the Avenue de l'Opéra and ordered a light dinner, to be prefaced as quickly as possible by two large cold gins and tonics. He drank half of his before speaking of his ordeal. He looked worn out, and the eyes under their dark brows looked more tired than she had ever seen them.

'I'll tell you now,' he said, 'and get it out of the way. As I expect you've guessed, it was all tears, tears and more tears. Those big blue eyes of hers were fountains, and I wasn't very far from tears myself. At one point she accused me of having saved her life only to deal her a death-blow eight years later. She was very bitter about you and pretended to think that the brother-sister story was just a cover-up, and I don't think she believed me when I told her I'd lately learnt that I was Constant's son. However, that hardly matters. I told her I was seeing Tizard tomorrow and would arrange for a settlement for her, a sort of *dot*. That had a somewhat cheering effect for a short time, then it was all tears again. When everything had been said that could be said, I went up to my studio and rang up Ferdinand Bloch. Luckily he was in. I told him the facts and he said he'd come and see her as soon as I'd left the house, in half an hour's time. We discussed Annette and I said that on no account must she be regarded as an obstacle to his marriage and that he could rely on me to keep her. When I told him I was settling something on Lucille so that she wouldn't go to him penniless, he brightened considerably, so much so that he at once offered to keep Annette until I sent for her. So I suppose things have gone as well as we could have hoped. But poor, bargained-for Lucille! I felt like a Sultan disposing of an unwanted female slave.'

'Yes, poor Felix,' Sibyl said. 'But what really does surprise me is that she seems so willing to part with Annette.'

'I don't know,' he answered. 'Remember what she's been through in the past. She knows, too, that the child is very devoted to me and she may honestly feel that she has more hope of making progress with us than with her.'

'Which is probably true,' Sibyl agreed, 'and I'm looking forward to trying to bring her on a little faster. I'm already fond of the child, and I think she has possibilities. It's only that unfortunate word-blindness that keeps her back. Also, luckily for her, she's pretty.'

They had finished their drinks. 'Another round?' he

asked, and she emphatically said, 'Please!'

Towards the end of dinner he brought his diary out of his pocket and looked at it to make quite sure at what time he had arranged to see Paul-Etienne Tizard the following day. He found the entry and then turned back several pages.

'I suppose you realize,' he said, in a voice full of amazement, 'that we have only known each other a little more than a week? A little more, did I say? Just two days more.'

They stared at each other as if confronted by something totally impossible and unbelievable.

She took her little red leather diary out of her handbag, looked for an entry and found it.

'I shall have to believe it,' she said. 'Here's my entry for the first day. "Left for Heathrow early. Good flight. Light lunch on plane. Landed at Orly airport. Took a taxi to the Petit Cercle. Started to unpack, then found Felix's number and rang him up. Liked his voice. Met him at the Fragonard for a drink at six. Feel immensely drawn to him." There it all is, the beginning of everything. Just one week and two days ago!'

'Yes,' he said, and she saw that his face was fast losing its exhausted look and the lines in it seemed less deeply marked. 'I have been in love with you for precisely that length of time – from our first meeting at the Fragonard. It will no doubt become a part of our private folk-lore. What did you find to do on Tuesday night?'

'Nothing at all. I went to bed, read a little, then turned out the light. I was tired, but I didn't sleep for some time. I was rejoicing in the dazzling knowledge that I had found a brother.'

'And the next day,' he said, 'you came and lunched with us, and poor Lucille cooked a very good meal.'

'Yes, and then,' she went on, taking up the tale again, 'you walked back with me to the Petit Cercle, and on the way you told me many things. And you said you knew of a nicer hotel and stopped in the Boulevard Beaumarchais on your way home to get me a room. May I see your diary? It looks like the very twin of the one that Hugh Beallby uses, the one that had your name and address in it, which I begged him to let me have, and at last he tore out the page it was written on and gave it to me. And he was so distressed and full of fears and doubts that tears came into his eyes. What a strange saga ours is!'

'About as strange as it could well be,' he agreed. 'But speaking of Hugh Beallby, I feel we should get in touch with him very soon.'

'We must and we will. I'll write a letter to him tonight. And now tell me what's happening tomorrow.'

'Tomorrow I'll try to do some work in the morning while Lucille is packing, and keep out of her sight in my studio. I'm working on that sketch I began in the forest of Fontainebleau, and I think I'm going to like it. Ferdinand Bloch said he'd call in his station-wagon between eleven and twelve and take Lucille and Annette and all their possessions away. So let's thank heaven for Ferdinand Bloch. I hope they'll marry very soon and it wouldn't surprise me if they invited me to the wedding.'

She said, with a smile, 'You know the French character better than I do, and I expect you're right. If they do ask you, I hope you'll go.'

'I will, and gladly.'

Later he walked back to the hotel with her, and as he left her there, he said, 'here ends our ninth day. Soon, please heaven, I shan't go back to an empty house, and soon too, please heaven, we shall begin to spend the rest of our lives together.'

CHAPTER XIII

The Tenth Day

The next day he worked in the morning as he'd said he would, and just before half-past twelve he rang her up, a call she was anxiously waiting for.

'They've just left the house,' he told her. 'I had no breakfast because I didn't want to risk seeing her again. Annette, of course, went with them, looking, poor child, as I could see from my window, lost and miserable. Ferdinand Bloch, sturdy little man, carried down one small trunk, five suitcases and a good many bundles, and stowed them all away in the back of the station-wagon. So that's all over. I wish I could come and take you to lunch, my darling, but that I can't do. Rita Villet-Rocca rang me up and insisted on my lunching with her. She says she wanted to see me about something important, and wouldn't tell me on the telephone what it was.'

'Good heavens!' cried Sibyl, 'you don't think she can have found out that she's made some ghastly mistake, do you?'

'Of course not, I don't think that for one moment. It's something else entirely. She spoke about a painting, but I was a little short with her because I wanted to be sure everything was going well downstairs. So she said, "Never mind. It's obvious that you're a little *distrait*. Come to lunch with me and I'll tell you then." And of course she added, "Thank God Lucille is going!" Which I fully expected her to say. All the same, I felt I ought to go to lunch with her and I said I would. We do owe her rather a lot – and that's an understatement if you like – and I didn't want to seem churlish. After that I'll see Tizard, and after that I'll come along to you. Would you like it if I were to ask Paul-Etienne and his wife, Marianne, to dine with us tonight, supposing they chance to be free?'

'But of course, that would be delightful.'

'Good. In any case, I'll be with you at about five-thirty. So au revoir, my darling.'

'Oh, one thing more,' she said. 'I've written to Hugh Beallby and posted the letter. So I think he may fly over to see us the moment that lawsuit is finished.'

She found a small restaurant not far from the Musée Cluny and had an omelette *aux fines herbes* and a cup of coffee. Then she went to the Cluny, to find out if there was a possibility of her being able to get work to do there, and was taken to see a pleasant, middle-aged woman with whom she had had some correspondence. She proved co-operative and friendly, and thought it quite possible, she said, that as Mademoiselle Matherson was proposing to live in Paris, work might quite well be found for her at the museum.

Encouraged by this – for she had told Felix she had no wish to remain idle after their marriage – she went back to the hotel to wait for him. In spite of his reassurances as to what Rita might be wanting to tell him, she felt far from happy about her. There was something unpredictable about that odd little woman, something tricky and far, far too clever, in a by no means pleasing sense. She waited for him downstairs by the front door where she had waited, such a short time ago, for Lucille, and suddenly the day darkened and rain came pouring down. People scuttled into doorways or drew their coat collars about their ears and ran, and the streets shone as they had not once shone during these past days in Paris.

At last Felix hurried through the door saying 'I've got soaked through. Let's go up to your room and I'll take off my jacket and hang it up to dry. I came by metro as I couldn't find a taxi.' They went up to her room and she unlocked her door with a heavy, old-fashioned key, then quickly helped him off with his jacket and hung it over the back of a chair, noting, as she did so, that there was something fairly heavy in one of the pockets. He took her in his arms, saying, 'Now, Madame Forbain, I can embrace you without getting you wet.'

'I love my new name,' she said, when he let her go. 'Now tell me quickly what your lawyer said. Will it take a long time? And what has to be done? And please sit in the little armchair.'

'Well, he assured me that it was quite a simple matter, and no birth certificate is required. It will be advertised that Felix Carl Matherson will in future be known as Félix Carl Forbain, and I understand there will have to be some sort of authorization from a court of law. Also that we won't have long to wait. I told him as much of the story as I felt he ought to know, and he was greatly interested. He said his father used to know Constant very well and had a certain admiration for him. He added that my use of the name Forbain as a nom de plume, or in this case a *nom de brosse* made things still easier, as it was already known. As it happens, he and his wife Marianne are free tonight and will dine with us. I proposed the Fragonard as it's a place of importance to us, and told him it would be a little celebration. I also booked a table.'

'I'm delighted,' she said. 'So far I've only met one of your friends, dear Henri. Some day I look forward to meeting his sister Louise, though I feel you have some reservations about her.'

'None whatever,' he answered, 'though I'd like you to know the facts first. After her husband left her, in a rather brutal way, she was in a state of despondency, even despair. I've always been fond of her and I did my best to console her, in a way I'm sure you'll understand. Then she wanted me to marry her, but that I felt I couldn't do. For one thing she's too rich and besides I could never have endured that boring social life she leads. So all that came to an end, but we remained friends and I'm always glad to see her.'

'I rather guessed something of the sort,' she told him, 'because of a remark or two of Lucille's. She wasn't in the least indiscreet, but what she did say gave me the idea.

Now, please, I want to hear all about Rita.'

'You shall, but I have the only comfortable chair, so come and sit on my knees. She's a most extraordinary creature. Since our last meeting on that never-to-be-forgotten Saturday when I went to her and asked her "Whose son am I?", she's been down at the château. It seems that Constant rang her up and said he needed her help. He told her that my mother was due back from Corsica on Saturday next and that before she came he wanted to please and surprise her by getting rid of a picture she hates, but that up to now he's never made up his mind to part with because it was given to him by his father. However, he's now decided that it must go. It's a portrait by Largillière and my mother has always loathed it because it resembles the only one of Constant's mistresses of whom she was ever jealous. It's of a pretty woman holding a basket of flowers and wearing a sort of shepherdess hat. Very typical of Largillière and very charming. Well, my old friend Raoul Sachs has long wanted to get his hands on it, so he and Rita flew down to Nîmes together, hired a car for two days, and drove to the château. Constant was delighted to see them both and got out his best Bordeaux for them. The picture was well wrapped up and they departed with it the next morning in the way they'd come. Raoul will either sell it to a rich collector in Paris, or take it to London to Sotheby's or Christie's. He'll get a handsome commission and of course Rita will get her whack. And my mother will be delighted.'

'Where was it hanging?' Sibyl asked.

'In the big salon. There was no problem, it appears, about what to hang in its place. It will be a portrait of my mother painted years ago by a pupil of Carolus-Duran, but he's so little known that I can't at the moment recall his name. Constant simply referred to it as "your mother's portrait". However, she'll be delighted.'

'And it was this that Rita was so eager to see you about?'

'Partly that, partly curiosity about us. Were we going to be married, and if so, when? I told her I was changing my name to Forbain and she seemed pleased. She then added, characteristically, what a great pity it was that I could never inherit my father's title.'

'Exactly what one would have expected her to say,' Sibyl observed.

'And she seems to have given us some sort of present, a kind of engagement present, or I suppose it's that. She slipped it into my pocket just as I was leaving, and told me to take good care of it. I've no idea what it is.'

'Shall we have a look?'

She got up and took it out of the pocket of his still damp jacket.

'Luckily she's wrapped it up well,' she remarked as she gave it to him.

It was a parcel about six inches square, and, as Sibyl had remarked, very carefully wrapped, neatly tied and sealed here and there with strips of adhesive tape. A letter was fastened to the outside of it. He pulled it off, saying, 'I suppose I'd better read this first,' and tore it open. He hadn't read far when he cried out, 'Good God! She must be mad. She really must be off her head. Can you guess what's in the parcel?'

One look at his horrified face told her.

'Your mother's diaries,' she said.

'You're right. She's "purloined" them, after all. This letter's written from the château. It begins:

Darling Felix,

I wouldn't do this for anyone else in the world, but you know I've always doted on you since you were a mere baby (and I knew whose!) and during all the many years since your mother brought you to Paris. So I'm doing this for you and Miss Matherson – or may I speak of her as Sibyl? I feel you'd both be happier if you looked at these girlish scrawls (which tell the whole story), yourselves. I also feel that, on the whole, I have a perfect right to do it. The only bothersome thing is that you'll have to put them back somehow before your mother's return from Corsica, which will be on Saturday. I'd take them back myself but I'm off to Malaga tomorrow to stay with friends. However, I've no doubt you can fly down to the château – your father complains that he hasn't seen you for weeks – and put them back where they belong. It's quite simple. Your mother keeps them in the bottom drawer of that big, handsome old chest of drawers to the right of the window that looks out on the lake. They were underneath some old fancy dresses that she hasn't worn for years and will probably never wear again. The little key (which I've attached to a label inside the wrappings so that you won't lose it) belongs at the back of a very small drawer in the right-hand side of her escritoire, under some old lavender-bags.

Raoul is delighted to have the Largillière and your mother will be equally delighted that it's gone. The flight, both to and from Nîmes was quite pleasant. You, I know, have often flown down there. I used to hate flying, but I find I'm rather beginning to like it.

Now I'm off to bed, but I'll ring you up tomorrow when I get back to Paris, and perhaps I can get you for lunch.

Much love to you, and good luck to you and Sibyl,
        Rita'

Both of them were shocked and dismayed.

'What an outrageous thing to have done,' Sibyl said with disgust. 'I can't even bear the thought of their being here in my bedroom.'

'Nor I. But they won't be for long. I think I'd better call off the dinner with the Tizards and fly down to Nîmes tonight, if I can get on a plane.'

'Oh, no!' she pleaded, 'not tonight! Why not tomorrow morning early, and by daylight? That will still give you time. I suppose you could get back the same day, but wouldn't it be better to spend the night with Constant?' (In time, she thought, she would teach herself to say 'your father', but not yet.) 'Then you could leave early on Saturday morning.'

He thought for a moment and then said, 'Yes, perhaps that would be better. I think it might be a good idea to ring up the old man now. He might not like my simply turning up without any warning whatever. I'll ring him up from here.' And then he added, 'He'll be having a birthday quite soon, on June 29th. I'll tell him that as I can't be there at the time, I'm bringing him a small present. That would help to explain my brief visit.'

'A good idea if you have something suitable to give him.'

'I have, as it happens. I was hoping to give it to you. It's a small pen drawing by Tiepolo. Constant lost one when some drawings were stolen from the château about six months ago, and I picked this one up fairly cheaply in an antique shop in St-Rémy. They didn't know what it was, and I wasn't sure until I got back to Paris. It will have to do.'

'I should think it would do very well. But, oh, Felix, what a bore the whole thing is for you – for both of us! Can't I come with you?'

He shook his head. 'There isn't even a suitable inn near by where you could stay.'

'Then that settles it,' she said. 'I certainly don't want to stay at the château.'

'Not even when you're Madame Forbain?'

'Not even then. By the way, I wonder what Constant will think of your change of name?'

'It won't surprise him – nor my mother. I've often said in the past that I'd like to change it. I felt I had no real right to the name of Matherson – having run away – and it was just one more link with the whole tragedy. Also, it will simplify matters in the future not to have the same name as my wife.'

He sat down on the bed, took up the telephone and put in a call to the château. There was some delay but when he finally got through the connection was so good that she could hear everything that was said at the other end.

Constant was evidently at his desk, writing, for he picked up the telephone at once.

'*C'est toi, Félix? Ah, bon, bon! Je suis enchanté que tu m'as telephoné. J'espère que tout va bien avec toi, mon fils.*'

The talk continued in French and Sibyl listened, trying to picture the man who was Felix's father. His voice was affectionate and warm, and he was evidently in the habit of calling Felix "*mon fils*".

'*Ta mère reviendra samedi prochain, Dieu merci!*' Felix then said that he'd lunched with Rita that day, and she'd informed him of that fact. She'd also told him about the Largillière. The older man laughed as at an excellent joke. '*Une jolie petite surprise pour ta mère.*' When Felix said he would like to spend the following night at the château if it was convenient, his father appeared delighted but asked, why for only one night? Felix then told him that he hadn't forgotten that he would soon be having a birthday, but that as he couldn't, alas! be there on the day, he was bringing down a small present for him. Unfortunately he had to return to Paris on Saturday morning. Constant had long since given up trying to bring mother and son together, knowing that if they did meet it had to be by agreement and mutual consent, and said that one night was better than none. He would clearly have liked to go on talking, so Felix brought the conversation to an end by saying:

'*Alors, cher Constant, vendredi vers une heure. À bientôt.*'

That settled, they felt happier. Felix had to go back soon to change, and said how strange it would seem to return to an empty house. All the same, he added, he could manage perfectly well. He had already contacted a Madame Georges who lived over the bakery in the next street and she had promised to come in for two mornings a week, which was all the help, he said, that he would require for the present. Sibyl decided to say nothing to him as yet about her visit to the Cluny and what had been discussed there. They could talk about all that later on when she hoped they would have more time to themselves. But she did say, because it had been working like yeast in her mind ever since Lucille's departure:

'In case we aren't able to discuss this before you go, I want you to know that I'm thinking, if you approve of course, of letting my flat in London, putting my personal things into storage and getting my dear Mrs Tronsett to come and live with us here in Paris. She'd be terribly lost without me, and she's the nearest thing I've had to a mother since I was three years old.'

'Well, bless her! What a wonderful job she made of it! I've been thinking about her too and what a joy it would be to have her here. My darling girl, I almost feel we're too lucky and too happy. Rita is the only discordant note in an otherwise perfect harmony, Rita and those wretched diaries. I must go now and get into dry clothes. It seems to have stopped raining so I'll come for you at seven-thirty and we'll have time to walk to the Fragonard.'

They clung together for a moment.

'I do hate your going away, even for one night.'

'Well, I'm not exactly looking forward to it. Put on a pretty dress. I want you to charm the Tizards though I know I can count on your doing that whatever you wear.'

It was a pleasant evening and she liked the Tizards, especially Paul-Etienne, and thought Felix in excellent hands. His wife, Marianne, was a writer and critic, and wrote articles for one of the two best literary journals in Paris. Their son and daughter – twins – were at school near Grenoble. Felix had painted a portrait of Marianne, one of the very few that he had done. She was clever, plain, sharp-featured and humorous, and so very far from being the conventional pretty woman, that he knew he would enjoy painting her. After dinner they went to the Tizards' apartment which was not a long way off, saw her portrait hanging over the mantelpiece, and stayed long enough to drink a little cognac.

The portrait, Paul-Etienne said, was one of their most prized possessions. Marianne was sitting at her desk, surrounded by newspapers, with a background of bookshelves, the books not too tidily arranged. She was wearing a striped blouse, and the whole picture was full of life, informality and movement. They didn't stay long because of Felix's early start the next morning and when he took her back to the hotel they found the parting so painful that they felt it best not to linger over it.

'I hate to let you go,' she said, clinging to him, for they had gone up to her room to say their goodbyes, 'and on such a hateful errand! I wish I could go with you, but I shall never want to see the château even when I am Madame Forbain. I shall only want to see it through your eyes.' She was determined, remembering Lucille, not to shed a single tear, but when he had gone and she had locked her door she felt that never until that moment had she known the true meaning of loneliness.

CHAPTER XIV

The Journey to Nîmes

He drove his hired car through the *allée* of *bigarades* – smelling almost the year round of orange blossoms – that led up to the Château Aubaine, and felt as so often before that it was home and yet not home. He loved it, but with an always uncomfortable love. What right had he to love it, or to be there? No right at all. But love it for its beauty, its situation, its elegance and charm, he must, and even at that moment, did.

'I'm jolly lucky to be living here, I suppose,' he had once written to a school friend in England when he was thirteen and staying at the château for the holidays, and the 'I suppose' expressed his true feelings. 'My stepfather is all right and I'm having riding lessons. In the spring and summer the hillsides are covered with yellow broom. I could easily get lost, but the gamekeeper always comes with me. He's all right too and I like him. His name is Bertrand. I don't speak anything but French here.' A few such boyish letters had passed between them and then the friendship had languished and there was silence.

He parked the car in a clump of mimosa. Bertrand could put it into the garage later if he liked, but it would make his early start the next morning easier if it could be left where it was. He went up the curving, double staircase to the front door, found it unlocked and went in, the wrapped-up Tiepolo under his arm and his light suitcase in his hand. He left both of them in the big main hall, and saw no changes since his last visit. He averted his eyes from the trophies of the chase on the walls – one huge tusked boar's-head that he and his mother agreed in hating – and saw that the paintings – some mediocre, some very good indeed – had not been added to. The door into the salon was open, and he caught a glimpse of the newly hung painting of his mother wearing a bright yellow ball-gown, a painting that deserved, he considered, only obscurity. Beyond was the library where his father was usually to be found. He was about to see, for the first time with new eyes, the man he now knew to be responsible for his existence, and he was about to reach his fortieth year without knowing it. Would he feel any differently about him? Would he see in him attributes he had not seen before, or had previously taken for granted? Perhaps he knew him too well to be struck, at this late date, by anything he might think resembled himself. In any case, it was a new and amusing experience. Unfortunately it was one his father could not share with him.

There he was, sitting at his big writing-table, and hearing Felix's footsteps he put down his pen, turned, showing bright dark eyes under bushy grey eyebrows, and a smiling, grey-bearded face, and held out both arms.

'Forgive me, my son, if I do not get up. The arthritis is very bad today. But never mind that. I am delighted to see you.'

'And I to see you,' Felix said, and bent down and kissed Constant on both cheeks, as was his custom. 'But I am sad, sad about the arthritis. Is it worse? Or does it merely vary from day to day?'

'It is daily, I think, a little worse.' They always talked to each other in French, though Constant's English was not bad. 'But all the same I can still write and I can still enjoy Ticina's excellent cooking and now and then I drink a little Chablis, or Bordeaux. And tomorrow, thank God! I shall have your mother with me. Look, my son, the drinks are on that table, so go and help yourself.'

'But you must have something too,' said Felix, 'so that we can drink each other's health. Shall I pour you out a little whisky?'

'I have never learnt to like it, though they tell me it is best for me. A little vodka, I think.'

Felix poured out a small glassful – he knew he liked to drink it neat – and gave himself a gin and tonic with plenty of ice in it, and they raised their glasses to each other.

'Did you have a good flight from Paris?' Constant asked.

'Excellent. It is wonderful how little time it takes. And the drive here from Nîmes is always pleasant. I am very glad to be here.'

'I have good news for you,' Constant said. 'Joyful news. The book is finished at last.'

'Well done!' Felix cried. 'Then we must drink to that too. I congratulate you. It has been a great task. How far did you take it? Just where did you decide to end it?'

'With de Gaulle entering Paris, though I speak of that only briefly. Shall I call it, *From the Goths to de Gaulle*?'

'Not at all a bad title! Now we must find a publisher.'

'I think that may be very difficult. However, that is of no importance, though naturally I would like to see it in print. What is important is the pleasure I have had in writing it. What a history Provence has had! Like no other in the world.'

'Bloodier, I am inclined to think,' said Felix.

'And I think you would be right. Yes, I have waded through blood to the very end. Please God no more will be shed in my lifetime or in yours.'

'A pious hope, and I join you in it. Now, Constant, tell me please, would you like to see the little present I've brought you, or shall I leave it wrapped up until the 29th?'

'I want it now, please. I am too old to like putting off such pleasures.'

Felix went into the hall for it and put it into Constant's hands.

'Unwrap it for me, my dear boy. My hands are very stiff.'

Felix unwrapped the drawing and gave it to him, whereupon Constant screwed a small magnifying glass into one eye and held it near to his face.

'A Tiepolo, I think. Yes, I do believe it is. Smaller, but not at all unlike the one that was stolen. The satyr is very similar. I am delighted, my son, and how clever of you to find it. Yes, I am quite certain it is a Tiepolo. For skies, and for such pen drawings as this, I think he has few equals. I thank you most warmly.'

'Where is Bertrand?' Felix presently asked. 'I hope he's well. I always look forward to seeing him.'

'He is away. He will be back later, this evening, I hope, to help me to bed. He has gone to see his sister at Alés, he fears she may be dying. As she is over ninety it is perhaps to be expected. He is just the same loyal old Bertrand, though a little forgetful at times. But Ticina, Blanche and Lulu are well. They have now been with me for more than thirty years. We are all growing old – except your mother, of course. I myself am growing old faster than anyone else. Who will keep this place when I am gone? Must it be sold? I do not know. I have no son to leave it to. Your mother would find it too lonely. She would prefer to live in Passy and take her holidays in Corsica. I wish you, my dear boy, would marry and bring up a family here.'

'I hope you have many years ahead of you still, so we won't talk about that,' Felix said, as he had often said before, 'and we'll hope that before long they may find a cure – or even perhaps an amelioration – for your arthritis.'

But for that, Constant had little hope. 'Ah,' he then said, 'here is Blanche to tell us that lunch is ready.'

Felix at once went to Blanche and kissed her wrinkled cheek. 'I am so happy to see you again, Blanche, and you look not a day older. Please tell Ticina and Lulu that I will come and see them after lunch.'

He went to Constant to take his arm, and Blanche quickly took the other. 'Two are better than one,' she said, 'and I am still, thank God, very strong.'

They got him out of his chair and into the dining-room, though he protested, as they went, that he could still walk quite well unassisted. The dining-room, like the library, was panelled, this room in pine, the other in walnut. From where they sat they could look out on the lake, lying placid under the serene sky, and beyond it to woods and hills. At this moment Felix was wondering if the opportunity would come after lunch for him to slip upstairs to his mother's room and replace the diaries, as Constant usually had an afternoon nap. But today there was no nap. He wanted to talk. He said that Felix's coming was a godsend as he had seen no one but the servants for nearly a week, and had felt very lonely. Their neighbours, like himself, were growing old and found visiting their friends more and more of an effort. 'All their young people prefer to be in Paris, or abroad. No one is left now but the farmers. Fortunately many of them are my good friends, but they are busy people. So I thank heaven for my book, and for your mother, for when she is here I feel almost young.'

So they talked on, chiefly about world affairs, growing unemployment, and politics, for though Constant had played no part in politics, he was highly critical of those who did. He was an entirely selfish though lovable being, and had devoted himself, throughout his life, to his own pleasures, though one of these was offering generous help to those who needed it. Felix was too fond of him to feel the contempt he supposed he ought to feel for his way of living. His two marriages had both been childless, which had caused him great sadness, but he lived in precisely the way he felt was suitable to a man of his birth and position. It would have been hard to find, Felix thought, a man who was less a figure of his own time. He was an anachronism, but no less charming for being so. He would probably have said, in his own defence, and truthfully, 'I have never in the whole of my life, so far as I am aware, done an unkind action.'

Once Felix excused himself and went upstairs. He took the diaries out of his locked suitcase and went very quietly, his footsteps muffled by thick carpets, along some corridors to his mother's room which was exactly across the hall from Constant's. He opened the door softly and looked in. There, sitting with her back to him, was a young niece of Lulu's, a frequent visitor because she was clever with her needle, stitching away on some dress of his mother's. He closed the door, without, he hoped, being heard, and returned the diaries to his suitcase. It would be safer, he thought, to wait for darkness and the night. He then went for a walk around the lake, his thoughts busy with Sibyl and their plans for the future, and returning to the library found Constant in his chair at his writing-table once more, making notes.

'There seems to be no end to a book like mine,' he said. 'I found I had forgotten to acknowledge some of my sources. But now I am ready to talk again.'

It was the same old Constant, but Felix, now so keenly aware of their relationship, could not refrain from searching for similarities and believed he had found them, chiefly in eyes, eyebrows and forehead, though they were not sufficiently striking to be observed by others. It was simply that it amused him to be on the watch for them.

Later Blanche came in and put out the drinks. Constant asked her if there was still no sign of Bertrand.

'None,' she replied. 'I think myself, Monsieur le Comte, that he ought to have a newer car. That old Renault of his is so old that it is forever breaking down. I expect he is somewhere on the road, trying to mend it.'

'Well, Blanche,' Constant said, 'perhaps you are right. We will see to it.' And as she went out he said to Felix, 'We will not, of course, change for dinner tonight. I find it too difficult without Bertrand, and we are quite alone. Help yourself to a drink, my son, and bring me if you will a little tonic water. We are having a very fine Bordeaux tonight in your honour, and two of our own ducklings. Ticina makes a very good orange sauce to go with them.'

'You are lucky in many ways,' Felix told him. 'For one thing having Ticina, who is the best cook ever to come out of Italy, and for having an excellent appetite as well.'

'And my dear Angèle, as my wife,' added Constant.

'That, naturally,' was Felix's reply.

At half-past ten, which Constant said was his bed-time, Felix helped him up the stairs to his room and, Bertrand still not having returned, assisted him to undress and got him into his bed. He had books on a small bedside table and said he usually read till midnight. So Felix decided that he had better postpone his visit to his mother's room until well after that time. Tired himself, tired of the whole unpleasing business, he undressed, put on pyjamas and a dressing-gown and lay on his bed, hoping to wake in a few hours' time when there would be no one stirring.

When he did wake he was surprised to find that it was half-past two. So much the better. He quickly got up and with the hated diaries – unopened and unread – and the little key, went softly along the corridors once more to his mother's room, using his electric torch to navigate the corners. Someone, probably on Constant's orders, had put a bowl of roses on the dressing-table. He pulled open the big lower drawer of the chest to the right of the main window, old wood protesting somewhat noisily against old wood, and slipped the diaries under a pile of tissue-covered dresses. With the aid of his torch he had no difficulty in finding the little drawer in the writing-desk and slipped the key in under the lavender-bags. All had been done according to Rita's instructions. With a long sigh of relief he closed the door behind him and went noiselessly back along the corridors to his own room. He had just reached his door when there was a loud and furious shout behind him. '*Arrêtez-vous!*' He was felled, much as the night porter at the Petit Cercle had been felled, but this blow came from behind, and he was at once stretched full length on the floor unconscious. Bertrand, recently returned, having seen a light moving from room to room and knowing nothing of Felix's presence, had entered the house with the old sawn-off shotgun he had kept, since the robberies, beside his bed, and had crept upstairs with it. Felix got almost the full blast of it. Then Bertrand switched on the lights and saw what he had done. He had killed his dear Monsieur Félix! His shouts and cries sounded all through the house. He bent down and tried to lift him, but his old heart, with the shock and horror of seeing the disaster he had caused, gave out, and he fell to the floor unconscious beside his gun and its victim.

Then Blanche, Lulu, Ticina, little Linette the sewing girl, all rushed to the spot from their various rooms in their nightclothes, with shawls or rugs about their shoulders, so appalled at the sight they saw that for whole seconds they could do nothing but stare in horror, their hands over their mouths. Then Blanche, the bravest and strongest, acted first. She dragged Bertrand, who was no light weight, off Felix's body, and putting the gun into little Linette's frightened hands, cried, 'Throw it out of the window!' Then she ran as if with wings on her feet, down the corridor and down the stairs, catching a glimpse, as she went, of Monsieur le Comte limping out of his room in his long nightshirt to go to the scene of whatever dreadful thing had taken place. She cried out to him, 'I will ring up the doctor. He must come at once. A terrible thing has happened to Monsieur Félix.' Then, down in the hall, came her ordeal. She dialled the number again and again and the operator did not reply. '*Aidez-moi!*' she cried down the telephone, sobbing. '*Pour l'amour de Dieu, aidez-moi!*' In time a sleepy voice answered; her call had got through to someone at last. She said there had been a terrible accident at the Château Aubaine. The doctor must come at once, and she gave the doctor's number. She heard it ringing and ringing, and at last the doctor's wife, Madame Clermont, well known to them all, answered. She woke her husband and told him there had been some terrible accident at the

Château Aubaine, she was not quite sure what, but there were two people in a very serious condition. They must go at once. She got him out of bed, got his clothes all ready for him to put on, fetched his medicine case from the place where he always put it, and was dressed and ready to go in minutes. His slowness drove her almost to frenzy. 'The Count himself may be dying,' she cried. 'Hurry, hurry! I will get the car. I will drive you there. Twenty-eight kilometres, but at least there will be no traffic.'

'Calm yourself,' he said, 'and ring young Retier. It seems to me that an ambulance will be needed. Tell him to bring one. When you have done that, I shall be ready.'

She did as she was told. In five minutes more she had got the car out and was waiting at the front door. Not for the world would she have let him drive himself. He got in with his usual deliberation, wearing an overcoat against the cold of early morning. She was a skilful driver and as she drove she thought how often, over the years, they had been sent for to go to the Château Aubaine and had got there in good time and had done what it was necessary to do. She dreaded these night calls, Louis was getting older, they were hard on him. But the Count was his good friend and one of the trustees of the hospital, also its most generous supporter. He would not have dreamt of delegating such an errand to anyone else. He would do well and faithfully, in spite of his age, whatever needed to be done, and she thanked heaven that few people were on the roads. It was beginning to be daylight – no, not daylight yet, but the dawn was coming. She wondered if the Comtesse was back yet from Corsica. Nothing was ever wrong with her, she was never ill. Once she had sprained an ankle, and this was all she could bring to mind. But the Count had suffered much in the past. Almost yearly he had influenza, once pneumonia and had nearly died; once he was poisoned by fish from the lake. And now there was the arthritis. And there was old Bertrand, often ailing, and Lulu who had once burned herself terribly, and there had been guests at the château who had had illnesses. Once the Count's stepson, Félix, was thrown from his horse and his collarbone broken. That was years ago. All these things she remembered and, to keep him awake, reminded her husband of them as they went.

Then Dr Retier, in the ambulance, overtook them, waving to them as he passed. The village was shuttered and silent, not even a dog to be seen. And at last there, ahead of them, were the iron gates, and then the *allée*, and then the château all lighted up and the front door wide open as the ambulance, its headlights still on, arrived first.

'Not Monsieur le Comte,' Blanche told them. 'It is Monsieur Félix, shot by mistake by old Bertrand, who now is suffering from a heart attack, and is probably dying. Thank God you are here.'

The two doctors between them lifted Felix, carried him into his room, laid him on the bed and undressed him, while Constant hovered round, still in his nightshirt but with a coat over his shoulders, and tears running down his cheeks. Félix, he told them, was bleeding everywhere, the women had been wiping, wiping, there was nothing else they could do. Doctor Retier attended to poor old Bertrand, who begged to be allowed to die and then lost consciousness again. They put him into a spare bedroom and told young Linette to sit by him.

Bertrand, it seemed, had aimed fairly low. The pellets had scattered widely and many were embedded in the walls. Constant was now made to go back to bed, and given sleeping pills. Everything, they assured him, would be taken care of. Dr Retier had already telephoned the hospital to prepare a bed and send for the surgeon to be there when they arrived. They would see to everything, nothing that could be done would be left undone.

Blanche helped Constant into bed and gave him the sleeping pills the doctor had put out for him, but he felt there was still something that he should do.

'Please go to my desk, Blanche, at seven o'clock, and look up the telephone number in Paris of our good friend Monsieur Henri Dumontelle. Ask him to fly to Nîmes and go to the hospital – he will know the one, he has been there himself – because his friend, Monsieur Félix is there, and badly injured. I know he will want to come. You were very clever, Blanche, to get the doctor as you did. You have done well. Now there is this one thing more. Telephone him at seven, remember, not earlier.'

And he laid his troubled head on his pillow.

Henri, still asleep beside his ex-wife whom he had decided to re-marry, got the call at seven and fairly leapt from his bed. He told his ex-wife, Béatrice, what had happened and said he must dress quickly and catch the first plane. She complained a little that it was only their second night together but on the whole took it well. Then, while he was dressing, he went to the telephone in the hall and rang up Sibyl at her hotel. He had been told the good news by telephone only the morning before that she and Felix were going to be married as soon as it could be arranged, and he felt that she not only ought to know, but ought to go with him to Nîmes, for her own and Felix's sake. He told her simply what had been told him by Blanche. 'Shall I meet you at the airport,' she said at once, 'or can you call for me here?' He said he would call for her at eight. She told him she would be downstairs, waiting at whatever time he came. Would they be spending a night in Nîmes? Probably two, he said. She then asked, hardly daring to speak the words, 'Is his condition serious?' And he said, 'Yes.'

Dear, blessed Henri, she thought, best of friends! Then, though she had been brought up as an intelligent, inquiring agnostic with no religious beliefs, she knelt down beside the bed – it was the old need, the old gesture – and prayed, begged, for Felix's life. With all her heart and soul she begged – call it praying or begging – for that life, far dearer to her now than her own.

Henri arrived promptly, driving the same small, fast car he had driven when they had dined in the Bois. They said little. He could tell her no more than had been told him by Blanche – that old Bertrand had shot Felix thinking him a robber. She remembered then the burglary at the château and the valuable drawings stolen. The Tiepolo Felix had taken with him was to replace one òf them. Could it have been that Bertrand, an old man now and perhaps nervous and excitable, had shot Felix when he was putting back the diaries, mistaking him for a robber? It seemed possible, more than possible. Oh, those diaries, Rita, the whole miserable, unnecessary affair! She could speak of none of this to Henri who would have to find some explanation of his own.

Henri put his car in the car park and rejoined Sibyl. He had booked seats on the plane early and by telephone, and a mention of the Quai d'Orsay seemed not out of the way in the circumstances, but he was anxious until the tickets were in his hands. They boarded the plane and found that they were able to sit together. But they were too distressed to talk much and sat trying to read the morning papers. When they reached Nîmes, which they did exactly on time, Henri called for a taxi. 'We'll get ourselves a self-drive car when we get to the town,' he said. 'We shall need one.'

They drove straight to the Cheval Blanc where Henri had once stayed after missing the last plane to Paris, and booked rooms. Then he telephoned for a car, and one was promptly brought from a nearby garage. 'So far so good,' he said. 'Now we will drive to the hospital.'

It was a modern hospital, certainly built within the last eight or ten years, and Sibyl got some comfort from the up-to-date look of it. When they inquired about Monsieur Matherson at the office they were told that he was in the operating room. It was very doubtful, the young interne at the desk said, that he could be seen today. He would say no more, so Henri went hunting for a nurse while Sibyl waited, her heart sinking lower with every moment that passed. But Henri had the good luck to be able to intercept a young woman who told him she was assistant matron of that wing of the hospital. She paused in her errand to answer his appeal for information. Yes, the patient he was inquiring for was still in the operating room, she had just come from there. 'You must be prepared to wait,' she said. He saw Sibyl and beckoned to her, and she came quickly to them. 'This young lady is his fiancée. I am his oldest and best friend. Would it be possible to see that Monsieur Matherson gets a note from me? It might help him.' He tore a page from his notebook and wrote on it, 'Sibyl and I are here. Love, Henri,' Yes, she said, she would see that he got it, and she advised them to come back tomorrow at about ten-thirty, then she hurried away.

Sibyl said as they left, 'What would I have done without you, Henri? I would have heard nothing, known nothing. Even that unlikeable woman, Rita Villet-Rocca has left Paris. I could have rung up Felix's lawyer, I suppose, and he would have made inquiries, but what ·agonies I would have gone through first!'

He stood for a moment on the hospital steps and took out his handkerchief to wipe his glasses, which had grown misty. 'I am so thankful,' he said, 'that Felix rang me up and told me you were going to be married. That was just before he left, to come here. How lucky that he did!'

'We both wanted you to know,' she said, 'before anyone else.'

When he took off his heavily-rimmed glasses he at once looked years younger, more as he had looked – and seemed– that evening in the Bois when he had told her about his ex-wife. Not at all the young diplomat on his way up the ladder. 'And Lucille?' he asked. 'There was no time to speak of her.'

'She will marry a lonely widower who has admired her

for a long time. But Felix and I will keep Annette.'
'That is like you,' was his reply. 'You are unselfish people, and I love you both.'

Then he put on his glasses again, and as he did so his youthfulness and vulnerability seemed to vanish and he became once more his public self. She liked both aspects of him. Then he took her arm and they went down the steps and over to where the car was parked.

'We must try to keep up each other's courage,' she said. 'Mine isn't what I would like it to be.'

'It will be a worrying time,' he replied, and opened the door of the car for her. 'He was so happy when he rang me up and told me the good news. I knew he had found everything he wanted and needed.'

'We both had,' she said. 'And now, this!'

He longed to give her comfort, but they knew nothing, and there seemed to be no comfort for him to give.

They had a light, late lunch, and after it he went to the telephone booth and rang up the château. He felt he must thank Constant for having sent him the message. It was wonderfully thoughtful and considerate. Constant spoke at once, at the other end, and his voice trembled with his anxiety. Henri told him he had already been to the hospital but was not able to see Felix, who was in the operating room. 'If there is anything I can do for you,' he said, 'please tell me.'

But Constant said there was nothing. His wife was returning, he was thankful to say, in the late afternoon. 'My good friend Dr Clermont will be keeping me informed about Félix's condition,' he said, and then added, 'You need not, my dear Henri, ring me again, though it was most kind of you to do so. The truth is I am in dread of the telephone. You will understand. But I thank you all the same.'

After that they went to the Jardin de la Fontaine and walked about in it for a time but took little enjoyment from trees or flowers or the sight of children playing. They sat on a bench in the shade and Sibyl said:

'Henri, you've told me nothing more about your ex-wife and how things are developing. We've had little chance to talk since our evening together. So tell me, please.'

'I will tell you. Things are arranging themselves. We are now living together "in sin" as they used to say, in my apartment, as she was finding her mother exacting and difficult. We will be married very quietly a week from now. Our little Andrea who was in poor health when she arrived, is now well again, and we are all three happy to be re-united. It is very strange, I think you will agree, how life sometimes seems to take charge, and we are simply like people in a play who have to discover what the author intends for us and so play our parts in an impromptu fashion.' He added, 'I find my wife in many ways improved, though that makes me sound a little like a schoolmaster.'

'Well, I'm very happy,' she said, 'that the author decided to end the play in the way he has. I'm sure it's the best way.'

After that they went to the Musée d'Antiques, but Henri was not much of a sightseer or an antiquarian, and they returned to the hotel. So that day passed. They dined together and said they would go early to bed. Sibyl took two sleeping pills and knew nothing more till Henri rang her up next morning.

'Time to get up,' he said. 'I have just sent for my breakfast. Did you sleep?'

'Thanks to sleeping pills, yes. I'll meet you downstairs in less than an hour.'

When they met in the hall below he thought that her pale-skinned face with its charming contours was paler than usual under the cap of smooth, shining brown hair. She had on the linen suit she had worn the day before.

'It's early still,' he said, 'but we can wait in the waiting-room if we must. I have brought the car to the door, so we will go at once.'

They drove to the hospital and parked the car where it

had been parked before. Just beside it was an English car, with a chauffeur. The chauffeur was sleeping, his cap over his eyes.

They went up the steps and into the office. The same young man was in charge.

'We would like to speak to the assistant matron,' Henri said. 'She knows who we are, and who we have come to see.'

'I will try to get in touch with her,' the young man said, and picked up a telephone. 'Meanwhile I suggest that you wait in the waiting-room. It is down that corridor,' he made a gesture towards it, 'and you go to the end.'

They did as he suggested, both wishing that he had said, 'The waiting-room is at the end of that corridor,' instead of saying, 'and you go to the end,' which had a hateful sound.

The room seemed full of people, but two couples were called for just as they arrived and hurried out, and then only one person remained, a woman. She was strikingly handsome and her gay, brightly coloured clothing seemed unsuitable to that place. The perfectly dressed hair looked as if it might have been 'done' by a hairdresser that morning. She was standing with an air of impatience and displeasure by the window as if saying to herself, 'Outrageous to keep *me* waiting here. Outrageous!' Sibyl, who had guessed at once who she was, felt a shiver go up her spine. She was standing almost face to face with her father's wife, with Angela, Felix's mother, but above all, at that moment, that tremendous moment of recognition, with the woman who had run away at the moment of her father's greatest need, and the mother of the child buried in that lonely grave. No wonder that Felix had disassociated himself from her. No wonder, no wonder! And then the woman's eyes fell upon Henri who had stopped dead, and was standing a little to the rear, near to the door by which they had come in. Her expression changed at once. Her handsome face put on a social look, a 'salon' look, and she came a step nearer.

'Henri Dumontelle! It's so long since I've seen you I hardly recognized you.' She did not, and Henri must have been grateful for it, hold out her hand. 'How kind of you to have left your Quai d'Orsay to come down here. Have you seen Felix?'

'No one has been allowed to see Felix yet,' he replied. And then, in all innocence but certainly not with the discretion Sibyl would have expected of him, he went on to say, 'Not even his fiancée, Mademoiselle Matherson, who has come from Paris with me, has been allowed to see him.'

'His – *what* did you say?' She might have been standing on a stage before an audience, so theatrical was her manner. She repeated her question speaking in English, 'His *what* did you say?' And then she turned on Sibyl. 'Miss Matherson, if she is the person I am sure she is, is the daughter of my first husband, Professor Matherson. She is therefore Felix's half-sister. There can be no possibility whatever of her *marrying* my son. If she is so much as contemplating an incestuous marriage with him, I absolutely forbid it. I will have it stopped. Now, young woman, what have you to say?'

'A good deal,' Sibyl unhesitatingly replied. No question now of keeping the facts from Henri. That simply did not in the least matter. Such a horror and contempt did she feel for this woman that she was strengthened by it, icily loathing her, icily despising her. 'I know perfectly well whose son Felix is,' she replied, her voice controlled and steady. 'He is *not* the son of my father, as no one knows better than you do. He is the son of your present husband. And Felix knows this too as well as you do, and as I also do. It is he who told me. If you attempt to interfere in any way we will broadcast the facts so that even your husband, poor deprived man, will know at last. If you leave us in peace, Felix and I will leave you in peace, with your wretched secret. So it's up to you. And I have nothing more to say to you except good-day!'

She turned swiftly and left the room at once, closely
followed by Henri, the door having been left conveniently
ajar. She was trembling now, but it was an inward
trembling, and she was determined that it should not
show. Henri shut the door of the waiting-room sharply
behind them, and was thankful he had, for coming
towards them was the matron, a big, grey-haired woman
whose uniform seemed barely able to contain her powerful body, accompanied by the younger assistant matron,
whom Henri had seen yesterday.

'Here they are, Matron,' the younger woman said,
'Monsieur Matherson's fiancée and his best friend. I will
leave them to you.'

The matron, both of them believed, was about to take
them to Felix, but instead she said, gently and with kindness, 'We cannot talk here. Come with me to my room.
We will talk there.'

They followed her, Henri holding firmly to Sibyl's arm.
He whispered to her as they went, 'I half guessed whose
son he was, long ago. Don't worry about that.' She
wasn't worrying about that, she was far beyond caring
who knew. Her heart was sinking, sinking. What were
they about to be told? That Felix could not be seen
today, or – the worst, the worst that could possibly be,
the worst, for which she was already, as they went on that
frightening walk behind the big, bustling, kindly woman,
half prepared?

The room was small, with many shelves and cupboards
and a big writing-table which took up most of the space
in it. The matron closed the door. There, looking from
one to the other, she spoke.

'I am extremely sorry,' she said with great gentleness,
'but I am afraid I cannot let you see him today. The
pellets have all been removed but he is very weak and is
now having a blood transfusion. I can assure you,
nevertheless, Mademoiselle, that all will be well with him.
He is a very healthy man. I think if you come tomorrow
at about half-past ten you can see him, but you must not

stay for more than five minutes. If I were to let you see him today, his mother the Countess would not be pleased. Her husband is one of our trustees and a good friend to the hospital and Dr Clermont is keeping him informed of our patient's progress. I must go now to the Countess who is waiting, I hear, with some impatience, and tell her that it will be best if she does not see her son at present. So, if you will excuse me – '

She went to the door and opened it to let them go through before her, then, struck by a sudden memory, she turned to Sibyl.

'When I was a nurse here, twenty-two years ago, before the hospital was rebuilt, your fiancé was brought in with a broken collar-bone. I nursed him and I thought him one of the most charming patients we had ever had. So I am happy to be able to congratulate you both, and most sincerely.'

She closed the door quickly without waiting to hear their thanks, and went hurrying, stoutly and heavily, across the wide hall and down the corridor to the waiting-room, while the two made a hasty bee-line to the front door, eager to get into the car and be away before the Countess could appear.

The sleeping chauffeur in the car next to theirs was now awake and polishing the windscreen. They felt they knew to whom the car belonged and made a quick departure. As they drove through the hospital gates, Sibyl said:

'I think that was one of the most likeable women I have ever met. I more than liked her, I loved her.'

'Yes,' Henri agreed a little plaintively, 'but she has forgotten me. Four years ago I was here with a bad attack of dysentery, and I saw her quite often.'

'Oh, poor, poor Henri!' Sibyl cried out, but her little involuntary burst of laughter was too near other and deeper emotions and the next moment she was beyond speech, beyond anything but tears, and sobbed into her handkerchief from the sheer relief and happiness that she had not been able to give way to until now. 'Forgive me please, Henri. It's all been too much for me. You'll understand, I know. But she did make it perfectly clear, didn't she, that he'll be quite well again? She did, didn't she? Oh, tell me she did!'

'She did indeed,' he said, and patted her shoulder with his right hand as he drove on. 'And you can stop crying because thank heaven there's nothing to cry about. On the contrary. But tell me when you can, my poor child, what you propose to do. I must get back to Paris tomorrow for the sake of my work but also for Béatrice and my little Andrea.'

She was wiping her eyes now, ashamed that even for that brief interval she had so entirely lost her usual self-control.

'Don't worry about me, dear Henri,' she said. 'I must find a cheap hotel and I will stay here till Felix is ready to leave. Then I shall bring him back to Paris. How long do you think it will be? A week? More than a week? Perhaps even two?'

'Perhaps two, I should think, but they'll be able to tell you that at the hospital. And what about your future mother-in-law? Though after your masterly attack on her I doubt if she'll dare to come back to Nîmes. That delighted me.'

'I prefer not to dwell on the thought of our relationship, and I trust I shall never set eyes on her again. But now, Henri, that you know so much and have been such a good friend to us both, I'm inclined to tell you more. It's a strange story, but you must please keep it to yourself.'

'You need not have asked me. If I were not able to keep things to myself, would I have kept my present job? But perhaps you think I talk too freely about my personal affairs. For that I blame my own honesty.'

Once more he had made her laugh, though at the same time she felt that it was true. She gave him a brief outline of their story, but omitted the tragedy and Felix's part in it.

'Now everything is much clearer,' he said, 'though I

find it extraordinary that no one but I myself, it seems, has observed the quite striking likeness between Felix and his father. And now, my dear, I think you should get in touch with your good friend and lawyer as soon as you can. He may be planning to come to Paris to see you. Ring him up tomorrow night when we will have, we hope, good news of Felix. Ring him up at about seven o'clock when he will perhaps be drinking his whisky and soda as a good Englishman should, and his little wife – I think of her as little – will be getting their dinner.'

'Bless you, Henri, that is exactly what I will do. I ought to have seen the wisdom of it myself.'

'You have had other matters to think of. And now that we are back at the hotel we will ask if they know of a cheaper one where you can stay, though I would be happy if you would stay here and allow me to be your absent host.'

But this she wouldn't hear of and within the next hour the hotel had been found and the proprietor of the Cheval Blanc vouched for its respectability and cleanliness.

'But you'll be so lonely,' Henri said, 'because tomorrow, after I have had a glimpse of Felix, I really must go. How will you get to and from the hospital?'

'Walk, of course. It's only about four kilometres, there and back. That's nothing to me.'

Then there was the problem of her hotel room in Paris. For this she needed Henri's help. He said he would go and see the proprietor, ask him to have all her belongings packed into her suitcase and keep it there for her until her return, when she could decide what to do next. 'He is a nice man and a friend of Felix's,' she told him.

'Don't worry about anything,' Henri said. 'You have quite enough on your mind. But what will you find to do all day when you are not at the hospital?'

'I have some work to do,' she said, and was thankful that she had slipped the *Timaeus* into her bag, together with her manuscript and her little Greek dictionary. 'And besides, Henri, have you forgotten that we are in one of the most interesting towns in France and the one that has the finest Roman amphitheatre in this country? My father and I only had time to go to Arles and Avignon. Now I'll be able to see the amphitheatre, the Roman tower – the "Tour Magne" – the Temple of Diana and a host of other things.'

He gave her a look of incredulity and amazement.

'You are an extraordinary girl,' he said.

They dined early that night and after dinner Henri went off alone to the cinema as he said he rarely had time to go to one in Paris. But the next morning he was packed and ready to start by ten o'clock and they drove to the hospital. On the way he saw a shop that sold perfumes and in spite of Sibyl's reluctance he insisted on her going into it with him and choosing a bottle of perfume for herself. She tried, unsuccessfully, to keep the sales-woman from spraying her with it. 'Most unsuitable for a hospital visit,' she protested. 'All the same, Henri, I shall treasure it. It's the most beautiful bottle of scent I have ever owned.'

They found the young assistant-matron and she took them at once to Felix's room. As she opened the door softly she said, a finger to her lips, 'Only five minutes, please,' and left them. Henri sat on a bench in the hall and Sibyl went noiselessly to the bed. She was at once surprised by the change in Felix's appearance. It seemed to her that all the lines in his face had been smoothed out, and he looked years younger. She knelt down beside him and laid her cheek against his. Then the dark eyes opened, but he made no movement. Her presence there was wholly and immediately accepted and a great wave of thankfulness and happiness seemed to flow from one to the other.

'What is that perfume you're using?' he asked in a whisper. 'I like it.'

'Henri bought it for me this morning.'

'Tell him what a comfort his little note was to me. I think it saved my life to know that you were here.'

'Tell him so. He'll come in for one minute.'

'I'm going to get well,' he said, and his voice was stronger now. 'I'm so thankful for us both.'

'My darling, I know, and I'm so happy. But don't talk now. I'll be here tomorrow and every day, and soon I'll be reading to you. When you're well, we'll go back together.'

'Together,' he murmured. 'That has a lovely sound.'

She kissed his forehead and got to her feet.

'Now Henri must come in.'

She tiptoed out and Henri tiptoed in. He was out again in one minute exactly, a happy smile on his face.

'Almost his old self,' he said.

That evening, at seven, she got through to the Beallbys' home in Surrey.

'Uncle Hugh, it's Sibyl. How are you? Is the case finished yet?'

'Yes. We lost. I'm feeling years older. You must write to George and congratulate him.'

'I shall, I shall. I'll write tonight. I must.'

'I suppose you're speaking from Paris.'

'No. From Nîmes.'

'From Nîmes? What are you doing in Nîmes?'

'I came here with Henri Dumontelle, Felix's best friend. Felix has had an accident and is in hospital here. I'll write you all the details very soon. Perhaps tomorrow. He's getting better, thank heaven, but he may be here for two weeks. Can you hear me clearly?'

'Perfectly. But as this is going to be a long talk, I'm glad you reversed the charges.'

'I knew you would want me to. And now for the facts, the real purpose of this telephone call. Uncle Hugh, we *know* that Felix is *not*, repeat *not*, the son of my father. He is the son of the Count. It's all quite clear now. Do you remember how Angela hurried home from Paris, saying she wanted to be married as soon as possible? She was pregnant then, with Felix. She and the Count were lovers, but of course he was married, and a Catholic. Her Irish friend, whom you never liked, helped her, and between them they "brought it off", the whole deception, very cleverly. So cleverly that they deceived everyone. My poor father, the doctor, and even you.'

'No, not me. Your father, yes.'

'So you're not greatly surprised at what I'm telling you?'

'Not really, no. I had my suspicions. I would say they were more than suspicions.'

'But my father never had, not for an instant?'

'Not for an instant. He was too loyal. Too completely loyal and trusting. It never entered his mind.'

'Well then, Uncle Hugh, Felix and I are going to be married. We love each other. He is changing his name to Forbain. His lawyer is seeing to it now. And I am absolutely happy – or I shall be, when he is well again.'

'And what of his little – his little companion?'

'She has gone away to be married to an old admirer. But we will keep her young daughter Annette with us.'

'Does that mean you will live in Paris? I fear you will.'

'Yes, but you must come to Paris often, you and Charlotte. Your favourite old hotel is still there, in the Rue de Rivoli.'

'But I must see you soon. Soon.'

'As soon as Felix is back in Paris, unless you would like to come here. Uncle Hugh, I must tell you. I have met Angela face to face. She has never told her husband that he is Felix's father. She was afraid that *tout Paris* would hear, so she has kept it secret. But I told her that Felix knows and that I know, so she will have to think things over and perhaps "come clean".'

'But do you really know? Can you be certain?'

'Absolutely.'

'But I must see Felix again just to be sure that someone

like you ought to marry someone like him.'

'There is no one like him,' she answered. And then, feeling that a little teasing would do him no harm in his present pontifical mood, she said lightly, 'What a pity that you never really studied your Plato.'

'He was never *my* Plato. And why do you say that? It pleases you to be cryptic.'

'Because if you had studied him you would have known that "The perfectly real can alone be perfectly known." And Felix is perfectly real. And therefore I am able to know him perfectly.'

'How like your father you are! But now, may I speak of less lofty matters? What will you do about your flat, and about Mrs Tronsett?'

'I'll let the flat furnished, put some of my personal things into a storage place, and bring Tronny over to Paris. She'll love it when the strangeness has worn off.'

'And now that we are speaking of practical matters, what about money? You must be running short.'

'Not yet. Felix has insisted on paying most of my expenses and I still have some travellers' cheques. I'll let you know if I need anything more.'

'Please do. And oh, my child, how I hope that you are doing what is best and right for yourself! You must be the judge of that. Nevertheless, I want to come to Paris as soon as you and Felix are back. I would like to see everything well and safely tidied up. I will see, with your agreement, my old friend and our representative in Paris, Vidal Masson. I've known him for many years, and he helped Lewis Petersen when he was making inquiries about Felix and the family on my behalf. I don't know French law as well as I would like to know it, so I rely on him. And perhaps Felix, when we have met again, will put me in touch with his own lawyer. Then, fussy old man that I am, I will feel happier.'

'When you see Felix himself you will have no more doubts.'

'I believe you, my dear, and I pray it will be soon. Well,

Charlotte is calling me to come to dinner. My fond love to you. One day I shall hope to say, "My love to you both," but that will come later. Goodbye, and how I shall miss you in London! Goodbye.'